*To Inge -
So nice to
chat over a drink.
Hope you enjoy.*

Patti Brooks

Fame and Deceit

Patti Brooks

Aberdeen Bay
An Imprint of Champion Writers

Aberdeen Bay
Published by Aberdeen Bay, an imprint of Champion Writers.
www.aberdeenbay.com

PUBLISHER'S NOTE

This is a book of fiction. Names, characters, places, and in-
cidents are either the product of author's imagination or are
used fictitiously. Any resemblance to actual persons, living or
dead, business establishments, government agencies, events,
or locales is entirely coincidental.

International Standard Book Number
ISBN-13: 978-1-60830-006-8
ISBN-10: 1-60830-006-4

Printed in the United States of America.

Dedication

Dedicated to horses present and past. Horses that gave up
their freedom to fight alongside of our soldiers in countless
wars. Horses that carried our pioneers and all their belongings
across the country, then lugged the logs that built their homes
and later plowed their fields and trotted them off to church.
And cow ponies that partnered up with ranchers to work the
big western ranges.

Dedicated to Today's horses that bring delight to their owners
from nine to ninety. They climb mountains, jump huge
hurdles, work on police forces, strut like peacocks or race like
the wind. The patient horses in theraputic riding programs
bring a sense of accomplishment to the handicapped. The
sensation of a velvety muzzle searching his owner's hand for a
carrot is prized by every horse lover. Winston Churchill got it
right when he said, "There's something about the outside of a
horse that is good for the inside of man."

Acknowledgements

A lot of inspiration for *Fame & Deceit* has come in the form of intriguing news articles read over the years and I contemplated ways to weave them together. Of course a lifetime of interacting with a wide range of horses influenced my writing. I also want to recognize the dozens of trainers (along with their support teams of farriers and veterinarians) who dedicated their lives to harness the power of horses into finely tuned atheletes. I turned to Scott O'Donnell, PFC of the Connecticut State Troopers to advise me on crime scene investigations. I also value the hours spent working with fellow writers in several workshops as they persistently in helped me get it right.

Most of all, I have my husband, Bob, to thank. Always a professional horseman, he did not mince words when he thought I wasn't absolutely correct about anything related to horses. He also turned a room in our home into my special place where nothing but writing is allowed. A computer, a thesaurus, but no phone, no Internet. Just a big desk under a picture window that looks out at our farm and pond.

I am grateful for my friend and professional photographer, Jan Lynick, for the beautiful cover photograph. Jan began her career as artist in 1980 as horse photographer. Since then her work has appeared in and on covers of not only national horse magazines but also mixed-media publications such as "Expressions" and "Somerset Studio." Currently Jan works on a cartoon for children called "Rail Talk" which appears in three national magazines.

Fame and Deceit

Given the lively twists and turns of the plot, the reader might not be expecting the kind of characterization Brooks delivers. Ike Cherney and the rest of the cast are not simply vivid; they possess real depth. In talking with friends about the novel, reader will have to remind themselves that the characters are fictional creations."

Mark Spencer, Dean
School of Arts & Humanities
University of Arkansas

"Brooks weaves a complex tale that has it all: money, corruption mystery, sex and suspense. She keeps you guessing until the end with her intricate plots and multifaceted characters. Then throw horses into the mix, and you have a must-read for fans of mysteries and equestrian fiction."

Jami Davenport
Author of "Who's Been Sleeping in My Bed"

"A fast-moving mystery. Brooks managed to capture the essence of the every day horse show world while unraveling a great fictional murder mystery bursting with twists and turns."

Fred Nava
Morgan Horse World Championship Show Mgr.

CHAPTER ONE

"Benalli ordered Lisa off the farm."

Ike startled at the man's voice coming out of the dark night.

"Help me with this tailgate, Harlan," he said as the farm's bulldozer operator appeared at his side. Probably a good thing Lisa left, he thought, unlatching the ramp to the horse trailer. He didn't need another harangue about being away at a horse show for the past week.

"Don't you want to know about that looney tune woman?" Harlan helped him lower the ramp to the ground. The horse in the trailer called out shrilly. Horses in the stable immediately answered the worried cry from one of their own. Now it wanted out and pawed and banged inside the trailer.

"First I want to get Annie off the trailer and put up for the night. Easy, girl," he crooned to the mare. "Besides, I think you just told me all I need to know about Lisa."

"What do you mean?"

"She's gone, right?"

"Right. So, did you win anything good?"

"She's one fine mare." He threaded a lead shank through the mare's halter and backed her out of the trailer. "We turned a few heads at that show, I tell you. You're home, sweet girl." Ike stroked the mare's neck.

Strident galloping in the distance broke into the conversation. Ike discerned that only one set of hoofs struck the ground heavily, which meant a single, mature horse raced about. How could that be?

When he heard the sharp clang of metal on rock, he knew the horse was shod–and headed directly for him and Annie. The mare snorted and pranced nervously at Ike's side. He snatched lightly on the chain across her nose reminding her he made the decisions.

"Harlan," he spoke sharply, "listen up." Harlan didn't know a horse from a cow. How could he get any help from him?

"Holy shit." Harlan said. "It's charging us." He dove behind the truck and trailer.

"Come back. Get me a whip."

"Get it yourself. You're the horse trainer."

"I can't. It's just inside the trailer door. I need your help." Branches snapped as the horse bolted through the woods. Ike saw Harlan reaching inside for the whip. "The long whip with a lash."

He stepped back out with the six foot whip and sprinted toward Ike.

The mare yanked so hard on the lead shank it felt like his arm pulled out of the socket. "Whoa," he commanded. He knew Annie took one look at the man running toward her with a whip and her fear over-rode his command to stand still.

The rampaging horse screamed a shrill challenge. In an instant he identified the yell as belonging to Warrior, the testosterone-laden stallion with only one thing on his mind. And it wasn't going to help that the mare was just coming in season. She'd smell pretty promising to the stallion. He had to get Annie out of there. Briefly he attempted to load her back on the trailer, but with her mind on the stallion, she wouldn't have any part of it.

His remaining option was to get her the fifty feet to the safety of the stable. Even if he was successful in getting the mare to run with him, he knew he wouldn't make the barn doors before Warrior reached them. No, he decided, he'd best stay put with at least the truck and trailer covering his back. No doubt it would be the battle of his life. He grabbed the whip from Harlan and prepared to meet the horse. "Harlan. Don't you dare leave me. Throw stones at him." Warrior broke through the woods, trumpeted again when he sighted the mare and bore down on them.

Ike snapped the lash on the whip.

The stallion never broke stride.

"Get out of here, you." He bellowed, backing it up with

9

a string of firework-like pops of the whip.
　　Warrior kept coming.
　　Annie whirled about, wrenching his arm till tears
streamed down his face. He must not let go. He knew the stallion
would chase her down till one or the other collapsed or broke a
leg tearing through the woods.
　　Before man interfered with horses' sexual life, stallions
learned to ask before leaping or risk serious injury. But when
man stepped in and introduced planned pregnancies, many
bold stallions took the chance of mounting when they learned
man could hold a mare still regardless if the mare wasn't full in
season.
　　Where the hell was Billie? His assistant must have heard
the ruckus. Harlan bombarded the horse with stones.
　　Warrior kept coming.
　　From twelve feet away, the horse made a mighty lunge
intent upon making good on his sexual urges. Thank god she's
not in fully in season, Ike thought. In this stage Annie's instincts
made her require a stallion to nicker to her gently, asking.
Not demanding. So, like any self-respecting mare, she reacted
violently to the stallion's intentions, squealing and letting both
hind feet fly catching Warrior in his chest. Shaking his head, he
dropped back to all fours.
　　"Kurwa!" Ike cursed Warrior's former owner who
encouraged the young stallion to breed every mare they hobbled
and held fast for him to mount. The stallion became a team
player real quick, learning that it was safe to jump a mare if a
man held it for him.
　　Harlan peppered him with stones but the horse stood
his ground. A little wiser and slightly more respectful of
punishment the mare's back legs delivered, he screamed and
pawed the ground waiting for his chance. The mare violently
swished her tail warning him away.
　　"Harlan! Listen up. Come hold this horse."
　　"No way in hell."
　　"Come on, Har. We're running out of time."
　　"I never held a horse."
　　"Simple. Keep tension on the lead shank. Stroke her

neck. Calm her down. But, *Kurwa,* don't let her kick." He handed the mare to Harlan.

"Wait!"

"No time. Don't let her kick." He looked for his chance then dove to the stallion's side, leaning his body into the horse's shoulder and grabbed his halter.

"Listen to me," he growled, shaking the halter to get the horse's attention. He pulled and shoved till the stallion turned away from the mare. Quickly he moved out of Annie's kicking range, all the while gripping the halter.

In a loud voice intended to instill respect in the stallion, he spoke words intended for Harlan. "Can you hear me?"

"Yeah."

"Don't let go." With his free hand he unbuckled his belt and looped it through the halter for more control. "I'm getting this bastard back in his stall. Then I'll come back for you."

"Listen to me," Ike shook Warrior's halter and punched his neck before walking purposefully to the barn.

#

"You took your damn sweet time," Harlan said handing the lead shank to Ike.

"I don't know what I would have done if you weren't here. We'll make a horse trainer out of you yet." Ike tried to lighten the situation. He wouldn't be surprised if Harlan peed his pants.

"Go to hell. I'm with Lisa on this. I don't want anything to do with these animals."

"Where's Billie anyway?" Ike asked.

"Don't know. I saw her leave earlier. Probably had a date." He raised his black cowboy hat and backhanded the sweat off his forehead, wiping it on his jeans. "you two are sick to actually choose working with these beasts."

"The things you want most in life usually come with some major stumbling blocks. Leastways I've always found it works that way." He wrapped an arm about Annie's neck as they walked to the barn. "But I don't mind admitting if all young studs were all like Warrior, I might look for a different career.

"If you call what that stud did tonight a stumbling block, then I know you're sick." He poked his hat back into shape and settled it on his head. "So, did you win?"

"*Kurwa*, Harlan, what do you expect? It was her first time off the farm. It's not always about winning."

"I don't think our boss feels that way. Thought one of those glitzy trophies might cheer up him up. Benalli's been hounding me. He's pissed you've been gone for so long and never called." Harlan flipped on the stable lights, and horses called out from stalls on either side of the aisle.

Ike snapped the chain cross ties to either side of the mare's halter and stroked her neck till she settled. He unbuckled her blanket and slid it off her back.

"If you had won," Harlan continued, "it might put him in a better mood. I have my own problems with Benalli without being the dog he kicks when he's mad at you."

Ike released the mare from the cross ties. Together they made their way down the brick aisle to her stall. "See you in the morning." He slipped the halter off the mare's head and latched the stall door.

"Thanks for your help," he said to Harlan as he turned off the stable lights. "I'll check in with Benalli first thing in the morning."

"I think you ought to hear about Lisa first."

"All right. What do you know about Lisa?" They stood in the stable door looking out at the soft May night. Sharp stars pricked the cloudless sky. Ike savored the smell of horses in a clean stable. The sound of them finishing up the last of their night hay never failed to soothe him.

"She was stuffing things in her VW when I came back from the gravel pits. I went over to help and tried to get her to talk." Harlan hooked his thumbs in his jean pockets as he told his story.

"She mostly mumbled under her breath, but before she drove off, she said– very loudly – she hoped she'd never have to smell another horse for the rest of her life."

"That about sums it up," Ike agreed as he watched the

barn cat scamper out of the stable and disappear under a bush. "She knew from day one that my life's career is training horses. But from the day she moved in, she started undermining it."

"You know, I used to envy you having a looker like Lisa, but now I'm sure as hell glad I never tangled with that woman. Didn't care who she hurt that stood in her way." Harlan wiped the toe of each cowboy boot on the back of his jeans. "Well I'm off to the pits."

"Someday you're going to explain to me why you do all the digging around with the dozer in the middle of the night." Ike could never reconcile the image of his friend wielding the big earth-moving equipment about the farm with the man who'd wet his pants if asked to touch a horse.

"That's a story you're better off not hearing."

Ike watched Harlan until the black night sucked him in. Now that the adrenalin rush surrounding Warrior's attempted rape abated, he felt thoroughly fatigued. Still, he wasn't eager to go to his empty house. Maybe she left a note, he thought, slowly moving toward the little ranch house set under a stand of towering pines. I'm glad she's gone, he thought, making a mental note to get the locks changed. If she was capable of attempting to poison Annie, stood to reason he might find a little something added to his orange juice.

Locks! That's what niggled at the back of his mind. How did Warrior get out of his double-locked stall? Billie had a palpable fear of the stallion. No way would she leave a stall door or gate unlocked. Could Lisa have slipped in after Billie left on her date and undone both locks? Didn't seem to be any other explanation.

He left his boots at the door and headed for the kitchen. Leaning against the counter, he raised a bottle of juice, hesitated, then poured it down the sink drain.

"I'm not going to take that chance, Lisa, dear," he spoke out loud. He took a clean glass from the cupboard and filled it with tap water. Only after quenching his thirst, did he find the courage to look for a note. Part of him hoped he'd find it propped against the sugar bowl. Less than a year ago it was on the tip of his tongue to ask her to marry him. Damn good thing he never actually did! But in spite of everything, he knew he'd miss the way she warmed his bed.

No note. He had no idea what she might write except that she left for good. He walked down the hall. As he turned on the shower, he checked the toothbrush holder. Empty. He tugged off his clothes and stepped into the steam. Minutes later he entered the bedroom passing a towel over his cropped hair, hoping to find clean shorts in the drawer.

There it was: the note. On his pillow. Resisting the urge to rip it to shreds, instead he set it precisely in the middle of the dresser. He needed to be clear-headed when dealing with Lisa. Hard to believe she actually set out to poison Annie. Although he felt obligated to read it, he couldn't see one good reason why he had to read it tonight. It would only serve to make him hate her more.

CHAPTER TWO

Ike woke to the smell of fresh coffee and sound of someone moving about the kitchen. Lisa's back. Maybe he should call the police, he thought, turning to look at the bedside phone. At one time, he loved Lisa. Of course the huge brown eyes in a delicate face almost overwhelmed by the cascade of long brown curls had a lot to do with it. He still couldn't connect this vision with the woman who caused Annie so much pain– and most likely unlocked Warrior's stall door. He had to follow through and make her leave. He couldn't afford to allow her to sweet-talk her way back into his life. He would send her on her way after breakfast.

"Lisa!"

"No...Billie." The tall red haired girl turned from the sink, a big smile on her face.

"*Kurwa*, Billie." Ike, with only shorts covering his body, jumped back. "You can't walk into a man's house like you live here."

"Don't use those Polish swear words on me. I made breakfast," she offered. "I thought you'd enjoy it after what I heard happened last night. Harlan said he was scared out of his mind. And I want you to know that no way I left Warrior's door unlocked. That horse scares me silly."

"I know you wouldn't. Let me get some clothes on." He turned back toward the bedroom. He never could resist the smell of bacon.

"Don't have to for my sake."

It took him a minute to find clean clothes. He stuffed his shirt into his jeans as he walked back to the kitchen.

"What is it with Warrior?" Billie poured coffee and set the mugs on the table. "If he even thinks there's a mare around the corner he goes berserk."

"We've got his former owner to thank for that." Ike brought his mug to his face and inhaled the strong coffee aroma. Billie sat down across from Ike.

#

"I'd like to hear that story." Billie shook her head. stirring two spoonfuls of sugar into her coffee. Part of her liked the way he dug into the breakfast she set before him. The other part wanted some conversation.

"Warrior's a nut case. By the way," she changed the subject, "Benalli wants you in the office ASAP." She held the coffee mug to her lips and watched him nod again as he shoveled eggs and potatoes into his mouth. Damnit! Talk to me!

"I hand-walked Annie this morning," she tried again. Talking about horses usually got his attention "Thought it'd be good for her after her ordeal."

He gave her a thumbs-up but kept his eyes down, smearing jam on the toast.

"Well good morning to you, too." Billie stood up and threw the frying pan in the sink, put the eggs back in the fridge, slamming the door so hard the cereal box on top toppled, spilling Fruit Loops all over the floor. The phone began ringing at the same time.

"The horses appreciate me more than you," Billie said. "Easy to see why Lisa left."

"Billie," he said. "Can't you see I do appreciate breakfast."

"That sounds like shutting the barn door after the horse ran off. I'd answer that phone if I were you. It's probably Benalli."

Billie grumbled aloud as she stomped back to the barn. "Why do I put so much effort into getting Ike to notice me as something other than a stall-mucker?" She reached up and tore a leaf off tree ripping it to shreds. "You'd think I might have learned something from Lisa." The resident cat, lazing in the barn door, looked up and bounded off for cover. "So much for making him a home-cooked breakfast with his eggs crispy on the edges just the way he likes it. Polish pig at the feed trough." She pushed the tack room door open, let it slam behind her and yanked a bridle off a rack, plunking it on a tack hook..

He's so damn nice to the horses, she mulled over for the hundredth time. I'd give anything to have him stroke me like he does a horse. She poured a glug of Lexol saddle cleaner over a bar of glycerine soap in a bowl and swiped it on the bridle. I really thought with Lisa out of the way, he might begin to notice me. Well, maybe it's all too soon. I've got to give it more time. Billie heaved a weary sigh, her heart returning to normal for the first time since she bolted out of Ike's house. She picked up a towel and gently rubbed the bridle.

#

Ike watched Billies' round ass. stuffed so enticingly into tight jodphurs, stride out the door. Then he turned his attention to the insistent ringing. His feet crunched on Fruit Loops as he went for the phone.

"What?" he spoke into the mouthpiece.

"Ike?"

"Morning, sir." He stood up straight at his boss's voice.

"We need to talk."

"Yes sir," he said again, but Benalli had hung up. He rubbed his jaw and decided he needed a shave.

Ike left the dishes in the sink and went to shave. Slapping on aftershave, he walked back to the bedroom where Lisa's envelope loomed on the dresser. He stared at it for long minutes before picking it up, knowing he'd be better off if he just tore it up. He would never allow her back, no matter what she said or promised.

"We've been over the issue so many times," he spoke softly to the letter. "I loved you, Lisa. You're the only woman I ever said that to." He stroked the envelop with his thumb as though it was Lisa's wrist. "But I never misled you into thinking I was going to be anything other than a horse trainer. And I know that doesn't make me easy to be around." It sickened him every time he brought to mind what she attempted to do to Annie. He became thoroughly convinced that she was behind Warrior getting loose. He sat on the bed, shoulders slumped, holding the letter in both hands. Then he closed his eyes and ripped the letter in half. Putting aside the last temptation to read it, he tore it quickly into tiny pieces.

CHAPTER THREE

The horse galloped through the night woods, his head low, intent upon the nuances of his prey.

He darted among the trees, changing directions as easily as a cat. The woman on his back smiled at her horse's ability. She leaned forward over his center of balance, bending into the horse's turns, holding the braided reins loosely in one hand. No need to guide him. He knew his job.

Fool, she thought, eyeing the naked man she'd set her horse to. Clothed only in black socks, he looked ridiculous in the moonlight trying to out maneuver Sir Golden Knight. Nothing had ever out maneuvered the golden gelding– after all he was a World Champion Cutting Horse. Granted they trained him to chase cattle, the woman reminded herself, and the staged event took place in a brightly lit show ring. And technically you'd think a man would be smarter than a cow.

"Please." The man turned to face the horse and rider, attempting to hide his nakedness behind a tree trunk. Sir Golden Knight skidded to a stop, instantly still. The woman knew he waited for the man to make a move.

She took great pleasure in watching the fear in the disrobed man of the cloth. He gulped at the night air, gasping. "What have I done?" He swiped at the sweat running down his face with a shaking hand.

I bet he preaches "Fear of God" every Sunday, she thought, ignoring his pleas. Being in complete control of the situation sent a thrill coursing to the pit of her stomach.

She might ask if he could guarantee her eternal salvation if she granted him mercy. But she simply waited patiently for the minister to catch his breath so they could continue this cat and mouse game in the woods. She glanced with disgust at the shriveled little thing he was so proudly going to poke into her earlier.

She urged the gelding forward. The preacher bounded off in a spurt of energy and she encouraged the horse to move in closer, hoping the man could feel his hot breath on his naked back. The preacher glanced over his shoulder. The woman laughed at the absolute terror in his eyes.

Suddenly, he collapsed in front of the horse. The gelding heaved his thousand pounds off the ground in a mighty effort to jump over the fallen man. She grabbed the saddle horn to keep her seat and pulled him to a stop as he landed. Together they turned to look at the preacher face-down in the pine needles, one black-socked foot twisted in a root. Blood flowed from the back of his head where an iron-shod hoof had cracked his skull.

The woman stroked the horse's neck with a gloved hand. "So, what do we do now?" The horse stood quietly, his breathing returning to normal. Only peepers could be heard in the moonlit spring night.

She slid to the ground, took the rope tied to the saddle, then moved to the lifeless body, nudging it onto its back with her foot. The fright-filled eyes, frozen open in death, stared heavenward.

"Not a chance, Preacher. You're headed the other direction." She hooked her thumbs in her belt loops and explored her options as she spoke to God.

"I'm not going to apologize." She raised her head toward the sky and stuck out her lower lip as though daring God to send a bolt of lightening. "Killing him wasn't intentional, but You can't tell me the world isn't a better place without him. Consider me a modern day Avenging Angel." Finished with her prayer, she looked back to the lifeless mound on the ground.

I'd be digging a month of Sundays, she thought, if I bury him here. She walked about kicking roots and stones. "It'd take a backhoe," She spoke. "And that would be like making a highway for the police to locate the body." She leaned against her horse's rump while formulating a plan. Perhaps she could dig a grave in the soft soil under the barn. And, she thought, warming up to this plan, the horse smells might throw K-9 dogs off the track.

Or, she continued to think about her choices, she could arrange a trash pick-up.

"You're way too heavy for me to get onto the saddle, Preacher. Prime example of 'dead weight.'" She chortled at her humor. So, I guess we drag you home. Kinda like pulling the Christmas tree home." The woman hummed "Silent Night" as she fastened the rope with two half hitches under his arms.

She led Sir Golden Knight through the trees and tied the other end of the rope to the saddle horn. Stepping back, she ran a finger down her nose as she surveyed her set-up. Making a decision, she untied her slicker from behind the saddle's cantle and laid it on the ground.

"No dog's going to trace your despicable body back to my barn." She folded the naked preacher into a fetal position and secured him on the slicker. Humming "Jingle Bells," she led the horse through the May night. She stroked her gelding's neck.

"Next time," she repeated, as though testing the words. "Far too satisfying not to have a 'next time,' don't you think, old boy? And," she said, turning her eyes toward the heavens. "I will take up the yoke of this burden and do my part in scourging the earth of these sinning men of the cloth."

Reaching the barn, she untied the body, lifted the heavy saddle off the horse's back and placed it on the rack in the tack room. She took the time to curry the dried sweat off the gelding.

After turning him loose in his box stall, she filled his water bucket and threw him a flake of hay before returning to the body. She tugged at the lifeless minister, struggling to drag the body into the workshop.

Once inside, she stood over him, hands on hips, her breasts straining at the confines of the low-cut jersey as she regained her breath. "No need to go to the gym, tomorrow," she quipped. "I can see this new game has lots of benefits, Preacher."

She went to the workbench, studying the tools arranged neatly in their assigned slots, picking up several before choosing a ten-inch flat-edge screwdriver and a pair of vise grips. Moving on, she searched for something else.

"Ah, here you are," she said spying the propane torch and matches. She fastened the screwdriver to the vice grips and dropped to her knees, she rolled the body on its left side. She lit the propane torch and held the screwdriver in its flame.

When the metal turned a dull red, she laid the shank of the screwdriver on the body's right butt. The acrid smell immediately accosted her nose. "Whew! You don't smell too good, Preacher." She re-heated the screwdriver again and again, placing it each time against the body's buttocks fashioning a crude "R."

She stood to scrutinize her artwork. "I'll have to work on that," she admitted, returning the tools to the work bench.

"Let's cover you up." The woman dumped several horse blankets on the body, arranging them so they'd look like a pile of dirty blankets waiting to be washed. "May nights can still be chilly, you know."

She picked up his trousers and searched the pockets, retrieving his key ring. Next she bundled his clothes together and turned off the lights, locking the workshop door behind her. She walked to the back side of a near-by maple tree and, running her hand up the bark, hooked the key on a nail.

CHAPTER FOUR

Ike took a deep breath as he stood at Benalli's wrought iron front door. He suspected this talk would be unpleasant. He felt like a school boy being summoned to the principal's office to report on his first show with Annie. Time and again he'd seen rich people buy expensive horses as a ticket to the social life of the big spenders. Winning mattered. They demanded nothing less from their trainers. Not presenting his boss with a blue ribbon would not make his boss smile.

He knew he took a big chance on talking Benalli into buying Annie. He placed his hopes of meeting his boss' demands on a young filly from unknown parentage. Only when he agreed to kick in his commission and become a part owner did Benalli agree. But he still had to find his boss a fiery stallion from a prestigious stable. That ended up being Imperial Warrior. And to think last night's fiasco could have permanently maimed both the stallion and Annie.

Benalli's angry voice cut into Ike's thoughts. Through Benalli's picture window, Ike caught glimpses of Benalli's wild gesticulating. Then Harlan took a step toward their boss. *Kurwa*! Har has balls. Not a good sign that his meeting would go well. He recognized Harlan's voice giving back as good as he got. Ike stepped behind a lilac bush so they couldn't see him listen in on their argument.

"Not only do I pay you good money, you owe me."

"If the law found out what you're doing..." Harlan challenged his boss.

"Better not let that happen," Benalli snarled. "Keep in mind you're in this as much as me."

"Someone's bound to check out the arithmetic. Just a matter of when."

Ike heard a door slam and knew Harlan got in the last word. Good for Harlan. Not so good for him. Harlan, his rusty-black cowboy hat pulled low on his face, strode past. Little prickles of doubt about what was going on every night at the gravel pit worked their way into Ike's consciousness. He frequently rode his horses along the farm road that led to the sand pit but only glimpsed the bulldozer behind the chain link fencing surrounding it. Up to now, he never gave it a second thought, but he couldn't shake off the bad feeling that his boss was up to something he'd like to keep a secret.

He stalled a few minutes before he knocked gently on Benalli's office door.

"It's open."

"Morning," He forced a cheerful note into his voice as he sank in the green leather chair facing Benalli's massive mahogany desk.

"Ike," Benalli said, the chair groaning as the beefy man leaned back. "We need to talk about Lisa. You know I had to tell her to get off the farm? Got a restraining order."

"Harlan told me she packed up and left"

"Carlos caught her in the stable in the middle of the night."

"I thought having Carlos bunk in the tack room while I was at the show would keep Lisa out of the barn."

"She's a troubled woman, Ike." He rested his arms on the desk. "I can't risk her causing harm to one of my show horses again. She needs to be locked up."

"She's not welcomed back in my house. I can promise you that. Did you hear about Warrior getting loose?"

"No."

"When I got home, he was running around in the night." He leaned forward across the desk to get his boss' full attention. "After I got the horses settled, I checked Warrior's door. Nothing broken. Someone opened not one but both locks. It was far from an accident."

"That's it," Benalli jumped up from his desk. "I'm hiring round-the-clock guards this morning." He paced in short heavy steps behind his desk. "I've have a major investment in these

Morgans that could be annihilated if that lunatic isn't stopped."

"We'll all sleep a little easier. Normally a little extra testosterone doesn't hurt when the going gets tough in the ring. But Warrior..." Ike shook his head, "that sucker cuts all communication with me when he sees a mare. It's going to be a long haul to get him to control that."

"I'm paying you good money to get it done. I expect great things from Imperial Warrior." Benalli stopped his pacing and stood in front on Ike, glaring down at him.

"It's going to take time." *Kurwa*! His boss was dense when it came to Warrior's shortcomings. "Remember you got such a good buy because his former owners could no longer handle him after encouraging the stud to breed every mare around – in season or not."

"Don't treat me like an imbecile. I do know a mare has to be in season to be bred."

"Technically. But Warrior learned that wasn't his problem. I suspect his owners didn't spend a lot of time determining if the mare was really ready to breed. If the handlers held the mare fast, he'd leap."

"So," Benalli said, sitting back down, dismissing the problem of Warrior's lack of manners, "tell me about the show." He took a cigarette from a pack on his desk then offered one to Ike.

"They liked your horse," he began with the positive. He lit the cigarette and took a long draw before he continued, making a full-fledged story as he talked about the big-name horse trainers who came up to him at the show and asked about Annie.

"They all asked about you and Crowne Stables. I told them you were determined to have only top-quality Morgan show horses." He handed his boss the professional photographs of Annie taken as she performed in her classes.

"I think this one would be great framed and set on your desk." He pulled out a picture where Annie, with head held high, ears pricked forward, trotted down the rail with the forearm of her front leg raised higher than level.

"She's a real mover," Benalli said. He smiled proudly as

he looked at his mare's high-trotting performance. "But don't you have one with a ribbon on her bridle?"

"The truth is," he snubbed his cigarette out in the Waterford ashtray, "we didn't win. You have to remember this was Annie's first time off the farm. She was leery of horses crowding her. It freaked her out when the spectator noise bounced off the walls of the coliseum. There won't be those issues next time."

"All right. I've put up with you playing around with that mare all spring. But now this is the way it's going to be."

Ike didn't like the anger he saw in the way Benalli ground his cigarette out.

"I conceded buying this horse because you were so adamant." He stood up and glared down at him. But you got to know I still can't see she has a chance of winning at the Grand National."

"But..." He stood up, not willing to let Benalli take control by looking down at him.

"Hear me out. I'm not so foolish to tell you to quit on the mare, after all as part owner, you do have a say in her career. But I can order you to devote equal time to my stallion." His fat fingers drummed on the polished desk. "You will get him qualified for the Grand National. Take them both. It'll up our chances of coming home with at least one winner." Benalli's black eyes stared at Ike. "I hope being a part owner of the mare won't influence how much time you spend with both horses. Face it, Imperial Warrior's name alone will make people stop and look."

"You're the boss," he said, ignoring Benalli's inferences. "I'll give it my best shot." But it takes a little more than a grand name to make a champion.

"Knew you'd see it my way."

Ike stood outside, his stomach churning. He drew a cigarette from the pack in his shirt pocket, simply holding it while looking at the lush green fields rolling away from either side of the brick mansion. Broodmares buried their muzzles in the May grass as their foals raced about on gangling legs.

He heard the phone ring in Benalli's office three times

before his boss barked a hello.

"You did what?"

He held his breath at the intense exasperation in Benalli's voice.

"*Merda*! What were you thinking?"

"I don't have to do anything. This...arrangement works both ways, you know."

Ike shoved the cigarette in his mouth and lit it. Nothing new about Benalli blasting out his anger. He could be heard from one end of the farm to the other. But who was Bennali talking to that caused such outright fear in his voice ?

"All right, all right. I'll send Harlan over this afternoon."

Imagine someone actually pushing Benalli into doing something he did not want to do? What could Benalli be sending Harlan for that caused such consternation? He puffed furiously on his cigarette. He suspected the fight between Harlan and Benalli figured into it somehow.

Soon the antics of two colts caught his attention and he spent a few minutes watching the foals, singling out the colt he thought had the best chance of being a great one.

But first he had to make Warrior a top priority. He brushed his mustache with a thumb, while some inner voice challenged whether he really was good enough to change Warrior's way of looking at life and make him a champion in just five months.

At the stable he found Billie in the tack room polishing bits. She was another one of Benalli's acquisitions. "She'll decorate the stable," Ike remembered him saying. Officially Billie was his assistant trainer.

Today Billie wore a light green button-down shirt with the stable's elaborate Crowne Stables insignia embroidered on the pocket. Several buttons were opened at the neck, and the shirt snugged her small breasts before a braided leather belt clasped it into the tight jodphur pants he enjoyed observing at breakfast. Certainly a different girl than the one that came looking for a job in a "Shit Happens" tee and dirty jeans.

"You look very professional, Billie," Ike said in lieu of an apology for not talking at breakfast. She had truly become an asset to Crowne Stable. He found he counted on her for some real help.

"Benny...Mr Benalli bought me a supply of these shirts and jods." She didn't even glance at him as she talked.

"We've have to start a rigorous training schedule for Warrior. Benalli wants him to qualify for the Grand National."

"Does that mean Annie has to stay home?" She stopped polishing to give him her full attention.

"No, she can go. Mostly to pacify me. He thinks Warrior is the horse that'll make a name for Crowne Sables. Annie doesn't fit his image of grandeur"

"Warrior is handsome, but Annie has what it takes. I'll have to talk to him about that."

"You have some special influence?" Ike teased. He picked up a halter and lead shank and headed for the stallion's stall.

"That's my business," she said as he walked away. "Some people actually appreciate me."

"How you doing, my handsome *ogier*," Ike spoke to Warrior as he entered the stall. "Boss says it's time you became a show horse." As he took a step toward the stallion, the horse snorted and rose on his hind legs. He back-stepped to avoid the flaying front legs.

"I'm not going to have a repeat of last night," he yelled. When the stallion landed, he charged Ike with ears pinned and mouth open. He ducked out, hearing the stallion's yellow teeth attacking the closing door.

"Billie," he yelled. "Bring the stud stick."

"I didn't much care for school either." He spoke quietly to Warrior while he waited for his assistant. "But that's the way it's going to be." Ike had doubts about overcoming the damage caused by the stallion's previous owner who allowed the youngster to pasture breed dozens of mares before he was halter-broke.

"Once we get a halter on this sucker," he said when she returned with a three-foot piece of two-inch plastic pipe. "No one is to leave him in his stall without it. You clear on that?

"Yes." She tucked her lower lip between her teeth.

"This horse wouldn't mind hurting someone. Our job is to establish the pecking order. Warrior thinks he's in charge." *Kurwa*, he thought, seeing the color drain out of Billie's face. She's terrified.

"You see it every day in our herd of yearlings. Who's the first one at the grain feeder?" Ike asked, trying to get his assistant to stop thinking of the danger of entering the stallion's stall.

"Houdini–the white faced colt."

"And I see you feed the chestnut with the long ears off by himself, right?"

"The others won't let him come up to the feeder."

"That because he's tired having the others push him around," He kept talking to the scared girl. Come on, Billie, loosen up, he thought. "The white faced colt is at the top of the pecking order. The long-eared one is at the bottom." He talked on till eventually her shoulders relax.

"Warrior is fighting for the alpha position. His testosterone really kicked in this spring and he's willing to challenge who's boss around here." Sure gave me one hell of a fight last night, he thought.

Warrior, apparently agreeing with Ike, kicked the stall door with both hind legs sending Billie diving for the other side of the aisle.

"I can't do..."

"Yes, you can. No way can we push him around He probably weighs eleven hundred pounds." Ike said, no compassion in his voice. I can't coddle her or she'll be worthless, he thought. "But we can outsmart him."

"How?" He could barely hear her whisper.

"First, you can't let him sense fear. Let him think for a second you're not totally sure who is in charge and he'll take over. That's where this stud stick plays a major role." The hollow plastic pipe made a loud noise when he rapped it smartly against his thigh. Warrior snorted. "It doesn't hurt much, but he feels threatened by the loud noise and gives me his immediate attention."

"Listen up, Billie, the second part is equally as important. You must immediately do exactly as I say."

She nodded, but he sensed she wasn't completely committed. Even more, he didn't like the way she tensed up as they walked into the stallion's stall. But that was all the attention he could devote to her fears. Now he must make sure Warrior understood he was not going to back down.

Warrior pinned his ears, and feigned a charge.

"Who do you think you are?" He spoke loudly, stopping the stallion in his tracks. The horse snorted, stood still for a second before making good on his charge.

He raised the stud stick, bringing it down hard on the stallion's neck. Bewildered, Warrior stopped and shook his head, sizing up Ike. Billie cringed behind him.

"Billie, get up here," Ike said in the same loud, angry tone, keeping his eyes on Warrior. The horse was sure the angry voice was directed at him...and it was. The words were for Billie. Unsure, the horse flicked his ears, trying to decide about this challenger to his position.

"Corner him....NOW!" Ike bellowed for the benefit of horse and assistant. Taking advantage of Warrior's indecision, he walked confidently to the stallion's left side, keeping the stud stick handy. He saw the stallion contemplate rearing but growled at him again.

"Whoa! You stand right there." The horse shook his head, but stood. Ike moved right in and slipped the halter on the horse's head and threaded the lead shank over his nose.

"Now you're going to walk out of here like a gentleman." He snatched the lead shank across the horse's sensitive nose a couple of times, to back up his authority. Warrior lowered his head and followed Ike out the stall where the trainer secured him on the cross ties.

"It's important this *ogier* learns I make all the decision in his life," he said as they curried the horse and picked the snarls out of his mane and tail. "Maybe he has enough spunk to make it after all. Let's hope he won't put all his effort into not working."

"What's this *'ogier'* you keep calling him?" Billie asked. Do you mean 'ogre' or is it another of your swear words?'

"Polish for 'stallion,'" he laughed. "Although 'ogre' fits him pretty well."

#

After an intense training session, he led Warrior back to his stall, pleased to see the stallion walk respectfully at his side.

"Good morning's work," he placed an arm around Billie's shoulder as they walked down the aisle. "Let's see if we can get Luke out here to re-shoe Warrior with heavier show shoes."

"I'll call him."

"Great," he smiled. Girls flocked to stables across the state the day the rugged blacksmith arrived. "Break for lunch?"

Billie checked her watch. "Sure. Then I have Ariel for a lesson."

"How's the kid coming?"

"She's the sweetest little girl. But her mom is tough on her. All the ministers' wives I knew were almost too sugary."

He laughed. "If you had to look in the mirror every morning and see the face Mary Ellen Crawford has staring back at you, you'd probably be sour, too."

"She expects so much of her and is getting even harder since that minister's gone missing. Ariel tries, but it doesn't come easy and she's only ten. Mrs. Crawford just doesn't cut her any slack. I have her riding Clyde. At least he's kind to her."

"Good choice. That horse builds confidence in the meekest of riders. See you later." He walked slowly back to his house trying to make sense of his eavesdropping outside Benalli's office. What issue had Benalli and Harlan screaming at one another? And who did Benalli talk to on the phone that sent him into such a frenzy?

CHAPTER FIVE

He opened the door to the rich, spicy smells of chili.
"Howdy, Horse Trainer," Harlan said. "Hungry?"
"What are you doing here?"
"I'm here to make a deal." The snake tattoo that ran from
Harlan's biceps down to his finger- tip writhed as he worked a
wooden spoon around a pot. "Come test my hell fire chili and I'll
tell you what I have in mind.
Ike washed his hands at the kitchen sink, wiped them on
his jeans and sat at the table.
"So, what's the story with Lisa?" He set the bowls on the
table.
"I never want to see her again. Benalli hired guards to
make sure she never steps foot in the barn again." He took a big
spoonful of chili and immediately reached for his Coke. "Good
stuff, Harlan. Burns all the way down."
"Good to see you thinking with your head and not your
dick. Lisa could have permanently ruined your horse and gotten
you fired for sure." He shook his spoon at Ike. "I think she has a
screw loose."
"Possibly." He didn't want to talk, or even think, about
the woman ever again, so he kept his mouth full of chili instead.
Be honest, you dumb Polak, Ike rebuked himself. He didn't
need the trouble that came with Lisa. Even so, he pictured the
college hangout where he often took Lisa for a Coke. She'd sit
across from him, admiration lighting up pretty eyes.
"Seeing you have an empty house," Harlan said,
"suppose you let me have the spare room and I'll make sure we
eat good every day."
"You cook more than chili?"
"You bet."

"Can you make pierogis?"

"You Polish, Horse Trainer?"

"Pure-bred."

"So that's why you're always spitting out strange stuff like that '*Kurwa*?'"

"Yeah."

"Ike Cherny can't be for real, then."

"Dwight Chernokowski," He held up his hands. "So, when can you move in? I never did learn to cook."

At the sound of galloping horses and shrill whinnying Ike bolted from the table, knocking his chair to the floor.

"Not again," Harlan said. "Count me out."

Ike hurried to the window to see the yearlings racing down the drive heading directly toward Benalli's manicured lawn. He hopped out of the house, pulling on his boots as he went. He saw Billie, her long legs taking great leaps in pursuit of the colts, a grain bucket swinging in one hand and lead ropes streaming out behind her. With the white faced youngster leading the way, the escaping colts dashed about, tails held high, tearing up Benalli's lawn and smashing through prize specimen plants.

He did his darndest to circle in front of the herd, hoping to alter their route and send them back to their pasture.

Benalli came out of the house frantically waving his arms and shouting in Italian. The colts turned on their heels at the sight of him, and, spying someone they knew with a bucket of grain, headed for Billie who turned and ran up the hill keeping a few feet in front of the colts.

Ike met her at the barn. Quickly he opened a paddock gate. Billie rushed in with eleven happy colts behind her.

"What happened? I don't see a broken fence." Was Lisa behind this, too? He wondered.

"No fence. Houdini again," she gasped, winded from her uphill sprint. "Not a gate that colt can't open."

"I pay good money." They turned to see a red-faced Benalli trudging up the hill. "Loose horses twice in less than one day. These things can't happen." He pulled a handkerchief from his pocket and mopped the sweat running down his face. "Grape vines. My wife's rose bushes. Trampled beyond saving."

"We'll double lock all the gates," Ike said.

"Just like you double-locked Imperial Warrior's stall door? If you can't do the basics of keeping colts in pastures and my stallion in his stall, what make you think you can train champions?"

Ike and Billie kept silent, properly contrite.

"It's high time I see some results of all the money I put out on this place. See it doesn't happen again."

"Hello. Am I interrupting?"

"Mrs. Crawford," Billie broke away from Benalli and greeted the minister's wife and daughter. "You're not interrupting. We're all set for Ariel's lesson."

"I brought a carrot for Clyde, is that okay?"

"Sure is." Billie reached for Ariel's hand then turned to the girl's mother. "Ariel will be riding in the big ring today, Mrs. Crawford. We'll be out as soon as Clyde is bridled."

"I'll walk out with you, Mrs. Crawford," Benalli smiled. "May I call you Mary Ellen?"

"Please do."

Ike smiled, watching the pudgy Italian and the hawk-nosed minister's wife walk toward the ring. Mary Ellen passed a hand over her brown hair pinned in a tight bun on top of her head. She was obviously pleased with Benalli's attention. Had to hand it to his boss; he knew how to read people.

Ike followed a distance behind Billie as she and Areil walked to where the lesson horses were stabled with their own tack room and cross tie area designed to keep them safely out of the way of the exuberant show horses. Usually Ariel skipped alongside, but today she hung back, hobbling along.

Ike watched Billie dropped to her knees and call out "Ariel! Are you all right?"

"I...fell off my bike. Mommy said I mustn't complain. But I don't know how I can get on Clyde." She blotted her eyes with the bottom of her tee-shirt. "Please don't tell I cried."

"Never. And I'll put you up on Clyde so don't worry about bending that knee."

He slowed his pace, letting Billie and her student have

some private time. By the time he reached the lesson barn, Billie had Ariel standing on a sturdy mounting block, her hands full of Clyde's bridle. The little girl's left hand was timidly attempting to stuff the bit into Clyde's big mouth while her right hand worked at pulling the bridle over his ears.

"Good job," Ike praised her when Clyde was successfully bridled. Ariel beamed. Billie placed her in the saddle and stood by while the child picked up the reins properly.

Billie's really good with kids, he thought, watching them walk sedately out of the barn. He followed behind and joined Benalli and Mary Ellen on the rail.

"So where is your husband's church?" Benalli asked as Ike joined them.

"We've been in Danielson for five years now."

"Do you know the minister that's been on the news?" Ike asked. "The one that's gone missing?"

"You must mean John Gibbens. Yes, Allen and John have worked on a number of projects together. Ariel," "keep your heels down," Mary Ellen admonished her daughter as she rode by. "You'd think after a year of lessons, she could have mastered that."

"There's a lot of things a young rider has to keep track of, Mrs. Crawford." Ike quickly defended Ariel. Why can't she just let the kid have a good time, he wisely kept this to himself.

Mary Ellen turned to face Ike. Her large breasts heaved menacingly. "I rode as a child, Mr. Cherny. I am well aware of the discipline it takes."

Ike swallowed hard, stunned by the chilling look in the woman's small eyes and mean curl to her mouth,

"Do you know Mrs. Gibbens, too?" Benalli changed the subject.

A full minute passed before Mary Ellen released Ike from her killer glare. "I don't know how many church suppers Beverly Gibbens and I organized over the years. She's not holding up well. It's been almost a month since he's gone missing." Mary Ellen stopped talking to study her daughter riding by.

"Her posture is atrocious. Can't Billie see that?"

"I'm sure she does, Mrs. Crawford," Ike mustered his self-control. "She also knows a big part of learning to ride is to gain confidence that she has complete control over a big horse."

"I do approve of Ariel learning control. Taking control of her life is a most important lesson. Girls especially must have the courage not to be pushed around."

"Look, see how Billie is asking Ariel to stop with her leg next to a specific point."

They stopped talking and listened intently to what was going on in the ring.

"Good job," Billie praised her young rider. "Now count eight steps and pick up a trot for just twelve steps, then walk."

"Is someone covering till Rev. Gibbens is found?" Benalli asked.

"Allen organized a few local ministers to fill in for him." Mrs. Crawford paused as Ariel rode by again.

"Good job," Ike called out, curtailing any remarks from the girl's mother. The woman looked at Ike, her mouth a grim narrow line.

"I worry any day now the church elders will look for another minister and Beverly will have to move out. She has three children," Mrs. Crawford said.

Benalli make a comforting sound.

"Beverly said he went out after supper to visit his parishioners in the Meadowside Nursing Home. Apparently it has been his habit to do this every Thursday night. He never came home."

"Do you think he was under pressure and took off?" Benalli asked.

"Everyone liked John," Mrs. Crawford said. "It's hard to imagine anyone would set out to cause him harm. He organized summer day camp for children no matter what church they belonged to. Spent hours every day making sure the young people had a good time along with bible study."

"The news said they found his car parked along Merrow Road in Tolland. So he didn't leave by plane or train," Ike said.

"I pray for his safe return every day," Mrs. Crawford said. "I'm afraid something terrible happened to him. Beverly doesn't think the police are taking this seriously. But John is a dedicated minister. He wouldn't abandon his parishioners."

CHAPTER SIX

"Billie!" Ike strode onto the stable floor. "Billie!" He headed toward the drone of the electric clippers and found Billie at the wash stall clipping the muzzle whiskers on a lesson horse.

Annoyed she pretended not to hear him, Ike pulled the clipper cord out of the socket.

"Benalli's bringing people to see the horses. He unsnapped the crossties and tried to hand the lead rope to Billie. "He wants a damn horse show. Get this horse out of here." He tried to shove the lead shank in Billie's hand again.

"Good morning, Ike" Billie smiled sweetly and continued to brush whiskers out of the clippers.

"For the last time, get this horse out of here."

Half hour later, Ike and Billie stood with Warrior on the cross ties waiting for word from Benalli. The young stallion kept looking for ways to bite his handlers or stomp on their feet. Warrior was a deep red bay with tiny ears peeping out of his sleek back mane. He wore a show bridle with a long shanked curb bit.

"Another minister's gone missing," Billie said, "from over at a church in Vernon."

"I heard that, too."

"Knock it off, Warrior." She belted the stallion in the nose when he tried to bite her. "Mrs. Crawford said that minister is 'a tad more zealous in comforting his female parishioners than is prudent.' Those are the exact words she used." She laughed.

"The TV news is making blatant innuendos that the missing ministers had an eye for pretty women."

"Really? You suppose there's some jealous women out there helping God punish the sinning roving clergymen?"

Ike heard voices and went to the stable door to see.

"Here they come." He hurried back to the stallion. "Now I'm going to keep Warrior in here," he pulled on his leather gloves, "to give you a chance to get to the end of the ring." He chose a whip and threaded the four narrow leather strips of reins through his left hand and steadied the stirrup iron in his right.

"Remember, use the rattle can and cracker whip to keep him animated." He vaulted lightly into the saddle. "But don't over do it, or the hoopla will become boring," he said to her back as she hurried out the stable door.

He waited a full minute before squeezing Warrior, letting his spurs press against the stallion's sides. He swished his whip and chirped. The stallion picked up his head and moved down the aisle.

"Lazy sucker," he muttered and let the horse feel the full force of his spurs at the same time as he smacked Warrior's shoulder with the whip.

The horse exploded into the sunlight, capturing the attention of Benalli and his friends.

He aimed his wildly trotting stallion toward the ring. High on the north bank beyond the ring, Ike and his horse caught sight of Billie waving a plastic bag tied to a six foot whip.

Warrior reacted by raising his head high and made a spectacular entrance. All eyes were on them. He caught a glimpse of Benalli, puffed up with pride.

Once around the ring and he felt Warrior lose interest and as soon as he couldn't sense a near-by mare, he reverted to his innate laziness. He jabbed the spurs into the horse's sides and he leapt forward. He didn't like doing this anymore and showed his displeasure by pinning his ears.

God bless Billie, he thought, seeing his assistant dance about the hill, cracking a whip and shaking the be-jesus out of the pebble-filled milk jug.

Warrior's spirits picked up a bit at Billie's efforts. Ike quit while the horse still looked good. He smacked his whip against his shoulder and trotted smartly into the infield. He tried to make it look like he had to demand the horse to stop when, in actuality, the horse was begging to stop.

He snatched lightly at the bit in an effort to raise the

tired horse's head. Exhausted, Warrior filled his lungs with air. Ike knew his flared nostrils could look wild if you didn't know the horse was simply gasping for breath.

After a moment, they walked over to the rail, allowing Benalli's friends to admire the handsome horse up close.

"Imperial Warrior is his name," Benalli said to a woman standing at his side. She wore a plain navy blue suit with a prim white collar and her blond hair was drawn fiercely into a french braid. She didn't seem to be Benalli's type, but Ike could see he gave her his full attention. "He'll be going to the Grand National in October."

"Good-looking stallion," the woman acknowledged.

"Eugenia has horses, too." Benalli told Ike when the woman stretched out a hand and stroked the stallion's sweaty neck. "Champion Quarter Horses."

By the time Ike rode Warrior onto the stable aisle, Billie had Annie on the cross-ties.

"Warrior made some good passes," Billie said as she picked out Annie's ground-sweeping tail.

"Never could have pull it off without your help." Ike unbuckled the throat latch and slipped the bridle off the tired horse's head. "Your dancing on the hillside kept his mind off working."

"Thanks." Billie lifted the saddle off. She mopped the sweaty underside with a towel before setting it gently on Annie's back.

"We're beginning to work like a team. You're anticipating what the horses need to look their best."

"I bet there's another way we'd team up pretty good." She cocked her head and batted her eyelashes.

"Come on, Billie. You know I'd lose this job real quick if Benalli thought we were fooling around."

"How many times do I have to tell I'm not sleeping with my boss?" She turned away from saddling Annie and looked at him. "The truth is he simply likes to look at me. I think the kick for him is having everyone believe he does more."

"No time for this now." He didn't like the implications of this conversation. Taking Billie out required some serious thought. Not that she wasn't easy on the eyes. "Benalli's friends are waiting for a horse show."

"Wait till Benny's gang sees Annie," she said, holding the off stirrup while he mounted from the other side. "He's sure to let you leave Warrior home from the Nationals."

"Don't bet your next paycheck on it."

"Well, I'm going to make her look great." She dashed out the stable, her long legs carrying her quickly up the hillside.

"Okay, my sweet *Lajkonik*," he crooned. "Let's show them a real show horse." He picked up the reins and the little mare pranced happily into the sunshine.

He could hear Billie whooping cheerfully from her spot on the hill. Annie puffed up and trotted into the ring.

No need for spurs and whip on this one! He held the reins lightly in his fingertips and guided her into the ring. He let her do what the mare loved most – show off. He came out of the far corner and felt Annie flag her tail. She raised her head even higher and snorted gaily in response to Billie's spirited shenanigans. When Benalli's friends burst into applause, the mare spiked her tail heavenward and trotted, as on springs, down the rail.

Ike urged her to cross the ring diagonally and reversed directionss. Annie didn't care where Ike directed her, there were people cheering her on, indicating she was great. Billie danced across the hillside, gaily waving the whip with the plastic bag tied to it.

"Atta girl," he spoke to his mare. "Boss has to be impressed with that show." He dropped his hands down to her withers and the pair made their way back to the stable. While Billie unfastened the bridle's many buckles and hooks, he took his saddle into the tack room.

He came back out to see Benalli running his pudgy hand down Billie's back as the girl had her hands full removing Annie's bridle. "Looked pretty tantalizing up on the hill, Honey. Hard to keep our eyes on the horse with you dancing about."

Ike slammed the door.

Benalli dropped his hand and turned to Ike. "Great job today, Ike. But I'm a little disappointed you didn't work Warrior longer. Was it an off day?"

"One of his best days."

"Best? Even I can see he was spent after once around the ring. Seems he lacks condition. Are you sure you're giving him top priority? Don't understand how that performance could be his best."

"Doesn't have the heart of a high-stepping Park Horse." He picked up Annie's flowing tail and separated it into three sections. "We have to resort to tricks to get the job done. Like a lot of lead in his shoes just to get every inch of motion. Basketball players often use that method in training." He began folding the mare's tail in a tight braid. "But he doesn't like the heavy shoes. Warrior doesn't appear capable of building up the muscles, so it tires him and he quits."

"What do you think – added supplements - more grain?" Benalli started pacing the barn floor. "Eugenia thought maybe more hours cantering might improve his wind."

"Can't force a horse to be a park horse." Ike said. Perhaps you'd like to hire Eugenia as your horse trainer, he kept to himself. "Attitude is the most important." He doubled over the braid so it was less than a foot longer than the mare's dock. "Warrior would shine as an easy-going Classic Horse. But those classes are limited to Amateurs." He wrapped the folded braid in masking tape and stepped away from the mare.

"Say ...why don't we get him ready for you to drive?"

Benalli stopped his pacing and faced Ike. His cell phone burst into the conversation. Ike watched the color drain from his boss's face when he checked the caller ID. He kept busy adjusting the leg straps on Annie's stable sheet, but still heard words like "Today?" "This is happening far too often." "We can't risk having one of our trucks pulled over."

Benalli snapped his phone closed. He turned to Ike, his eyes burning back coals.

"Get Harlan," he commanded.

"He's probably sleep..."

"Wake him up. I want him to have the dozer up and running in one hour." He strode out of the barn, walking briskly toward where Eugenia stood at a pasture fence watching the yearlings at play.

Ike left Annie in Billie's hands and jogged over to wake Harlan. He turned at the sound of Benalli's enraged voice as it rose up the hill. He knew from his boss' arm-flailing and head-bobbing, that he wasn't exchanging pleasantries with the pretty blond woman. He stopped for a moment. Something about the blonde. Sure, he suddenly realized, she was the same woman he met at the feed store, but that day she wore jeans and a plaid shirt. Not the school marm get-up she wore today. He hurried on to wake Harlan, wondering what kind of relationship she had with his boss.

This job held the hope of him earning a world class trainer reputation. He could not afford to piss-off his boss by fooling around with any woman Benalli might have an interest in.

CHAPTER SEVEN

With his arms full of Chinese take-out, Ike kicked his truck's door shut, He stood still under the pines listening for the dozer. Nothing except the incessant cry of the Whippoorwills. When he heard the dozer working all afternoon, he knew he better figure out something else for dinner. If he found Harlan in the house, he planned to learn more about what was going on. "More," he said out loud. "I don't know squat."

He fumbled with the door knob and pushed through, taking the food straight to the kitchen. Harlan sat at the table, his nose just inches from the paper he wrote on. At a quick glance, you'd think the tattooed snake that circled his arm moved the pen. Crumpled balls of paper lay about.

"I got Chinese."

"Give me a minute." Harlan continued writing. "Almost done."

Ike set out plates and took beers and soy sauce from the frig. He opened cartons and jabbed a big spoon into each.

"Done. Got an envelope?" Harlan said, folding a bulky pile of papers into thirds.

"Under the TV." He set the food on the table while Harlan pulled out a drawer and found an envelope and stuffed the handwritten papers into it. He ran his tongue over the glue and carefully pressed the envelope closed.

"I need you to keep this for me," Harlan said waving he envelope in front of Ike then placed it on the counter. He picked up the crumpled papers before pulling up a chair to the table.

"You got pork-fried rice. Good." He picked up the carton and a fork and started eating.

"Hey! Stop pigging out."

"Sorry," Harlan took a long swig of his beer. "I was

still thinking about my letter." They ate hungrily for a time. Finally Harlan pushed back from the table and retrieved the envelope."Listen up, horse trainer." He sat back down, tapping the envelope on the table.

"I'm listening." Ike put his fork down and looked at Harlan.

"If I should go missing, I want you to get this letter to my mother."

That got his full attention. *"Go missing?* Look, Harlan, since you're sharing my house, I have a right to know what's going on. Working a dozer in the dark of night. Then today Benalli got a message that sent you to the pits in full daylight. And what about last week's phone call that almost gave Bennalli a stroke?"

"You're better off not knowing. When the police come you'll be clean."

"Police?"

"Forget I said that. Look, will you get this to my mother or not?"

He nodded, never taking his eyes off Harlan.

"Thanks. Her address is on the envelope. But here," Harlan said, opening his wallet, "You ought to have her work address as well." A color snapshot of a smiling little girl fell out. Ike picked it up noticing right off the girl had the same narrow face and straight black hair as Harlan.

"Now that's a happy smile," he said. This had to be Harlan's kid, he thought as he handed the picture back.

"Yeah," Harlan's face softened. "And I know what you're thinking, she's mine."

"She live with her mom?"

"Mom's long gone," He drained the last of his beer. "Thanks to me. Now Janie lives with my mom." He got two more beers and sat back down.

"So, your wife just up and leave?" Ike tried to get him talking.

"Not so simple. I was responsible for killing her." He shoved away from the table and started dropping dishes into the dishwasher.

"*Kurwa.* Harlan, did you just tell me you killed your wife?"

"It was an accident." Harlan picked up the half finished take-out cartons and found a place for them in the frig. "I loved Caroline."

"You can't keep feeding me one half-story after the other." He spoke to his roommate's back as the dozer man stood at the kitchen window looking out at the night. "Come on and finish your beer and fill me in." Ike saw his shoulders droop. He turned and sat back down.

"Caroline and I married right out of high school," he began. "I had been working summers for Benalli. He offered me full time after I graduated. Taught me how to handle the big dozers." He took a long swallow of beer before continuing.

Neither of them, Harlan confessed, had the slightest idea of how to handle money and before long they had debts up their gazoos.

"So I thought if I could hit a couple of convenience stores, I'd pay off the largest debts. Just enough to get back on track." The snake on his arm writhed as he clenched his beer bottle.

He talked about how he chose carefully, locating one without a surveillance camera. Determined the right time to hit it. Went off without a hitch.

"If I had let it go at that I wouldn't be sitting across from you today. But no, I needed one more...withdrawal to pay off my debts and wouldn't you know Caroline wanted to come along."

Ike pulled the caps from two more bottles of beer and set one in front of Harlan.

"Before I got out of the car, I told Caroline to wait for me." Harlan pushed away from the table and paced around the kitchen. "This time the clerk waved a gun. He told police that he pulled the trigger hoping to scare me off. Instead it went right into Caroline's head. To this day I don't know what possessed her to follow me into the store."

Ike patted his shirt pocket and pulled out a pack of Camels. He stared at Harlan and stuffed a cigarette in his mouth, letting it hang there.

"Don't you ever think about the cancer you're smoking?"

"Try not to. So why aren't you in jail?"

"They let me walk right out of there the next day," Harlan continued, "and there was Benalli waiting in his car. As he drove me here, Benalli said he could make all the charges go away if I would work for him on the farm and keep my mouth shut."

Ike stood up and located his Bic on the counter. "What kind of man holds power like that?" He drew deeply on the Camel.

"I didn't much care to question that."

Ike watched Harlan's knuckles turn white as his friend clutched the beer bottle.

"But I sure knew I didn't want to go to jail. When he saw he could count on me to...take care of certain things, he doubled my wages. Mom doesn't have to pay out anything for Janie. You make a habit of smoking in the house?" He waved a hand to dissipate the smoke. "I've been wanting to talk to you about it. Not good for you."

"Yeah, that's what Lisa said." Ike held the cigarette away from Harlan.

"Got to give her credit for that."

"You made your point." He snubbed out the Camel.

"Back to this letter- one phone call and Benalli will have me behind bars and I won't be able to support Janie. But, if something happens to me and you get the letter to my mother, she will have what she needs to bring down Benalli."

"What could happen to you?"

"Truth is I don't really know. I do know that someday someone may find life easier if I'm not around. You'll have to take my word that it doesn't have anything to do with the horses. But if it happens, it will be the end of Crowne Stable. Keep the letter in a safe place. If you don't find dinner on the table some night, get it to my mom."

Harlan's confession dumbfounded Ike. They drank their beer in silence for a time. So, my roommate is a criminal. He pushed back from the table. And responsible for getting his wife killed. He picked up a dish rag and cleaned the soy sauce and spilled rice off the table.

And my boss pulled some strings and Harlan walks free. What did I do? Go to work for a man who obviously holds something over the heads of the police? And Crowne Stable will close if Benalli is charged with....with *what*?

He pulled on his boots and walked out into the night. It felt so right to have a stable of good horses to train. Morgan Horses he could turn into something special. He held the smoke from a freshly lit Camel for a long minute before slowly exhaling. It's Benalli's dirty money paying me...and the hundreds of expenses for keeping a horse farm. And who called Benalli that churned him into a frenzy?

He walked to the stable, heeling out the cigarette before entering. He heard Billie passing out the night hay. Never understood why Benalli wanted all the horses stabled every night when it'd be so much better for them in the pastures on a nice May night. Ike pointed out it'd save a lot of stall cleaning dollars, too. But Benalli couldn't be persuaded. Wheelbarrows were pushed up a specially laid out ramp and emptied into a farm truck and dumped down at the gravel pit daily. Had to admit moving the manure daily did keep flies away. But cleaning thirty stalls every day? Not terribly efficient. Was it somehow related to Harlan's work at the gravel pit?

"Got a minute?" Billie dropped a flake of hay in a horse's stall and slid the door shut.

"Sure."

"Come sit outside with me."

He pulled out a cigarette as soon as they sat shoulder to shoulder on the park bench.

"When are you going to quit that filthy habit?"

"If you brought me here to lecture...." He sprang up and prepared to walk away. It made sense not to smoke in the house, but he'd damn well light up outside whenever he felt like it.

"Don't be so thin skinned. Can't you see what it's doing to you?"

"No, I don't"

"Why do you suppose you're coughing so much?"

"*Kurwa*, Billie. It's May in Connecticut. The air is full of pollen. Plenty of people cough this time of year."

"And what grew in snow last February that made you cough most mornings?"

"Is there something you want to talk to me about? If not, I have things to do."

"I apologize for caring. Yes, I want to talk to you about Ariel."

He sat back down and stuck the cigarette back in the pack.

"Something's not right with Ariel and her mom. You know how hot it was yesterday? Well they both wore long-sleeved shirts buttoned up to their necks. When I asked Ariel if she'd like me to roll up her sleeves, she jerked her arm away. Whimpered. And the other week I know she wasn't telling the truth when she said she fell off her bike."

"You think someone is beating on them?"

"Well, yes. Mrs. Crawford is terribly rough on Ariel. She never gives Ariel the tinniest bit of praise. But on the flip side, why would Mrs. Crawford be wearing a long-sleeved shirt, too? And Ariel's dad is a minister, not a wife beater. I don't know what to think."

"There's nothing we can do but keep an eye on Ariel." He recalled Mary Ellen demanding perfection from Ariel the day he stood on the rail with her. "I'll try to be around for her next lesson."

"Thanks for listening." Billie stood up. "I was beginning to wonder if I was just being paranoid."

"No, you're being observant and caring. Two good traits in my book."

Billie went back to haying the horses and Ike walked down the aisle stopping in front of Annie's stall, his thoughts returning to the possibility of closing down Crowne Stable.

The mare nickered softly and came to greet him.

"But how could I leave you behind, my little *Lajkonik*?" He stroked her velvet muzzle. I can't afford to buy out Benalli's share. He leaned against her stall, running a hand across his jaw. "We've got to make it to Oklahoma, you and I." Should he believe Harlan when he said Benalli's activities did not involve the horses?

"See you in the morning," Ike called out to Billie. He glanced toward a rustling in the bushes as he walked out of the stable. Deer, he thought.

#

Billie slid shut a stall door and watched Ike walk out the barn. She loved his straight shoulders and the cocky angle in which he carried his head. His ears stuck out a little bit. Quite a little bit. "All the better to keep my hat on," he said when she teased him about it.

CHAPTER EIGHT

Ike gulped his morning coffee and hurried to the stable. Something was wrong. Horses banged around their stalls, striking the walls, calling out. He glanced at his watch. The horses should be quietly finishing up their breakfast at this time. Were there loose horses again?

"Billie?"

"Down here...in Warrior's stall," Billie sobbed.

"What happened?" He unlatched the door, and Billie tumbled out into his arms.

"After you left last night I stepped inside Warrior's stall to straighten his blanket." She clung to Ike, crying into his neck. "Someone locked the door on me."

"You spent the night in Warrior's stall?" He envisioned the terror she experienced, locked in with an unruly stallion that scared the hell out of her in the best situations. She smelled like a dirty horse.

"I stood in a corner all night. I didn't dare shut my eyes."

He took a step back and smoothed the tangled curls off her face as he listened.

"Who did this?" Her freckled face was splotchy. Tears streamed from her bloodshot eyes.

He shook his head and clamped his mouth shut, not wanting to blurt out that Lisa was a likely candidate. That noise he heard in the bushes as he left the stable– must have been Lisa lurking outside waiting for her chance to cause Billie some harm.

"Why don't you go shower," He picked hay out of her red hair. "Get some sleep."

"The horses...."

"I'll feed them. Meet you back here after lunch and we'll

work a few horses."

#

"Who do you think you are telling me how I train my horses?" He challenged Billie. "I know you had a tough night locked in Warrior's stall, but I still make the decisions around here." He had planned on jogging both the Oklahoma-bound horses around the farm's dirt roads.

"You need to stay away from the sand pits if you'd like to keep your job," Billie said, sitting on a tack trunk gently rubbing glycerin saddle soap on a saddle. "Benny told me not to go near the pits till he gives us an all-clear."

He stared at her, unwilling to back down. "What do you know about all this traffic? I see Department of Environmental Protection cars and State Police cruisers. "

"From what I've picked up from the drivers, one of the Benalli trucks was pulled over for some silly thing like a missing tail light. When the troopers checked the truck's log, something didn't add up right, so they escorted the truck to the nearest weigh station." Billie selected a clean towel and rubbed the saddle. "DEP decided they needed to look at all the paper work since January. Just before you got here two troopers came out of the house carrying ledgers. The men you see are going over every inch of all fourteen trucks looking for defects." Billie swung the towel over her shoulder and stood up, carefully placing the saddle on the metal rack.

"Harlan must know what's going on," she said. "What does he say?"

"Haven't seen him." He leaned against the door jamb and watched her hang a bridle on a harness hook. "Remember that day Benalli sent me to wake up Harlan in the middle of the day? The day we showed the horses to Benny's friends? She nodded.

"Something was really eating at him. After dinner he handed me a letter to keep for him. He wants me to give it to his mother if something happens to him."

"What could happen to Harlan?" Billie stopped saddle-soaping the bridle and turned to face him, her eyes wide with alarm. "Where is he? We have to find him."

"It's all right this time," he said with more assurance than he felt. "Harlan told me the next morning he needed to take a few days off. He was packing a duffle bag when I left for the stable." That could be it! Harlan is burying toxic waste behind the chain-link fence. That would explain why they're checking the trucks' logs and examining the gravel pit. He felt like a rusty screw churned in his gut. He tuned back in to Billie's prattling.

#

"I really like this job." She picked up a tube of metal polish and squeezed a dollop on a small rag. "Do you think Benny's done something terribly wrong?"

"Still like it after being locked in with Warrior?

I'd like working anywhere if you were near-by, she thought, inhaling the sent of his cigarettes. She hated that he smoked so much, but it was getting so that a whiff of smoke made her body come to attention knowing Ike was close at hand. Holding the shank of the curb bit, she rubbed in the polish. "Could they shut Crowne Stables down?"

"I don't know what to think. Harlan keeps telling me whatever hot water Benalli is in doesn't involve the horse farm. But it's the trucking company that pays for the horses, so I've been worrying, too."

"Well let's enjoy them while we still can. How about taking Annie for a little walk?"

"All right." His shoulders relaxed. "Saddle her up. We'll probably need a traffic cop to make our way through the cars."

#

"Problem?" she asked when Ike returned, just minutes after he rode the mare out of the stable. Annie was jittery, switching her tail and noisily chewing on her bit.

"So damn many cars it was like riding on the interstate. There's an army of men with clipboards climbing all over

Benalli's trucks. We were doing okay until some jackass blew his air horn." He vaulted off and threw the reins toward Billie. The mare snorted and twitched her ears at the rough treatment.

"Don't take it out on her."

"You'd better stop telling me what to do." Even so, he came back to calm Annie, but when he reached out a hand to stroke her neck, she tried to bolt from his touch.

"It's all right, girl," Billie crooned to Annie while she scolded Ike with her eyes. The mare settled but never took her big eyes off Ike, her nostrils flared.

He glared at Billie, then strode out of the barn.

#

Twice he tried lighting a cigarette only to have the hilltop winds blow it out. On the third try, the cigarette took and he inhaled deeply. He felt the tension ease and sat on the park bench outside the stable door. He watched as car after car drove down to the pits and then back out. Most of them were dark sedans with state license plates.

Too many coincidences. What kind of man was Benalli? Part of him didn't want to go there. He felt like he had come home when he took this job. A real chance of making a world class trainer reputation for himself and putting Crowne Stable on the map for Benalli.

How could he turn his back on all the little things that kept popping up? On the other hand, how could he pass up this real chance at a World Championship? If the law had something on Benalli he hoped it wouldn't go down till after the show in Oklahoma.

"Luke's here," Ike called out to Billie when he saw the blacksmith's blue truck turn in the drive. The diesel pickup rumbled to a stop in front of the stable.

"How you doing?" the tall blacksmith said, shrugging out of his flannel shirt. "Hot for May." Wearing a navy tank and worn jeans, Luke adjusted his cowboy hat and strode to the back of the truck, propping open the three sides of his blacksmith-shop-on-wheels.

"Billie said you need show shoes for the stud."

"Yeah. We could use a little magic, too, if you've got any of that in your truck. Benalli's disappointed Warrior can't make it as a Park horse." Ike gawked at the ease at which the blacksmith picked up the solid iron anvil and set it on a stand. "Got to pull all your tricks out of the bag to get decent motion for the English Pleasure Division."

"Hi, Luke," Billie led Warrior up and snapped him to the cross ties.

"Hey, Red. You're looking good."

Ike glanced at Billie and agreed. Somehow since he spotted Luke's truck, Billie had scampered off and did girl stuff with mascara and a deep red lipstick. A few red strands of hair pulled loose from her pony tail and curled around her freckled face. And the way those snug jodphur pants hugged her butt. A man could get carried away. If his career wasn't at stake.

Luke stooped to pick up Warrior's left fore, examining the shoe. "We can try a toe-weighted shoe. That should help him lengthen his stride."

"Benalli's obsessed with motion."

"If we raise the angle of his hoof over the next couple of shoeings, that's the best way to increase the height of his foot's flight path." Luke took out a six-inch ruler. "But we can't go with a longer foot. He's already the full four and three-quarters inches." He dragged his toolbox over, chose the nippers, cut the nail clinches on Warrior's shoes then yanked the shoes off. He dropped the nippers and picked up a knife to pare the hoofs and clean out the old packing. "But," Luke stood up and faced Ike.

"I know, I know," Ike said, well aware of Luke's familiar lecture. "You can't make a silk purse out of a sow's ear."

"How about sweeping the floor, Red?" Luke asked. He stepped back and watched Billie pick up the barn broom and sweep the hoof peelings around Warrior. "Doing anything tonight?"

"I don't know what Red's doing, but I have lessons till five," Billie said.

" 'Spose I hang around and we go for pizza or something when you're done...Billie?"

"I'd like that." Billie smiled, tugging the long tail of her hair over her shoulder as she walked off to the lesson barn.

"Must be nice," Ike said, watching him flex his sweat-glistening muscles for Billie's benefit. He was confused about his sudden feeling of...was it jealousy? "Sort of like a girl in every stable?"

"Got to beat them off at times," Luke grinned. "I hear you sent Lisa packing."

"Actually Benalli did." He explained how Lisa almost killed Annie.

"Sick. Who'd of thought it of such a cute, cuddly thing?" Luke went to his truck to choose the right shoes. "How's the little mare doing?" He stuffed a hoof with tar and oakum.

"Scares me how good she's going." Ike pulled a canvas director's chair from the tack room and sat down. "Wish the show was tomorrow. My biggest concern is keeping her neck sweated down. She doesn't set up well if there's even an inch of flab."

"Great length of neck on her. Who'd you say her sire was?"

"Aristook something."

"Home bred? Did you see him at the farm?" He finished nailing on the last shoe, reached for the hoof stand and set Warrior's hoof on top.

"No, why?"

"Just trying to figure where your mare got that long neck from. Don't usually see it in the Morgan Horses." The blacksmith was quiet while he rasped the hoof.

"Really has a Saddlebred-y look," he said, setting the hoof down and moving on to the next. "Have you heard what they're saying about Peggy O's colts? I was at Mountain Sun stable yesterday. You know Jill?"

"Probably not as well as you."

Luke grinned. "She says she ran into Ken Lipman at the last show who said he knows for a fact the last three colts were really out of a Saddlebred mare but registered to Peggy O." He straightened his back and pushed the hoof stand to the side. "And those colts are raking in the blue ribbons with their lofty

Saddlebred looks."

"Can't happen with blood typing and DNA. Probably just sour grapes at coming in second to them. Peggy O's colts are tough to beat."

"The word's coming from too many directions," Luke shook his head in disagreement. "Someone's found a way to play games." He draped an arm across the stallion's neck. "Finished with Warrior. Anything else while I'm here?"

"I'd like you to tighten the clinches on Annie." Ike stood up and passed the lead shank over Warrior's nose, snapping it to the halter.

"Take another look at the necks on Peggy O's kids. Ever see those swan-like necks in the Morgan breed?" Luke swept the floor as Ike led Warrior back to his stall. "Not at all like Peggy O's," he continued when Ike returned with Annie. "Sure as hell not like that chunky Morgan stallion they breed everything to." He stood back and took a good look at Annie. "I'd like to see her sire." He picked up Annie's left front hoof, set it on the hoof stand and tightened the clinches.

"Come on, Luke. Annie's a Morgan. Yeah, she's got a long neck, but her Achilles' heel is she doesn't like carrying it perpendicular to the ground like most Saddlebreds can."

"Isn't that Aristook farm in the same town as Dr. Clints' American Saddlebred farm?"

"Think his stallion jumped the fence?"

"Wouldn't be the first time someone took advantage of a weak link in the fence."

CHAPTER NINE

"Let's see how Warrior likes his new shoes," Ike said the next morning to Billie when he arrived at the barn to train horses.

"Luke said he did everything he could and still keep Warrior legal," Billie said, picking up a halter and lead shank.

"Some blacksmith pillow talk?" He teased.

"Wouldn't you like to know?" Billie shot back and left to get the stallion saddled.

"This is the plan," he said while mounting the stallion. "I'll jog a couple of times around the ring to make sure he's happy with his new shoes. We'll put him away while he still likes it; before he tires and it becomes a chore."

Warrior raised his head as he pranced down the aisle. A beautiful May morning, not hot and sticky like summer can be in Connecticut. The young stallion blew softly through his nostrils, clearly enjoying getting out of the stable, testing the air for any scent of the mares in near-by pastures. He kept Warrior in a controlled jog twice around the ring till he felt the horse pick up a rhythm with his heavier shoes and action chains. He signaled Billie, and by the time they reached the far corner of the ring and turned, he saw Billie pick up a flag whip and rattle can.

But Warrior didn't see Billie. Ike knew his mind was on stallion things.

He trotted on, excited at catching a glimpse of mares and foals. As they neared Billie, she started whooping and waving the flag whip. The stallion stopped dead, and Ike nearly toppled over his neck.

"*Kurwa*, Billie. I can't ride and tell you what to do. Think, girl. What do you suppose a horse will do if you step out in front of it and crack a whip? He thrust his feet back in the stirrups, headed back to rail and picked up a trot. Warrior responded but with clear head bobbing when his right front hoof touched the ground.

Ike pulled him up and leapt from the saddle. Billie vaulted over the ring fence and ran to the horse's head.

"What happened?" She placed a hand on either side of the stallion's bridle.

His anger couldn't find words. He lowered the injured hoof and turned to face Billie. "What happened is you cracked the whip in front of Warrior face while his attention was on the mares. His reaction was to get away from you. Therefore," he said slowly and carefully, his eyes demanding Billie's full attention. "he did what his inborn instincts told him to do – flee. He lost the rhythm of his stride, and stepped on himself. It'll be a week before he's happy about working."

He continued to stare at Billie hoping to see some sign that his words hurt as much as the hurt she caused to the stallion. The girl had to understand the seriousness of her actions.

"Geeze, I so sorry."

"Put him away. Soak that foot is cold water then use Ickmathol on it." He watched Warrior hobble back to the stable. Handsome sucker. Sure had a low pain threshold. He patted his shirt pocket for a cigarette. Lit it in one try and inhaled deeply.

He calculated the time remaining before the Grand National entries were due. The horse isn't even qualified yet. He'd have to work his tail off to be ready in time. He ran a hand across his hair and made his way back to the park bench outside the stable door.

He saw Mrs. Benalli in her flower garden stand up and wipe a gardening glove across her brow. She smiled at him and waved.

"Morning, ma'am." He smiled back.

"Can you help with Warrior?" Billie asked. "He won't stand still for the medication."

Together they walked into the stable where Warrior stood quietly on the cross ties. He stooped and picked up the injured foot. The two-inch gash was clean and cool to the touch but Warrior tried to pull his hoof away when Ike gently poked it.

"Let's get a light coating of Ickmathol on this."

She held the horse still as he gently massaged the black ointment into the wound. "Repeat that again tonight."

"Ike, I'm really sorry."

"Good morning." Ike and Billie turned to see Eugenia standing in stable doorway.

"Hello! This is a nice surprise," he said, enjoying the sight of her dressed in jeans and cowboy boots, her blond hair clasped simply at the base of her neck.

"Thought I might catch you working horses," Eugenia said.

"Just finished our first one. Billie," he turned to his assistant. "Why don't you put Warrior away and bring out Duffy?"

"Yes, boss."

"I'm glad you stopped by," he said after Billie left. "I didn't recognize you the other day dressed in a suit and your hair pulled back." He gently tugged the silky hair on Eugenia's neck. "You looked a little different from the woman at the feed store.

"I have to look official for my job."

"Which is?"

"Department of Environmental Protection Commissioner."

"I'm impressed. So that's how you know Benalli."

"Should I saddle Duffy?" Billie interrupted as she secured the colt to the cross ties.

"Sure," he said, noting his assistant's scowl. He'd have to talk to her later about being more cheery when clients were in the barn. "Here," he tossed a brush to Eugenia. "No watchers, only workers in this stable."

Soon the young gelding stood saddled and bridled.

"Okay," he spoke to both women. "I've only ridden Duffy a few times. My goal is to get him around the ring on all fours. No rattles cans and hoopla."

Billie placed her right hand on the youngster's nose

and held Ike's stirrup with the other to keep the saddle from slipping. Duffy snorted and tried to move off before he settled in the saddle.

"Let him go," he said softly. She quietly took a step back, and Duffy moved nervously down the aisle. He stopped the colt before the door, turned and walked back coming to a stop next to Billie. He relaxed in the saddle, hoping the horse would do the same.

She patted him on the neck. When he felt the horse loosen up, he turned again and this time walked out of the barn and aimed for the ring.

By the time Eugenia and Billie reached the ring, Duffy trotted erratically down the rail, learning to balance Ike's weight and trot at the same time. He felt the colt strain to keep his balance.

Suddenly Duffy reared. He hugged the colt's neck to keep from jerking the reins and pulling him over backwards. With Ike's weight over his neck, the horse returned to all fours and tried to bolt off. He settled quickly in the saddle and pulled the colt back. When he did, the horse inadvertently struck one hoof against another.

Mad at the man on his back and hurt in his hoof, Duffy started serious rib-cracking bucking by leaping into the air and landing hard on all fours.

"Exciting as a rodeo," Eugenia said. "He's good."

"I'll ride like that someday," Billie said.

Soon Duffy tired and Ike urged him into a trot, keeping the horse well collected and balanced, using his legs to urge the horse up into the bit. He felt the horse tiring and made the decision to quit before the youngster got sloppy and started hitting himself again.

"Whoa," he said. Duffy eagerly acquiesce. They stood for a minute, giving the colt's heaving sides a chance to quiet. Then he asked the horse to move off at a mannerly walk. The tired youngster happily complied.

"Cool riding," Eugenia said once Ike had dismounted. "I wouldn't want you to get hurt, but it was great to watch you."

He smiled as he cross-tied Duffy. Glad I stayed on--this

time, he thought.

Billie removed the saddle and took it back to the tack room. He picked up a towel and rubbed the sweaty horse's head.

"No watchers."

Eugenia laughed, took a towel off the bar and rubbed on the horse. "This has been fun. But I'd better get to work."

"So what do you do after work?"

"What do you have in mind?"

"We could get something to eat."

They settled on a time and place.

"Bye," she called to Billie and draped the towel back on the metal bar. "Thanks for a good time."

"She likes you," Billie said when Eugenia walked out the stable door.

"You think?"

#

Checkered tablecloths, candles in old Chianti bottles–perfect setting for a first date. Ike and Eugenia talked about horses from the salad right through the spaghetti. They finished off a bottle of wine as the evening played out. He enjoyed every minute of getting to know Eugenia and found the attention she paid to what he had to say very gratifying. Much different than Lisa, who cut him short if he mentioned "horse" more than once an hour.

"I understand you've been seeing someone pretty seriously," Eugenia said.

"How'd you know I was thinking about Lisa?"

"I didn't," she shrugged, "but if she's still in the picture..."

"She's not." He reached for her hands. "I never should have gotten involved with someone who didn't care for the horses. She couldn't understand the commitment it takes to develop a horse into a world champion." He held her hands lightly, running his thumbs across her knuckles. "Lisa considered Annie competition for my time, rather than the vehicle to make a name for myself and the stable."

"Must be Lisa never heard that 'There is something about the outside of a horse that's good for the inside of man.'" She pulled her hands away from Ike's and picked up her wine glass in a salute.

"I think every horseman has committed that quote to memory," he said, raising his glass and clinked it against Eugenia's. "Churchill hit it right on."

"What about Billie?"

"That's strictly a working relationship." He finished off his wine, not looking at Eugenia.

"Maybe for you, but I see things in the way she looks at you."

"Naw." He reached for her hands and held them lightly. "A horse trainer has to work closely with his assistant. We cover each other's backs in tough situations. That's all."

"A woman can sense these things."

"No."

"As long as you're not fooling yourself." She pulled her hands away and picked up her napkin. "There's a cool bar down the street that has good music on Thursdays," she said.

"You're on." He reached for his wallet.

Music blasted as he held open the Bull & Whistle's door for Eugenia. Dozens of small tables filled the dim room. Dancers packed the tiny space in front of the band. He grabbed her hand and pulled her behind him to an empty table off to the side. They ordered beers.

"What are you staring at?" he asked.

"Something about that woman at the bar. See? The bartender just set a drink down in front of her."

"The one in the brightly colored jersey...several sizes too small?"

"Made you notice, didn't it?" She teased. "She kinda looks like someone I know from my barn."

"Clearly offering an invitation to that man." He couldn't see much more than the jersey and long dark hair. The woman pressed herself closer to the man next to her.

"If it's who I think it is, she as pushy with men as she is with her horse."

CHAPTER TEN

She tossed back her mane of black hair and pushed opened the door to the bar with the other. Squaring her shoulders, the woman thrust out her chest till the snug jersey had no more give. She squinted in the dim light, searching for something–someone. Finding it, she sauntered toward an empty stool at the bar. Her ass did not go unnoticed as she wound her way through tables of beer-drinking men.

The man on the left smiled and made room for the woman.

"Thanks," she smiled back, perching on the stool. She looped the long strap of her small shoulder bag on the stool back.

"Vodka tonic," she ordered and heaved a lusty sigh.

"Tough day?" The man asked.

She nodded, turning her eyes toward the man. "I got laid off and I don't have any savings." Heavy mascara coated her eyelashes.

"Why don't you tell me about it."

"I don't want to spoil your night."

"I'm a good listener. It's part of my work."

"I can't pay...."

"Just talking to a pretty woman is pay enough. Where did you work?"

"A nothing job at a Cumberland Farm." She drank deeply from her glass. "But I was trying to save up to be a nurse. I'd really like to help people get better, you know." She caressed the smooth sides of her glass as she spoke.

"There's always work for nurses. Care to tell me why you were fired?"

"The manager's wife accused me of hitting on her

husband. And let me tell you, a woman would have to be pretty hard up to hit on that toad." She took a long swallow of her drink then placed the glass on the bar. "You know it's a curse... being pretty. Men are all over me. Women don't trust me. It's a damn curse. I should put on twenty pounds and throw away the make-up. Maybe then I'd have some friends." She picked up her drink and drank till it was empty. She rattled the ice cubes and raised the glass to her lips once more. She set it back on the bar with another chest-heaving sigh.

"But you're nice." She smiled up at him through her crusty eyelashes. "I got to get work or I'll have to sell my horse."

"You own a horse?" The man sat sidewards on his chair, giving the woman his full attention just as she gave him her best views.

"He's my best friend."

"Isn't keeping a horse expensive?"

"I work it off–muck stalls, give riding lessons." She looked at her watch. "And it's my turn to check the horses tonight. So I better go. Thanks for listening to my woes." She slid off the bar stool and jammed a hand in her jean pocket, fishing out money.

"Listen, you ever need to talk, give me a call. No charge in my line of work." She took the card he offered and looked at it.

"My God." She flung a hand to her breast. I've been talking to a minister...in a bar. Are you allowed to be here?"

The minister shrugged.

"Well, goodbye."

#

The minister and every other man in the bar set their drinks down and gave full attention to the attractive woman sashaying out. When the door shut, there was a collective sigh of appreciation before drinks were picked up and conversations renewed.

Soon the minister reached for his wallet to settle up. When he did he saw the woman's purse where she had hung it on the chair back. He threw some bills on the bar and hurried out with the purse.

Bursting onto the street, he searched the sidewalk. He caught a glimpse of her far up the street about to get in a car.

"Wait! Your purse!" he swung the handbag in the air.

She turned and started toward him. "I couldn't go far. My keys are in there," she laughed. "Thank you. Say, unless ministers have a curfew or something, would you like to come see my horse? You can ride with me. The stable isn't far from here."

"Sure."

#

They walked through the grass and into an old barn. Slatted oak stalls and a tack room were at the far end. Two dangling light bulbs lit their way.

"Here's my horse. He's a Quarter Horse." The horse raised his handsome head over the stall door at her voice.

"He likes you. I can see why. You're a very lovely woman." In one quick movement, the minister gathered her in his arms and pressed his mouth down on hers, demanding entry.

Suddenly she pushed back and the minister found himself looking at a small pistol.

"I knew you were one of those."

"One of what? My God, woman, I'm sorry. I just got carried away. Please put that away, I didn't mean any harm."

"No harm? Like not meaning any harm to Karen?"

"Karen?"

"Are you telling me that trying to get in Karen's pants during the Sunday school picnic has slipped your mind?" She felt the satisfaction of seeing the preacher's face turn red.

"You're..."

"Yes, I'm the one who just so happened to walk down to the river before you forced yourself on that girl. Now I want you to feel what it's like to get naked in front of someone you were taught to respect. I assume you have respect for this." She waved her gun in his face. "Take your clothes off."

"Think what you're doing...."

"I'm given it considerably more thought than you gave to almost ruining Karen's life." She cocked her head and took aim with the 380 semi-automatic gun. "Take them off...now!"

"Please be careful. You wouldn't want it to accidently go off."

"How do you know I don't?" She smiled, pleased to see his hands shake as he fumbled with the shirt buttons."

"Hurry!" She scowled and took a step closer. He shrugged out of his shirt and let it fall. "Get out of those pants," she commanded.

"Can't we talk?" He unbuckled his belt, hesitated the merest second before she wave her gun again.

"As a matter of fact, I would like to talk about how many other girls there have been."

"My God, woman, do you think I've made a habit of it?"

"Don't call God in to witness your lie. Last time: Drop-Your- Pants," she demanded. "That's a good boy," She smiled sweetly when the pants finally dropped to his ankles. "Shorts, too. Don't be ashamed of your shriveled little pecker. I'm not here to judge."

"I promise to never..."

"Think you can talk me down, Preacher? This is revenge. Pure and simple. Take off your shoes." He hopped on one foot as he tugged a black shoe off first one foot than the other. "After all, I'm just doing what the Bible says. Are you familiar with Judges 15.7? Let me quote it for you: '...Since you've acted like this, I won't stop until I get my revenge on you.'"

"Surely you must know Romans 12:19?" The minister shot back. "'Vengeance belongs to me; I will repay, says the Lord.'"

"No sermons, preacher. I'm running this shindig." Horses snuffled nervously when she fired a shot through the hayloft. Keeping the pistol trained on him she tied him up and secured him on the cross ties, shortening them with double-ended snaps so his wrists were high above his head.

She led the horse from his stall and snapped the horse's halter to the other set of cross ties. She brushed his golden coat.

"You really like that horse, don't you? How long have you owned him?"

She stopped brushing and faced the naked minister. "Look, preacher, I've had it with your Psychology 101. I'll tape your mouth shut if you keep it up." She turned back to her horse.

"Shit!" She stooped and picked up the horse's right forefoot.

"Something wrong?"

"He's missing a shoe." She stood up, hands on hips, staring at the barefoot hoof. "Guess this means the main event is canceled for tonight. I was so looking forward to it." She glanced at the man, seeing a glimmer of hope on his face.

"Don't think you're getting off so easily." She returned the horse to his stall.

"If you'll excuse me for a moment, I'll prepare for the second phase of this little party," She went into the tack room, ran a hand over the door jam and retrieved a key. Dropping to her knees, she opened a metal trunk. Moving a few things around, she located her new branding iron and propane torch and carried them back to the trussed minister.

"What are you doing." A pleasant thrill ran though her body at the fear in his voice

"You've heard of the Scarlet Letter?"

"Yes."

"This is my personal Scarlet Letter. 'R' for rapist."

"For Christ's sake, woman."

"It's time to pay for playing with children."

The woman took great pleasure in watching the terror rise as he tried to dance away from the branding iron. This time she made contact and the minister screamed. Horses moved nervously in their stalls.

She lit the propane torch again. Not quite as much fun as chasing him, but it had its moments.

"Please no, not again." The minister fainted as the molten iron sunk into his flesh. He sagged on the cross ties.

She frowned and placed a tarp under the limp body and went for a pail of water. She threw it in his face and watched him struggle to wipe his face with his tied hands and watched the fright set in as the memory of the night came to him.

"You need to be awake for the finale, preacher." She picked up her pistol and aimed it at the man.

"No, no... please don't."

She concentrated on her aim and pulled the trigger. The man's body writhed as the bullet bit into his right knee. She looked at the contortions on his face, like one might enjoy a sunset, as he twisted about on the cross ties attempting to cradle his knee. And the screams...like adding surround sound.

"Please." She loved hearing him beg. She felt on top of the world knowing the man's life was in her hands. She watched the blood gushed from the artery in the back of his knee.

"Let's see if we can get a few more spurting geysers. " She took aim at his belly and sent two bullets to open it up. "'... to avenge the blood of his brother Asahel, Joab stabbed him in the stomach and he died.' Recognize that one, preacher? Part of Samuel 3:27. You're not dying." she frowned.

"Please," he whimpered.

"Party's over minister. I have to get some sleep. I'm expected to be at my desk by 8:00."

"But you were fired?"

"Good story, huh?" She trained the pistol at his face, lingering as she enjoyed the agony and fear. The control was almost sensual, it brought such joy. "Was it good for you, preacher?"

This time the horses didn't even move in their stalls when the woman pulled the trigger.

She unsnapped the cross ties and let him drop to the canvas, then gave each horse a flake of hay and topped off their water buckets.

CHAPTER ELEVEN

"I understand horses travel better in a van than a tag-along trailer," Benalli spoke to Ike a month after the state Departments of Environmental Protection and Transportation, and the State Police crawled all over the farm. Benalli surprised Ike with a new green four-horse van with the Crowne logo splashed in gold on both sides.

He walked up to Ike, reached up and swung an arm around his shoulder. Together they read the lettering on the door: Owner: Agosto Benalli, Trainer & Farm Manager: Ike Cherny. "I want Harlan to show you how everything works. Take it for a long drive."

"He got you the best, Horse Trainer," Harlan enthused. "Your horses will be riding in a Cadillac. He sat in the driver's seat going over the dashboard indicators. "Two-speed rear end, air, leather seat with heat."

"Can I take this to mean last month's troubles went away?" Ike asked.

"Leave it alone. Just be happy you've got this beauty to take you to Oklahoma. Don't ask where the money came from. Let me show you about all these gadgets on the dashboard."

"Will I have to use all of them?" Sure the horses would enjoy plush traveling, but his experience with truck driving was limited to a standard pick-up. This dashboard lit up like a super jet's.

"You need to know how to handle the truck you'll be driving across the country, Horse Trainer. At least it doesn't kick and bite."

Ike leaned forward and studied the dials.

"Benalli had them install a second fifty-gallon gas tank."

Harlan pointed out a toggle switch. "Watch this and learn how to switch from one tank to the other. Don't let one run out before you switch because any sediment in the bottom of the tank could cause you to stall."

Ike reached for the one feature he recognized: the radio. But even that had symbols unknown to him.

"Can you believe he had the dealership install the XM Radio – something like two hundred stations. Even piped it back for the horses. Listen, here's four just for country western. Let's hit the road."

Ike crept down the drive, getting the feel of the powerful truck.

"Hey, Horse Trainer, take a breath." Harlan laughed.

Ike gasped for air, realizing he had been holding his breath. He eased out the farm gates and gripped the wheel as he prepared to negotiate the winding country roads.

"Take it on the Interstate," Harlan advised. You've got to feel the power at cruising speed." He turned up the entrance ramp, checking the outside rearview mirror for traffic.

"Give it a little gas. You'll find it a lot more responsive than one of your horses," Harlan teased.

He stepped on the throttle and the van surged forward. Harlan talked him through changing the rear end till he finally got a feel for it.

"Nudging 75 and feels more like 40 or 50," Ike said.

"It drives like a sports car, but don't be fooled. It won't corner or brake like one. You have to plan way down the road with a truck like this."

An hour later Ike brought the new van home, downshifting to ease between the Crowne Stable stone entrance.

"You'll have to get a Class 2 license to drive this," Harlan said. "What's she doing here?"

Ike didn't understand the cause of the alarm in his friend's voice. He saw Benalli standing next to Eugenia watching the yearlings play in their pasture. Although they leaned on the white board fence, Benalli's head bobbed vigorously. Experience told him Benalli was unhappy about something. He turned his attention to Eugenia, amazed how the woman turned a simple

outfit of red gingham shirt and jeans...albeit very snug jeans...
into something so seductive.

"You mean Eugenia?" How could she be threatening to
Harlan? He noted how rigidly his friend sat in the truck seat.

"She's not who I thought," Harlan mumbled.

He didn't buy that. If Harlan knew something about
Eugenia, he needed to know it, too. Maybe Harlan would open
up after a few beers. He had been dating Eugenia for awhile and
had every intention of continuing to do so.

They had so much in common. They talked about horses
endlessly, and she was the first woman he ever took a shine to
who understood the dedication it took to make a horse a winner.
Eugenia was acquainted first hand with what it took as she had
a world champion Cutting horse. Sure there were countless
girls– like the group of horse-girls who chased the muscled
blacksmith– in awe of his ability to work with fractious horses.
But he sensed it was much more with Eugenia.

And look at the other things they had in common. They
both ordered their steaks blood-red and firmly believed fish
belonged in the sea and not on the table. He recalled the first
time they went to UConn's dairy bar for homemade chocolate ice
cream. He thought he was introducing her to this Connecticut
wonder only to find out she had frequented the dairy bar since
her college days.

But most significant to a horseman, was the fact that, in
spite of their difference in height, they set their stirrups at the
exact same length. That was a real omen.

He drew the van to a stop beside the stable, and by the
time he slipped off the seat, Harlan was already gone. He made
his way down to Eugenia.

"Ike...you remember Eugenia?" Benalli said when he
joined them.

Eugenia winked at Ike. Guess that meant she didn't
want him to know they'd been going out. He decided to play
along.

"Yes, ma'am. I noted you had a good eye for a nice
horse."

"Eugenia would like one of our two year olds." Benalli

said. "I told her she could have her pick."

"Yes, I'd like the gelding with the four white stockings. I like his flash. Agosto wasn't sure of his name."

"Crowne Jester. Nice colt, ma'am. I suspect he'll mature out over 15 hands."

"That's what I thought. I like to place him in training with you. Break him to harness. I want to try my hand at driving."

"Great. We can start him in a bitting rig tomorrow and move onto long lining in a couple of weeks. We can make a goal of hooking him before winter sets in."

"I'd enjoy watching my colt work. Would it be all right if I stopped by from time to time?"

"Sure," he said. You bets your boots it's okay, he thought. "Let me know, and I'll save his day's work-out for when you're here."

"Today the phones were ringing," Eugenia said, "but the sun was shining, so I decided to sneak out of the office. I brought lunch for everyone." She held up a brown bag in each hand. "Grinders okay?"

"You bet," Ike said.

"There's enough to share," she offered Benalli.

"No. No thank you. I'm sure Gloria has my lunch on the table" Benalli turned and headed down the hill.

"Benalli doesn't seem very happy to see you," he said as the two walked shoulder to shoulder to Ike's house.

"Oh, he's put out that I asked him for a personal favor. Nothing to lose sleep over." Eugenia opened the grinder wrappers and placed them on plates. "I'm surprised to see how much you kowtow to Benalli."

"He is my boss." He filled two glasses with Coke and brought them to the table.

"But he doesn't own you," She sat down.

"He holds the purse strings." He sat across from her. "Men like Benalli need to wield the power their wealth enables them to." He filled his mouth with grinder.

"How can you live like that? You're not destitute. You're a talented horse trainer and should be treated with respect."

Whoa, girl! he thought, glad his mouth was too full to blurt something out without giving it a lot of thought. It's one thing to have to put up with Benalli but he sure as hell didn't need a controlling girl friend as well. If she thinks she's going to train me, she has another thought coming. He didn't train easy. She better learn that real quick.

He wiped the crumbs off the table as Eugenia put glasses and plates in the dishwasher. Homey-type scene, he thought. But after her agitating remarks during lunch, he wanted to put some distance between them. Living with Lisa's determination to eliminate the competition for his attention made him leery of whatever quirks Eugenia might have.

"Hello?" He picked up the kitchen phone on the second ring. Perfect! It was Billie reminding him he promised to talk to Mrs. Crawford. Just the excuse he needed to walk away from Eugenia.

"They just drove in," Billie said.

"I'm sorry I have to run to the stable," he said when he clicked off the phone. "I promised to look in on a lesson. Mary Ellen Crawford's daughter."

"Okay if I tag along?"

"If you'd like." Couldn't really say no. He wished Eugenia would go away. He hoped this might get the conversation safely established on horses and away from bars.

#

Ariel trotted by, concentrating on her posting, when Ike and Eugenia walked up to the ring. Eugenia smiled a big hello to Mary Ellen.

"Eugenia bought one of our two year olds and she's leaving him here for us to break to harness." He hoped this might get the conversation safely established on horses and away from bars.

"Is this your first horse?" Mary Ellen asked.

"No, I had a horse most of my life." Eugenia propped her arms on the top rail of the ring fence and watched Ariel.

While the women talked, he took delight in studying

Eugenia's body. The animal attraction was there all right, but something about Eugenia's attitude nagged at him.

"I had a horse when I was a teenager," Mary Ellen said. "However when I married a minister, I had to 'put away the things of a child,' as the Bible instructs. But I manage to slip out occasionally and take a friend's horse for a ride."

He picked up on the bitterness in Mary Ellen's voice that over-rode her thin smile. The iron-handed minister's wife seldom found something pleasant to say. But he had promised Billie. No use putting it off. He moved closer to the women and cleared his throat.

"Ariel's riding well today," he said continuing quickly before Mrs. Crawford had the opportunity to attack. "It's my opinion that Ariel could benefit by joining group lessons." Both women turned to Ike.

"I much prefer my daughter to have her instructor's undivided attention."

"I can understand that, but Ariel has reached a stage where she needs to think for herself, be in charge of maneuvering her horse around a ring full of kids and horses." He knew Mrs. Crawford liked that "be in charge" phrase.

"I suppose we could try a group lesson or two."

"It's the right decision, Mrs. Crawford. You won't regret it." Mission accomplished, he thought.

"Your daughter looks good on a horse," Eugenia said, most effectively breaking the tension. Everyone turned their attention to inside the ring where Billie instructed Ariel to trot Clyde over parallel poles laid on the ground.

"Trotting over cavalletties is a good exercise," Eugenia said.

"The horses are good for Ariel." Mrs. Crawford responded positively to the other woman's observations. "Being a minister's daughter can be very demanding with all the eyes of the congregation on her, wondering if she might be less than perfect."

"Tough on ministers' wives, too?"

Mary Ellen rolled her eyes. "There have been difficult times. Not every man of the cloth is a saint."

"It must be a scary time for the Connecticut ministry." Eugenia said. "I heard on the radio driving up from Hartford, that the wife of another minister has reported him missing."

"It's unprecedented. No communications. No bodies, God forbid. Ruth Wilkins called us at two o'clock this morning. Hysterical. It's her husband who's missing."

Well, Ike thought walking away from the women, Eugenia has moved Mary Ellen away from the topic of Ariel's lessons. Plenty of work waited for him in the barn. And he wanted to mull over what Eugenia was really getting at during lunch.

Ike wondered about the women in his life. Cuddly Lisa who turned into a demon when she felt he spent too much time with other females. Even when the female was a horse! And Billie, the resident redhead, always trying to ignite his interest. He was interested. And it didn't sit well with him to see her flirt with the blacksmith.

No way would he touch Billie as long as they both worked for Benalli. He would not throw away this great opportunity of making a name for himself. Come to think of it, his need to defer to Benalli is what Eugenia questioned. She must see me as Benalli's servant.

Every successful person made sacrifices and concessions along the way. If I want to make my dreams come true, I can't stop trudging toward it every day. Someday I will be a World Class Trainer. Till then I have to let Benalli call the shots.

"Good thing I have you," he said, reaching Annie's stall. "My little *Lajkonik*. Together we will create a lifetime of luck for both of us." He opened the mare's stall door, reached out to pushed her foretop out of her eyes, then stood there quietly admiring her.

As a young boy, he asked his mother time and again to tell the story of the *Lajkonik*, a hobby horse fastened to the waist of a warrior. During the spring celebration in Krakow, the *Lajkonik* pranced around chasing people. If he touched you, it brought good luck throughout the year.

#

An hour later Ike still puttered with adjustments to
Warrior's bridle. He looked up and saw Eugenia saunter toward
him down the dim stable aisle. The sight of her took away his
resolve to keep some distance between them.
     "Hi," she smiled, looking up at him, her eyelashes
shading her blue eyes.
     Kurwa! This woman really bewitched him. Ike smiled
down at her and continued fitting a new bit in the bridle.
Eugenia possessed a most important quality: she loved to "talk
horse." He wanted to see more of her, but her conversation over
lunch disturbed him. Maybe if they could sit quietly somewhere
he could explain why he deferred to Benalli. He figured it'd have
to be someplace public–preferably with a table between them so
they wouldn't get carried away before he said his piece.
     "Do you keep your horse far from here?"
     "At my dad's. In Coventry," Eugenia cocked her head.
Ike saw she wondered where this was going.
     "And guess what I just learned? Mary Ellen told me the
horse she rides is at the same barn. We've never run into one
another. She can't slip out until after dinner."
     "I'm about finished here for the day so what do you say
you take me to see this horse you don't stop talking about?"
     "I'd like that," she placed a hand on his arm. "Could it
be tomorrow afternoon instead? I promised Ariel I'd watch her
softball practice this afternoon. She's a sweet little girl, but you
know...there's something not right."
     "Like?" Watching Eugenia's eyes alter their hue from
blue to gray intrigued Ike. He tried to decide if her mood
determined the shade or it was simply a trick of the light.
     "Someone is hurting that child."
     He observed her eyes, clouded by bewilderment, become
definitely gray.
     "Maybe Mary Ellen is as harsh with her hands as she is
with her words. But she is a minister's daughter."
     She opened her mouth and stared at him.
     "Eugenia....what is it?" He touched her shoulder as she
clamped her mouth shut and turned away.
     "You look like you saw a ghost."

"More like the devil," she mumbled, cupping her elbows in her hands. "Got to go. Don't want to make Ariel late for her game."

CHAPTER TWELVE

"So...this is where you grew up?" Ike asked the next afternoon as Eugenia turned her Ford Explorer onto a dirt drive. Through the tangles of multi-floral rose bushes and ropes of bittersweet vines, he caught glimpses of a small Cape.

"Yes. My sister and I had some great times roaming the State Forest on our horses." The Explorer bumped and lurched down the rutted drive, past the house and headed for a weatherbeaten New England bank barn.

"You never told me you have a sister."

"Had. Serena...died. Murdered, actually," she said, pulling the Explorer to a stop in front of the lower level of the barn. I was eleven. Serena, seventeen."

Ike looked at her profile, seeing her pull her lower lip between her teeth and grip the steering wheel.

"Still hurts?" Ike reached over and softly ran his hand down her arm. "Care to tell me?"

Eugenia took a deep breath. Seconds passed before she released the air and reached for Ike's hand.

"Reenie...Serena...went on a weekend church trip to New York City. She went missing. They found her in a motel room days later. Raped and murdered."

Ike squeezed her hand and brought it to his lips.

"It's been over twenty years and they haven't found the killer. Nobody listened to me, but I know who did it." She pushed her hair off her forehead and told him how the sisters participated in the same church youth group.

"Our minister constantly touched Serena, finding reasons to hug her, run his hand through her hair. He gave me the creeps." She shivered and hunched her shoulders.

"Why didn't the police listen to you?"

"He supposedly had a great alibi. I was just a kid and everyone thought I was trying to get attention. Sound important. But I know it for a fact."

"How?"

She yanked her hand away. He flinched at the hate and anger in her eyes when she turned to face him. She's daring me not to believe her, he thought. She thinks I'm like her father. Eugenia studied his face before continuing.

"Our wonderful preacher took it upon himself to console me. Even got my father's permission to give me private sessions to get over my grief." She picked at her pink nails as she spoke. "Want to know how the sessions went?"

"I have a pretty good idea." He really did not want to hear any more, but he sensed she needed to tell the whole story.

"Right in the rectory, behind the locked office door. He told me I probably felt as I did because of the attention he had given to Serena." She opened the console and pulled out a tissue. "He apologized for neglecting me and would never neglect me again. And, of course, if I ever told, something terrible might happen." She pressed the tissue against her eyes.

"You're the first person I've ever told this to."

"*Kurwa*, Jeannie, how have you held it in all these years?"

"And you're the first person that has ever called me Jeannie," She gave him a watery smile. "I think I like that."

Ike wanted in the worse way to hold her in his arms and kiss her full rosy mouth. He knew it had to be soft. But with the SUV console working as an effective bundling board, he settled for bringing her hand to his mouth and kissing it.

"My horse is responsible for keeping me sane all those years till I left for college."

"You never told your parents?"

"There's just Dad. Mom died years before. And the day Serena died, Dad turned into zombie. He sits in front of the TV all day. Won't talk about anything but beautiful, talented Serena."

Ike heard anger creeping into her voice. Can't blame her.

Nobody gave a damn about her.

"Hardly knew I existed. Never came to see me compete in barrel racing. Did rouse himself to come to high school graduation – but came with pictures of Serena."

Ike couldn't think of what to say. He patted her shoulder.

"I thought he'd be so proud he had a daughter appointed a State Commissioner."

"Come on," he said. "No more sad stuff. We set out to have a fun afternoon." He opened the car door. "Show me this wonderful horse."

He watched her mouth curve upward immediately, the bitterness in her eyes turned into a lively twinkle. Did they turn a little bluer, too?

"Where would we be without our horses?" She popped her seat belt and opened the door.

She proudly led her champion gelding down the aisle and cross tied him. "Probably doesn't mean anything to a trainer of high-stepping horses," she prattled on, "but you're looking at an undefeated champion– for two years." She picked up two brushes and handed one to Ike. "No watchers," she teased. Together they brushed the golden coat.

"He's a good looking horse," he said. "Nice long neck."

"Didn't think you'd appreciate a neck that didn't rise straight up out his withers."

"Necks like that are for the high-steppers. A neck straight out in front of him is just what Bucky needs for his job of speed and chasing cows."

"Annie has the longest neck I've ever seen on a Morgan." She said. "More like my idea of an American Saddlebred neck." She put the brush back in the grooming box.

"It's one of the things that first attracted me to her," he tossed his brush in the box and followed her into the brightly lit tack room. "How the neck is attached to the body determines what the horse will be best at. Wow! I guess Bucky has been right good."

Championship ribbons hung on every available wall. Shelves supported dozens of trophies. Photos everywhere of a smiling Eugenia in snug western gear. He liked her image in a cowboy hat. He stepped closer to a big color picture of Eugenia on her horse smiling into the camera, a tri-color championship ribbon fluttering from Bucky's bridle. He checked her eyes in the picture. Definitely sky-blue eyes that day.

"He's been my once-in-a-lifetime horse." She hefted a silver-trimmed western saddle off a rack. "I know I'll never have another as great."

Cinched and bridled, she led the horse out into a fenced training ring.

"Storm's on its way." Ike looked up at the black clouds gathering in the sky.

Half a dozen goats raised their heads when the horse came into the ring, then bounded toward a small lean-to at the far end. A motley group of horses in the nearby pasture raised their heads for a moment. A bright sorrel nickered and took a few stiff-legged steps toward the ring before dropping his head to graze the early summer grass.

"I keep goats to practice with," Eugenia said as she swung quietly into the saddle and moved her horse toward the goats. "Which one would you like me to cut out?"

"How about the black one?" He never saw the subtle signal she gave her horse, but he moved quickly, and suddenly the black goat was separated from the others. The horse, his head low, riveted his attention on the goat. Although the Quarter Horse wasn't Ike's kind of horse, he appreciated the talent and training as he watched the gelding dart side to side, changing directions more quickly than the surefooted goat.

"He's a real athlete," he said as they hurried back to the barn just ahead of the full force of the storm.

"I'll never have another like him," she said as she removed his saddle and bridle. "That's why I bought Joker. I wanted something entirely different so I wouldn't be constantly comparing."

"Who owns the horses in the pasture?" he asked when she returned from the tack room.

"They're mine. All six of them." She toweled her horse's sweaty face. "Mostly senior citizens their former owners wanted to get rid of. The Appaloosa's totally blind."

"That's a lot of horses to store." He stooped to take off the rear skid boots.

"When Bucky started winning big time I invested his prize money. My retirees are living off that. Horses have been good for me. I consider this my pay back."

"That's a really nice thing to do, Jeannie." He set the skid boots on a hook, impressed at her sense of giving back.

"How'd Ariel's ball game go?" He changed the subject. Damned if her eyes didn't just turn gray.

"I don't think she finds it much fun." She put her towel back on the rack and chose a mane comb from the grooming box. "It was *déjà vu*, Ike. That coach never missed an opportunity to touch Ariel." She shuddered and hugged her horse.

"Surely Mary Ellen must see it."

"She does." She pulled the comb through her horse's short black mane. "But her husband won't let his daughter be a quitter."

"I can relate to sticking with something but not at the expense of placing Ariel in danger."

"He actually told Mary Ellen not to make a ruckus because the coach is a minister, too." She tossed the comb back in the box. "Said he'd find a time to talk to him privately." She chose a carrot from a bucket, snapped it in several pieces, and offered them one at a time to Bucky. "Meanwhile Mary Ellen won't let Ariel spend one minute around the coach unless she is there. I'm glad she understands being a minister does not make a man a saint."

"Maybe you're going a little overboard because of your experience with a minister. It isn't reasonable to place all the clergy in the same boat."

"I'd love to put them all in the same boat and send them over Niagara Falls."

"Ah, Jeannie, I know you had a rotten time as a kid, but look at what you've accomplished. State Commissioner, World Champion Cutting horse."

"But it came in spite of countless nightmares and working my tail off." She snapped a lead under Bucky's halter and turned to put him away.

"That's a good looking horse," Ike said as a palomino popped its pretty head over the stall door. He had to get her out of this bitter funk. He didn't like the woman it turned her into. The horse nickered softly and tapped the door with a front hoof. "Yours too?"

"No. He belongs to Harriet Stilton." Eugenia snapped another carrot and fed the pieces to the palomino. "Had some good cutting horse wins on the Connecticut circuit a few years back. Just does trail riding now. This is the horse Mary Ellen rides when she can get away."

#

The Explorer's wipers beat furiously at the pelting rain later that evening. "Do you need to do a night check?" Eugenia asked as she drove through the Crowne Stable gates.

"Billie's handling it tonight. Come on in for awhile. Give this storm time to pass before going back to Hartford." Not many chances left to get Eugenia to talk about her lunch-time lecture of kowtowing to Benalli. He hated the thought of changing the mood of this great day. And be honest, you dumb Pollack, he lectured himself, you're afraid you might see a side of Eugenia you don't like.

"Any chance of a cup of coffee?" They ran to the house, kicking off their wet shoes just inside. He expected Harlan would be home because of the storm, but didn't see his cowboy boots in the usual spot. What drove him to be out working in a storm?

"How do you take your coffee?" He pulled the Folgers from the cupboard, placing heaping tablespoons in the coffee pot basket.

"Strong and sweet."

Ike turned to see her fluffing her golden hair, shaking out the rainwater. What a treat to see her this way! So much nicer then the rigid french braid she wore for work.

He brought the tray of coffee things over to the blue plaid couch where Eugenia had snuggled in one corner.

"Oreos," She smiled as Ike set the tray on the coffee table. "My favorite."

"Comfort cookies." He poured coffee into mugs and offered her one. "Good for a stormy night." He sat next to her.

"I love storms."

They sipped coffee and listened to the wind whistling through the pines and the rain peppering the windows making a music designed to encourage snuggling.

Okay, he lectured himself. Now or never. He set his coffee down and placed an arm across Eugenia's shoulders, his fingers playing with the strands of her still damp hair. He took her coffee mug and set it on the table, determined to get into the reasons behind her sharp words at lunch.

"Jeannie...," he turned her face toward him. *Kurwa* he couldn't bring it up now! He ran his thumb across her lips. He felt her shoulders rise as she caught her breath. He closed the door on what needed to be discussed as she melted into him and raised her mouth to meet his.

CHAPTER THIRTEEN

He's an athlete, the woman thought as the naked man sprinted in front of her horse.

"We might be running into overtime tonight." She spoke to her horse as he snaked through the woods, head low, focused upon the man he had been set to chase. She allowed the man to stay well in front wanting him to feel he had a chance.

The preacher altered his direction, and the woman realized he must have seen the old cabin at the woods' edge. Multiflora rose bushes had staked a major claim to the structure, wrapping it in a thick tangle of piercing thorns.

He fell into the door like it was home base, struggling to get a grip on the door through the thorns. It held firm. He yanked and kicked at the door. He rammed it with his shoulder, crying out when the thorns bit into his flesh. Rusty hinges screeched as the door gave way and the man somersaulted inside. The woman vaulted from the saddle as the horse slid to a stop.

"Don't you know 'vengeance is mine, says the lord,' preacher?" The woman quoted the Bible.

"What have I done?" The man's muffled voice asked.

"Drape your slimy arms around little girls." The woman frowned. The voice didn't sound at all winded. "I know your kind." She heard the sounds of something being dragged across the wood floor. She tried pushing against the door he had slammed shut, but the thorns tore at her bare hands. The little game was fast losing its enticement. Seeing the terror in his face was by far the best part. Interesting how insignificant he became when he shed his clothes and stood trembling in front of her, pleading for mercy, embarrassed with his puny white body. "Puny" wasn't the right word, she admitted. "Adonis" kept floating through her mind ever since he stood naked before her in the barn.

She still sense a stirring coursing her body at the memory of his broad shoulders and muscular biceps and pecs. But the memory of what she had seen the fully-clothed preacher do brought her back to the job at hand.

"Preacher?" What was he up to? She heard him moving around inside.

Then silence.

Did he have a heart attack or something? Damn. "You're making me mad, Preacher." She didn't like losing control of her little party one bit. Yanking the lariat off the saddle she tied one end to the door, the other to her saddle. In one quick motion, she swung into the saddle and jabbed her spurs into her horse's side. He leapt forward, quickly taking up the slack in the rope. The door popped open in a spray of splintering wood. She spun the horse on his hindquarters and sprinted back. Taking the 380 semi-automatic out of the holster, she leaned forward in the saddle, peering into the dark cabin.

Then she saw the gaping hole where the window should be. Shit! She darted to the back side of the cabin and scanned the hay field stretching out for acres.

She spotted him racing toward the river. She spurred her horse into a gallop, gaining on the naked man with every step. An uneasiness nipped at the woman at the possibility of the preacher escaping.

She saw him hesitate at the river's edge and turn to face her. Hoping to wing him, she fired her gun.

Missed! She fired again. Simply not good enough to hit her target while on a galloping horse.

"Damn!"She hauled her horse to a stop and watched the man dive into the river.

CHAPTER FOURTEEN

Daniel sank far below the river's surface; the current aided his escape as he swam down stream away from the crazy woman. He ached to fill his lungs, his heart thudded from the race across the hayfield. Unable to bear another second, his head broke the surface. Gulping air, he gave himself up to the swift current. He heard the woman galloping her horse along the far shore.

No sooner did he see a bridge up ahead than he heard the horse's metal shoes ring out on the cement. The woman hauled him to a sliding stop, the horse almost sitting down on his haunches. In an instant she slipped out of the saddle and peered over the side of the bridge. The moon, three days past full, glinted off her revolver.

Good God what could he do now? The river bank offered no overhanging brush he could grab. The current forced him to move forward...directly under the bridge where the woman waited for him with drawn gun. He filled his lungs with air and swam to the bottom of the river, gambling the night-dark water kept him shielded.

When he felt his lungs would burst, he shot to the surface, praying the current had carried him under the bridge. Treading water, he turned to face the bridge and saw the woman, with her back to him, search the river. Safe...for a moment, he thought, letting the current carry him further from the woman. Thank God she hadn't seen him pass under the bridge. He caught sight of a thicket on the eastern shore and mustering up his last vestiges of strength, swam toward it.

His thorn-torn hands grabbed a branch. His body cried out to let go, but he knew he couldn't pass up the chance. As he tried to get a foot hold on the muddy bank, the branch broke, sending him splashing back into the water. He swam against the current to return to the clump of bushes. He reached out to grasp another branch, but the second he stopped swimming, the current pulled him away.

Weak and cold, he knew he'd have to swim upriver past the bushes. He concentrated on swimming efficiently, but his weary arms and legs splashed about. Finally survival drove him on and he swam just upriver from the shrubs.

As he headed down river again, he kept his eyes on the bushes, deciding to try for a Bittersweet vine that wove itself around the riverbank vegetation.

Don't quit now, he demanded his body. He managed to grab it, wincing as he wrapped the vine around his injured hands. Hanging on, he pulled his legs to the shore, securing a toehold in the bittersweet roots. He looked up the steep bank, judging it to be about fourteen feet. What now?

Naked. Exhausted. Well past midnight. Pretty much lost. How far would he have to walk for help? And Good God, Christ Almighty, he prayed, would a stranger open his door to him?

From stone to root to branch, he clawed his way up the bank.

Acres of two-foot corn stalks stood before him as he inched over the crest of the river bank. Crouching on his heels, he scanned the horizon, looking for lights or buildings. Got to be at least a barn somewhere. A jolt shot through him at the thought of the last barn he was in...with the crazy woman.

As his breathing slowed, he listened intently to the night sounds. A light breeze whispered through the corn stalks. In the distance a dog barked. He needed to find a road.

"It's not going to get any easier," he spoke out loud, and the Reverend Daniel Riker stood up and made his way through the rows of corn stalks.

How had this happened? Daniel tried to reconstruct the night. The crazy woman, called herself Sheila, sounded so sincere.

"Great actress," Daniel spoke softly into the night. He never gave it a second thought when someone called for help. Goes with the job, he told his wife every time he left their bed in the middle of the night.

How dumb could he be? The rough corn stalk leaves grabbed at his bare legs while he trudged down the row. Daniel berated himself for getting into a car with a strange woman just because she wanted to talk. *Refused to talk in my office–didn't want to disturb my family.* He shook his head at his gullibility.

Once inside the barn, Sheila turned into a...demon. *Never saw such venom spewing out of someone.* Hard to understand what she ranted about, he shook his head, trying remember exactly what had her so upset. *I guess she saw softball practice the other day. Did she really think I'd molest one of my kids? Yeah, I pat them on the head for encouragement. Sure as hell doesn't go any further.*

"Good God!" He came to an abrupt halt, a chill coursing his naked body. His wife forever reproached him for this. *Touching the kids.*

Gail! What would he tell her?

Daniel stood in the cornfield, hugging his arms to his chest, shaking in the cool night air coming off the river. A rustling caused him to look to his left. Several does and their fawns browsed through the cornfield. In the distance Daniel saw headlights blinking on and off as a car moved along a tree-lined road.

Encouraged by signs of people, he changed directions and moved off toward the road, plowing through row after row of corn stalks.

"Oh!" he cried into the night. Thrusting his arms in front of him he fell forward, his face crashing into corn stalks. Daniel rolled on his side, clutching his right ankle. He lay there, groveling in the dirt till the pain in his twisted ankle subsided.

Eventually he hauled himself upright and gingerly put weight on the injured foot. Trembling, he hobbled along, smudges of the dark earth clinging to his naked body.

Approaching the road, he saw a house across the street with a barn behind it. He stopped behind a tree and sorted through his possibilities, finally deciding to cross the road as quickly as his ankle would allow and go directly to the barn. Perhaps he could find a scrap of something to cover his nakedness before approaching the house where it appeared everyone slept.

Dressed in a ragged strip of blue plastic tarp fastened to his waist with a spring clamp, he took a deep breath, raised a bloody hand and knocked on the front door.

Minutes later, with his knuckles raw from knocking, a light came on and an old dog barked.

"Please, God," he prayed, "help me through this." He heard shuffling, like slippers on bare floors, and the distinct click of a dog's nails. The outside light over Daniel's head came on.

"Who's there?" A man's voice demanded.

"Daniel Riker, sir. Rev. Riker from the United Methodist church. I need your help." He heard a dead bolt moving, fumbling with the door knob and the door slowly opened.

A skinny old man in plaid flannel pajamas stood before him. Unkempt white whiskers covered much of his face. His tan hound dog barked twice, wagged his tail and sat down as his master's feet. The man's small eyes studied Daniel from his curly head of hair to his bare feet.

Daniel gritted his teeth, enduring the scrutiny.

"Minister, eh?" The man smirked. "She worth it?"

"No, sir. You've got the wrong idea."

"Whatever. Come on in." the old man took a step back and opened the door wide enough for Daniel to pass through. "Suspect you'd like to use the phone."

"Yes, sir," Daniel hobbled inside, following the man to the kitchen. The hound dog sniffed along at Daniel's heels. "Good of you sir, to let a stranger into your home in the middle of the night."

"Not much else to do with you banging away at my door." The man opened a cupboard and took out a bottle of Schenleys. "Pull up a chair." He ran water over a couple of glasses in the sink. "I could use a good story." He set a jelly glass in front of Daniel and poured in the whiskey. "Name's Charlie, by the way. Drinking buddies ought to know one another's names. Do I call you Reverend?"

"Call me Daniel. I don't drink–Charlie." Daniel held his hands up in front of him.

"Isn't drinking. It's medicinal. Drink." He scraped a wooden chair across the linoleum and sat down.

"I'd like to use your phone." Daniel picked up the glass and let the whiskey touch his lips.

"It can wait a little longer." He waved a hand in dismissal. "I want to know how you came to be walking around in the middle of the night naked as a jay bird." He took a swallow of Schenley's, closing his eyes as the whiskey slipped down his throat. "The truth now," he sniggered. "Ministers got to tell the truth. So," he prompted, "did you get her naked, too? What happened then? You didn't like what she offered and couldn't get it up?"

"Please, Charlie. That crazy women had murder on her mind, not sex."

"I hear tell there are those that get off on murdering."

"All right. If you stop the conjecturing, I'll tell you what happened." Daniel raised his hands trying to stop Charlie's train of thought. "Then, please, allow me to call my wife."

"Yeah, yeah."

He started at the beginning, considering it good practice for whatever he'd say to Gail, when he woke her up.

"That's as good as story as I've heard in a while. Ought to be a movie or something. Sounds like something that Stephen King wrote." Charlie drained his whiskey and pushed his chair back on its rear legs. "Now, who are you thinking of calling at..." he squinted at the clock over the sink, "...at 3:15 in the morning? Phone's on the wall." He pointed toward the fridge.

"Gail, my wife." Daniel stood up, adjusting his blue plastic skirt.

"Don't you think you should be calling the police?"

"I'll go down to the station in the morning." After I get some clothes on, he thought.

#

The phone rang several times before Gail surfaced from a deep sleep, and groped for the bedside phone. She cleared her throat and ran her tongue over her teeth expecting the caller to be a parishioner with a problem. Where was Daniel anyway?

"Hello, Rev. Riker's residence." With her free hand she clicked on the lamp and retrieved a pad and pencil from the night stand drawer.

"It's me babe."

"Daniel!" She swung her legs over the bed, immediately tuned into the urgency in his voice. "My God, where are you at three in the morning? Are you hurt? Has there been an accident?"

"No accident. But I've had...quite an adventure."

"This is hardly the time for games." She stomped a bare foot on the carpet. "Where are you?"

"Take it easy, babe. It's been an unbelievable night. Not one pleasant moment in it. I hate to ask you to go out at this hour, but I really need a ride home."

Gail scribbled down the directions to Charlie's.

"Charlie said the number is on the mail box and he'll leave the front porch light on. "Bring a set of my clothes, too. Please hurry."

CHAPTER FIFTEEN

"Good Morning, Daniel," Sgt. John Leary offered Daniel his hand. "Pull up a chair," the state trooper pointed to a padded metal chair on the other side of his gunmetal-gray desk.

"This is difficult, John. If one of my parishioners ever told me what you're about to hear..." Daniel shook his head. "A woman tried to kill me last night."

Sgt. Leary stopped organizing his desk and stared at Daniel. He sat down, and rested his folded hands on the crisp maroon desk blotter.

"Go ahead," the trooper spoke softly. His lean face took on a professional demeanor. He looked poised to memorized every word. At the same time, he managed to convey he had whatever time it took to hear the entire story. Daniel wondered if his parishioners felt the same about him when they came to unburden their souls.

"About eight o'clock last night I received a call from a tearful woman." He sat on the edge of the chair and looked at "Wanted" posters tacked to the wall behind Sgt. Leary's desk. The minister wet his lips and took the trooper through his ordeal of being made to strip, attempted to outrun a horse, then took cover in a thorn-covered shanty and finally jumped into the river as the woman on horseback shot at him.

"I could use some coffee." Sgt.Leary pushed back from his desk after Daniel finished recounting his ordeal. "How about you?"

"Black."

"How's Gail taking it?" He set a thick mug in front of Daniel and returned to his chair.

"Saint." Daniel blew on the coffee and took a sip. "I'm really blessed, John. How many wives would have accepted a tale like that?"

He watched the trooper pull a yellow pad from a drawer. Next he picked up a pewter cup, carefully chose a pen, then set the cup back on the desk turning it so the engraved plaque faced Daniel. He glanced at the inscription: "Putnam Gun Club Champion Marksman."

"There is additional information I need."

"Ask away. I believe if I hadn't jumped in the river I'd be the next name on the list of missing ministers. This Shiela is clearly a disturbed and vengeful woman."

"You're right. This is the first real clue to the missing ministers with any meat to it."

Daniel answered his questions, and watched the trooper pen precise notes while they drank coffee.

"Let's take a drive," the trooper finally said. He stood up, taking his Stetson from the coat hook, and settled it firmly over crew-cut blond hair.

#

"I'm pretty sure this is the road," Daniel said. "It was dark and I didn't pay of lot of attention. I had every reason to think Sheila would be driving me back to the rectory. There! I remember those high tension wires."

John slowed down. They scanned the sides of the rural road.

"This looks right." Daniel jabbed his finger at a narrow dirt drive on the left. The squad car came to a stop.

"No name or number on the box." John studied the battered black mail box. "That could be a sign on the ground." Leaving the car running, he got out and strode toward a homemade plywood sign pushed in the ground. He stooped to push the roadside weeds aside. Red letters proclaimed "Horses Boarded."

"All right," John said, settling back in the car. "If there's someone here other than horses, I'll do the talking."

Thorny bushes grabbed at the squad car as it bumped down the drive. The brambles gave way to a clearing. A small cape staked a claim to the far corner. On its roof, a blue tarp fluttered in the summer breeze.

"I'll see if someone is home," John parked the Crowne Vic, settled his Stetson on his head and started out toward the torn screen door. He heard a television droning from somewhere within the house. He knocked loudly on the door jam.

"Hello," he called out and knocked again. This time he heard heavy footsteps coming toward him.

"Good morning," he introduced himself. "Are you the owner?"

"Yeah. I'm Will Jordan." He chewed on a toothpick while he talked. "What do you want?"

"I'm hoping you can help me out here. I've got a man with me who claims a woman on a horse chased him."

"Don't surprise me none," he chuckled. "Horsewomen are a strange lot." Jordan hitched up his pants from where they dropped below his belly. "What do you want from me?"

"To be honest, I don't really believe this guy, but it is my job to check it out. He thinks the horse might be stabled in this barn."

"Not impossible," Jordan said, sticking his yellowed white hair behind an ear. "Flock of them horsewomen took over my old barn."

John looked in the direction Jordan jabbed a finger and got a glimpse of a old barn snugged into a hillside.

"My daughter, Eugenia keeps her horses here."

"That'd be Eugenia Jordan? Commissioner of the Department of Environmental Protection?"

"Yeah. That's her. Harriet Stilton runs the barn. Her daughter helps her out now that she spends all her time taking care of her looney son." Jordan spoke through the screen door. He turned his head occasionally probably when something on the TV caught his attention.

"Where was I? Oh yeah, only worthwhile one in the lot is Mary Ellen Crawford. She cares enough to stop in and see how an old man is doing. More than I can say about Eugenia. Always too busy to find time for her old man, that one." He took the toothpick out of his mouth and sucked air between his teeth.

"She does have important work in Hartford," "Sgt. Leary offered."

"Finds time for her horses, but not her dad. But the Crawford woman always brings a desert with her. I'd be ready to sell my soul for her devil's food cake, I tell you. Her husband's a mighty lucky man having a woman like her putting dinner on the table regular-like. He's the pastor up at Christ Lutheran in Danielson. Preaches a right fired-up sermon, I tell you. Beefy man with a booming voice. Puts the fear of God in you, that's a fact."

John listened patiently. "All right with you if I take a look around the barn?"

"Be my guest. But don't go opening none of those stall doors." He wagged a finger in warning. "Those women won't give me no peace if you let a horse loose."

"Thank you Mr. Jordan. We'll be careful." Leary turned and walked back to his car.

"Let me know if something comes of it." Will Jordan called after him.

"Looks like this could be the right barn," He said when he got back in the car. "Old man said there's a group of women with horses here." He started up the squad car and drove slowly down to the barn. "His daughter keeps horses here. Eugenia Jordan." They got out, slamming their doors simultaneously.

A radio played soft music as they entered the barn. They stood in the dim aisle, letting their eyes adjust from the harsh summer sun. He located a light switch and two dangling light bulbs lit the aisle.

"This is the stall Sheila took the horse from." Daniel walked to the third one on the left. Empty. He opened the door as though the horse could be hiding in a corner. Leary looked over his shoulder and observed the stall had a thick layer of clean white shavings. The hay rack and water pail were empty.

"There are a number of horses in the barn," Sgt. Leary said as he walked down the dirt aisle, glancing over stall doors. "Could you pick out the horse?"

"He was a dark golden color."

"Sure it was a male?"

"Sheila referred to the horse as a 'he.'"

"That narrows it down to three. Can you remember what color tail the horse had?"

"You can't be serious." Daniel peered into each stall.

"We have a choice of white, black and light brown."

"Good God, John. I don't know."

The trooper opened the door to the tack room and flipped on the light. They went immediately to the wall of pictures...of a dark golden horse.

"What do you think?" Sgt. Leary asked.

"Could be." Daniel passed a hand down his face. "And the rider is a blonde, just like Sheila, but that cowboy hat gives her a totally different look."

Leary turned off the tack room lights and shut the door. They walked down the aisle one more time not sure what they looked for.

"I doubt we'll learn anymore here. I'll go see this Harriet Stilton and see what she can tell me about the owners of the three golden horses."

CHAPTER SIXTEEN

Ike put the curry comb down when he heard angry voices coming from the ring. He knew Billie was in the middle of her lesson with Ariel. Was Mary Ellen hollering at her kid again? He put the horse he had been grooming back in the stall and went to see.

Sure enough he saw Mary Ellen, but even from a distance he realized the woman wasn't yelling at Ariel. She waved her arms, bobbed her head – furious at something. As he neared, he saw Benalli place his arm around Mary Ellen's shoulder. Immediately she stopped talking and swiped at her eyes. Benalli whisked a handkerchief from his shirt pocket and handed it to her. Mary Ellen blew her nose and Ike saw her body relax.

How does he do that? Two or three words, a pat on the shoulder and Mary Ellen becomes a pussycat.

"Good job, Ariel," Ike spoke as the girl rode by on Clyde. He decided to act like he didn't hear Mary Ellen's tantrum. Ariel rode without reins, relying on her legs, voice and other body language to communicate with the horse.

"I don't understand the value of this exercise," Mary Ellen said, turning her attention to Ike. "There certainly is no real life situation where a rider would be rein-less."

"I agree," Ike said. "But look what it teaches."

"I'm looking."

"Ariel is developing excellent use of her legs to clue the horse." What a obnoxious woman. "See where Billie has her doing figure eights? Ariel is turning the horse around those pylons by leaning slightly in the direction of the turn." He pulled a pack of Camels from his shirt pocket. "And see that? She just dropped the opposite leg back and pressed it against Clyde's barrel so he made a nice rounded figure eight."

"She certainly could have accomplished that with reins."

"True." He tapped a cigarette on his hand and stuck it in his mouth, letting it hang there as he talked. "This exercise helps Ariel build better balance. In all other athletic endeavors, people freely use their arms for balance." He turned down wind to light the cigarette, took several quick puffs before turning back to Mary Ellen.

"You don't have the freedom to do that on a horse. Ariel can use her body and her legs to keep her balance, but if she resorts to holding on with her hands she will inadvertently jerk the reins and give her horse a wrong signal. That leads to frustration for the horse and Ariel."

By the time he finished, he knew Mary Ellen had grasped the theory. She even smiled when Ariel completed her last figure eight and then firmly put her heels down and sat deeply in the saddle.

"Whoa," the child commanded and smiled proudly at her mother when Clyde complied.

"Well done, Ariel." Benalli clapped, and Ike joined in.

"This is so much fun." Ariel beamed as she walked by the group on the rail on her way back to the stable. "Billie said I can ride with my hands on top of my head next week."

"I don't want you to be offended, Mr. Cherny." Mary Ellen waved the smoke from Ike's cigarette away from her face. "But Ariel looks up to you. I hope you don't smoke around her. It's a nasty habit." She trailed along behind her daughter.

"What a miserable person," Ike said to Benalli after everyone was out of hearing.

"She can be grating." Benalli removed his sunglasses and ran a pudgy hand across his eyes. "Mary Ellen had a particularly bad day."

"Let me know when she has a good day." He took the drag on his Camel. "I swear she must drink vinegar for breakfast."

"Be a little understanding. The State Police questioned her about the missing ministers."

"Mary Ellen?"

"She hasn't been very coherent, but I gather a minister told the police that a mad woman on a horse shot at him and chased him into the Quinnebaug River." Benalli jiggled the sun glassed then set them back on his face. "So of course they think that woman may be involved with the other missing ministers. Somehow the trooper learned Mary Ellen rides, so I gather he thought she might be a good place to start looking for answers."

"I didn't know Mary Ellen owned a horse," Ike said.

They turned their heads at the sound of horses whinnying in the mare and foal pasture.

"*Merda* Ike. That better not be loose horses again."

Ike quickly saw that a foal had wandered away from its dam and raced about, yelling its head off.

"Take it easy, Mr. Benalli. It's just a foal that lost track of his mom."

"Good thing. Getting back to Mary Ellen, she rides a friend's horse occasionally. I agree with you that she is caustic. I'm not blind. I see the signs of abuse on both mother and daughter. So logic says Rev. Crawford would be the minister Mary Ellen would like to kill, not those other poor devils...ah, clergymen."

Benalli's cell phone jangled.

"You know the horse she rides is at the same barn where Eugenia keeps her horses," he said as he fished his phone out of his pants' pocket. "None of my business, but I think you ought to take it slow with Eugenia. We don't need another Lisa on the farm. I need to take this call,"

Ike knew he was dismissed. He made his way back to the stable in a daze. It disturbed him to think that Ariel's mother- the wife of a minister – was a suspect in the missing clergymen thing. He'd been to that barn. There had to be at least ten horses. Why Mary Ellen and not one of the other horse owners–like Eugenia? It sure sounded like Benalli thought something wasn't right with Eugenia.

Kurwa! Eugenia told him a minister abused her and killed her sister. A sour taste rose in his throat.

"Knock it off," he upbraided himself as he walked back

to the stable. Having a horse in the same barn didn't make Eugenia a suspect. But hating clergymen did.

Billie snugged up the girth on Annie's saddle as Ike walked onto the stable floor.

"You hear the latest in the clergyman saga?" she asked, making sure the curb chain on the mare's bridle lay flat.

He nodded. "What do you think?"

"It's not hard to picture Mary Ellen chasing someone with a gun." She swabbed the horse's neck with the special glycerine-iodine mixture used to spot reduce Annie's neck.

He reached for the box of plastic wrap and covered the horse's neck with several foot-wide layers. Next he covered everything with a neoprene wrap, gently pulling Annie's ears through the holes on top.

"Price of being beautiful," He spoke to his mare, stroking her neck. "Can't risk letting your neck pile on flab." He released her from the cross ties and picked up the reins. Billie held the stirrup, to keep the saddle from slipping while Ike mounted the mare and settled in the saddle.

"Visitor." Ike spoke softly as he saw a man silhouetted at the stable entrance. "Hey Jake," he said, recognizing the horse trainer. He stepped off Annie and handed the reins back to Billie. "What brings you to Crowne Stable?" He met Jake Paggette half way down the brick aisle and shook hands.

"Luke said if I was ever near-by I should stop in and see this special mare you're working." Tall, lean, with curly black hair and thick black glasses, Jake was one of New England's most popular trainers. In his hands horses became multiple champions. "This looks like the horse Luke raved about." Jake walked toward Annie; giving her the once over.

"That's Aristooke Annie."

"That a fact?" Jake cocked his head scrutinizing the mare more closely. "Never saw such quality come from that Aristooke farm. "No, sir, never did. Her sire can't be Aristooke Barney B."

"Papers say he is. And with DNA on every foal..."

"Been my experience folks will try anything if the stakes are high enough."

"I was about to work her. Care to see her go?" Annie

pawed, bored at standing still so long. "Don't think you've met Billie." He took the reins from Billie and place his left foot in the stirrup. Billie held the saddle steady from the other side. "Great assistant," He smiled down at his assistant as he settled in the saddle.

"Billie this is Jake Paggette. He's made more champions than anyone I know." He pressed his legs against Annie's sides and moved off into the afternoon sunlight.

"I've had a few," Jake squared up his shoulders and nodded in agreement. "Yes sir, there's been quite a few."

"Honor to meet you, Mr. Paggette," she said. "I think you'll enjoying watching Annie work." She picked up a cracker whip and darted out of the barn to her spot on the hill beside the ring.

Ike never sat a horse that sensed she had an audience like Annie. Real high-stepping show girl! Reins threaded through his fingers held shoulder high, he headed the mare into the ring. The mare stepped lightly and blew softly through her large nostrils. By the time she rounded the far turn Annie spotted Billie on the hillside, making the whip pop like firecrackers.

He felt Annie raise her tail and glanced at their shadow created by the afternoon sun and saw the mare trotted with her forearm way above level.

"Got one that can beat this, Mr. Paggette," he spoke quietly. That's when Billie shook the plastic milk jug filled with pebbles as she scampered across the hill.

If Annie could talk, he knew her response to Billie's antics would be, "What fun!" The mare spiked her tail straight up and paraded down the straight away.

He pulled her down to a show walk, kept her collected with head held high. As they came out of the next corner, he asked for a canter and Annie picked it up effortlessly.

Quit while you're ahead, he told himself. He brought the mare back to a show walk and headed out the ring gate.

"Well done," Jake admitted when everyone returned to the stable floor. "Talented mare. Yes sir, talented mare."

"We're partial to her around here." He slipped from the saddle and reached for a halter. "So what brings you to the neighborhood?"

"Delivered a horse to U Conn. One of my owners- you probably know him–Becker?"

"Sure. He owns that good stake horse." He took Annie's bridle off and slipped it up his arm while he buckled the halter on.

"Right. Hilltop Redman. Should be my star at Oklahoma." Jake leaned against a stall. "Anyway, Becker donated a gelding to U Conn. I just delivered it. The students have a good polo team and this horse might fit in well. Back to your mare," Jake pulled a pack of gum from his shirt pocket and offered Ike one.

"No, thanks," Ike picked up towels and threw one to Billie.

"That mare would fit right in Becker's breeding program. Miss?" Jake offered gum to Billie.

"Sure." Billie took the gum. "But Annie's not..."

"Annie's still a junior horse," Ike frowned at Billie and shook his head. He'd do the talking. "Just coming into her own. If she continues to improve, Aristooke Annie's going to worth a lot of money."

"Wasn't suggesting you give her away." Jake stuck the gum in his mouth. "Course there'd be something in it for you, too."

"Thanks for your offer, Jake. The mare's not for sale."

"Hmmm." Jake pushed himself away from the wall and stroked Annie's neck. "Keep it in mind." He held out his hand to Ike. "Good luck with her." They shook hands and Jake Paggette walked out of the stable.

"If you sell Annie," Billie threatened, hands on hips, glaring at Ike, "I'm going with her."

"Don't worry about that. Annie's a keeper."

"I don't like that man," Billie said. She picked up a pail of warm soapy water and washed the neck sweat mixture off Annie's neck. "He thinks Annie might not be sired by a Morgan."

"I've got the papers that say she's purebred."

CHAPTER SEVENTEEN

"Harriet Stilton?"

"What the hell do you want?" A slim woman with grizzled black hair, a mean down-turned mouth and the prettiest round blue eyes Sgt. John Leary had ever seen, stood on the other side of the wooden screen door.

"Just a few questions about the horses in the stable you rent from William Jordan." Experience had taught Leary that the more hostile the greeting, the more likely he had knocked on the right door.

"You got something against horses?"

"No, ma'am." This wasn't going to be easy. "I just wondered who owned all the horses in the barn. If one got loose..."

"That's a crime? You going to send my horse off to jail, too? For jay walking?" Harriet laughed raucously, slapping her thigh. "Wouldn't that be a crock?"

"Ma," a voice from inside cried out. "I got to pee."

Leary watched Harriet's face as she struggled to make a decision.

"You might as well come in. Yeah." Leary saw her warming up to the notion. "Come see what your brother state troopers did to my son. Bastards. Every one of you."

Leary removed his Stetson and stepped inside the dim house. He followed the woman into the living room where a grossly overweight man slumped in a lounge chair. Lank black hair hung in his eyes. Harriet pulled a rag from the waistband of her polyester pants and ran it over his face. Leary watched as she cupped his face in her hands, making him look at her.

"Pull the handle, Peter," she said.

He smiled and saliva ran down his chin.

"Peter." She gently shook his big head, looking directly into his eyes.

The man finally did as he was told and the lounge chair folded and then the rear pushed forward, helping the man get to his feet. He towered over Harriet.

"No, Ma!" Peter screamed, pointing a finger at Leary. "I won't go," he sobbed. The front of his khakis pants turned brown followed by a trickle of something dripping on the wood floor.

"Shit." Harriet glared at Leary.

She thinks I caused this, Leary thought, trying not to recoil at the mixture of urine and garlic and unwashed bodies.

Peter tried to shuffle away, but Harriet Stilton grabbed hold of his tee shirt. The man flailed his arms as though swimming upstream. Leary instinctively moved to assist.

"Stay away," she said and he backed off. He watched as she pushed and dragged the man to a couch placed next to a fireplace. She hooked her leg behind him and at the same time pushed on his chest. Peter dropped to the couch. With practiced motions, she laid him flat.

"Please, Ma, don't send me away." Peter pleaded, tears mixed with snots and ran down the sides of his face into his ears.

She grabbed a syringe off the mantel and plunged it into his arm.

"Please Ma, no. I'm a good boy."

She picked up his arm where it fell off the couch when the medicine put him to sleep. She stroked it several times before laying it across the immense belly.

"Get the picture of how much you're liked around here?" She cleaned up her son's face.

"I had no idea, ma'am."

"Come over here," she commanded. Leary followed her to a wall next to the dining room table.

"This is Peter. Before you bastards sent him to jail for something he didn't do."

He stared at the wall of pictures of Peter–in football uniform. Peter–dressed in safety orange standing in deep snow, grinning for the camera while he held up the head of the four-point buck. Peter–in a bow tie and dinner jacket placing a wrist corsage on a pretty girl in a strapless pink gown.

"Handsome," he said, studying the confident smiling black-haired boy. He looked a little closer. Blue eyes under thick black brows. Same as his mom's.

He stared at a picture of little-boy-Peter holding hands with his mirror image wearing a frilly dress and with the same thick black hair reaching her shoulders. Peter has a twin, Leary thought.

And one more picture; the one of most interest to Leary. He studied a picture of Peter on a horse...a dark gold horse... holding up a blue ribbon, smiling underneath a cowboy hat.

"You know what this says?" Harriet tapped her finger on a framed letter. He moved away from the horse picture and read that Peter Stilton was granted a full scholarship to U Conn.

"You sons of bitches made sure my son didn't get to be a fucking college graduate."

"Peter rode horses?" He hoped he could get Harriet back on track. He moved back to stand in front the picture of the dark gold horse.

"Didn't just ride. Peter was a champion."

"Is that the horse you have in the barn."

"Something wrong with our horse?" He turned to see a slim, feminine version of Peter walking into the house. A really feminine version. He assumed it was the same little black haired girl holding hands with Peter in the picture.

"Sgt. John Leary," he said.

"Paula Stilton." She said. Her blue eyes wide and watchful.

"Keep your damn hands off her," Harriet said.

"Ma." Paula scolded her mother and smiled apologetically at Leary.

"I'm trying to locate the owners of the golden horses stabled at William Jordan's farm." Leary turned his back to Harriet and spoke quietly to Paula. Pretty lame excuse to stop by, he thought. Hoped she didn't question it.

"*Golden* horses?" The young woman laughed.

Leary noted the high-pitched nervousness in the harsh

laugh.

"Guess you're not into horses. Horse colors are sorrel, bay, palomino–words like that."

"Those golden horses, whatever they're called, caught my eye." He fudged, not ready to give the real reason he stopped by. "They looked valuable and I thought I should know who owned them in case they got loose."

"There's three." She counted them off on her fingers. "Goldy is my brother's Palomino–blond with a white mane and tail. Eugenia Jordan's horse is a buckskin–that's gold with a black mane and tail. And then there's the old sorrel with a mane and tail the same color as his body. The summer sun bleaches him to gold. He's one of Eugenia rescue horses."

"Does anyone ride your brother's horse?" Leary watched Paula's mouth clamp shut before she looked away.

"Oh, Ma," Paula said, as though she didn't hear Leary's question. "Don't start. It's only two o'clock."

Leary followed Paula's gaze and saw Harriet sitting at the kitchen table pouring some kind of alcohol in a glass.

"I'll do as I damn please. Only time I have to myself is when Peter's out."

"What happened to your brother?" He'd have to get back to who might ride the golden horses later. Paula stared at Leary. He thought she was either going to cry or strike out at him.

"You really don't know?" she finally asked.

He shook his head. He knew. It was public record. But it didn't hurt to hear the family's version.

"Stop talking behind my back." Harriet swirled the alcohol in a glass of ice. "You going to talk about Peter, say it to my face."

Paula joined her mother at the red enameled table. He followed, pulled out a chair and set his Stetson on the table.

"Get that filthy thing off my table." Harriet glared at Leary.

He set it on the floor.

Paula spread her hands out in front of her and studied her nails. She swallowed hard and spoke: "Peter's a registered sex offender."

"Goddamn minister to hell." Harriet put the glass to her mouth and took several big swallows.

"Two months before he would have graduated from high school," Paula began, "Peter was sent to prison for raping and killing a girl."

"Of course they found her DNA in his car–they'd been dating since sophomore year." Harriet's voice brimmed with venom. "The conniving attorney found witnesses willing to say they saw Peter and Sophie fighting that afternoon." Harriet drained her glass and filled it till the vodka spilled over the rim. "Do I have to spell it out for you?"

"What's that, ma'am?"

"How the other prisoners treated eighteen-year-old Peter. I'd be glad to tell you."

"Ma." Paula laid her hand on her mother's arm.

"Sodomized. Tortured. Every day."

"Ma." Paula's face turned a splotchy red. "Peter finally lost his mind."

"And then the truth came out." Harriet raised a hand, pointing it at the ceiling. "After they ruined him. A well respected man of God who was about to die, confessed to everything." Harriet rested her head on her hands. "Said," her words slurred after several cups of vodka, "he had to come forward and tell the truth before he died. If there is a God, that man's in the deepest most painful hell."

Leary watched Paula take the vodka bottle and hide it behind the toaster.

"You have my sympathy, ma'am." Leary picked his Stetson up off the floor and stood. He saw Paula would like him to leave.

"Please don't judge mom too harshly." She followed him out the door, closing it softly behind her. "These have been terrible times. She used to love managing the barn, riding and talking horse with everyone. Once she started to drink she forgot to feed the horses, so I took over."

"I understand. Does anyone ride your brother's horse?" He watched a dozen thoughts flash across her eyes before answering.

"I do occasionally. Sometime after work Goldy and I wander through the state forest especially when there is a full moon to light the way. It's a whole different world by moonlight."

He had to stop staring at her vivid blue eyes framed with black lashes. He found her very attractive.

"And there are times Ma takes him for a ride at night if I'm home to look after Peter. That horse seems to look out after her if she's been hitting the vodka. It's the only time she comes home smiling."

"Do you remember the last time your Mom went for a ride?" Harriet Stilton certainly had motive. Violent, embedded hate. And she rode a golden horse. Paula had the same reasons to hate clergymen and she was noticeably on edge when he questioned the golden horses.

"Last week, I think," Paula scrunched her face up trying to remember. "I remember her saying it was almost like daylight with the moon just about full."

Paula looked nervously over her shoulder at the closed door. "Ma would freak out if she knew I let a minister's wife ride Peter's horse. Mary Ellen Crawford comes by to ride once in awhile. Her husband is a minister in Danielson." Paula stroked her arched nose.

Suspect number three, Leary thought.

"We don't take kindly to preachers in this family, Sergeant. But even though she is a minister's wife, Mary Ellen doesn't think much of them either. I'm pretty sure that holier-than-thou husband of hers beats on her. Escaping for an occasional trail ride is about the only pleasant thing she has to do. She can't let her hair down among the parishioners.

"Thank you for your time." Leary settled his Stetson on his head. "If you think of anything else, you can reach me at these numbers." He handed her a business card and headed for his car.

CHAPTER EIGHTEEN

With the World Championships in Oklahoma barely two weeks away, Billie and Ike spent hours packing the horse van. Show harnesses and Ike's saddle, bitting rigs, spare bits and bridles, liniments and leg wraps, light weight sheets and warm winter blankets. Plus all the gear to set up a fancy tack room with the new green canvas drapes, plus tables, chairs; even a cot for a quick nap in the tack room. Hay and buckets–buckets for drinking water, wash water and grain.

"All this for two horses," Billie said, releasing her hair from a scrunchie and raking it with her fingers. "How do stables that bring ten or more horses do it?"

"I don't see whips checked off yet," Ike said.

"You can check off saddle and harness whips. They're packed." She looked over his shoulder at the clipboard holding two pages of items that needed to be packed. I'll get a cracker whip now." she hurried to the tack room, binding her hair back up as she walked. How was she going to run Crowne Stables without Ike? What would it be like not to even see Ike for three weeks? Maybe it will be a good time to wean myself of him while he is gone. I'm never going to get him to notice me. I could pull all the stops out and make a special bloody-steak dinner that he enjoys. At least I can count on him to sit up and take notice of that.

#

Where has the summer gone, Ike thought, waiting for Billie to return to the van. More to the point, are my horses up to this? Sure like not to fall on my ass at my first Grand National.

He worked conscientiously all summer on sweating

Annie's neck till it was as lean and flexible as her conformation allowed. He tried various scenarios to determine how Annie should spend the fifteen minutes before a class. Attention to the tiniest detail made the difference between the tri-color ribbon and an also-shown.

But leaving Billie home to take care of the farm bothered him. Could he get along without her? She understood Annie and Warrior's needs better than him. There, he admitted it. Billie had become an intuitive horsewoman.

She was pretty good at the "woman" part, too. If he could just keep his eyes and mind off her and give himself fully up to the horses, he would reach his goals. Then he could thumb his nose at Benalli and pursue Billie. As long as Luke hadn't taken over by then. And, there was Eugenia to consider although his gut told him something wasn't quite right there.

He noticed Mrs. Benalli making her way to the stable pulling a garden cart of flower pots. The handy man followed behind with another cart filled with corn stalks tied with big green and gold bows.

"Let me do this for you, Mrs. Benalli." He took the cart from her.

"Hello, Ike," Gloria smiled. "Agosto tells me the stables go to great lengths to decorate their tack rooms." She fussed at the white urns with tightly budded golden chrysanthemums. "I thought these might help. If you water them along the way, they'll reach full bloom during the show."

"They're beautiful," he said. Just what I need, he kept to himself. Flowers to water. But he couldn't say no with Gloria so pleased with her offering.

"I thought the corn stalks would be a nice touch, with it being October."

"I'm sure they'll fit in." And they don't need watering, he thought, watching Gloria walk back down the hill.

"Here comes Eugenia," Billie said. "Are we finished with packing for today?"

"Yes. Can you bring out Joker? She's here to watch him go." He watched Eugenia park her Ford Expedition and walked toward him. He never tired of watching her walk. She took long strides for a woman, yet her hips swayed so enticingly. Hardly gave a man a chance to enjoy watching her beautiful large boobs.

"You look so good," he said reaching for her hand and pulled her along to the shadows of the stable. Gently he pushed her against the wall and pressed his body against hers.

"I brought you a present," she said when he released her.

"You sure did!"

"No, silly, a real present," She giggled like a school girl and held out a small box wrapped in silver paper.

"It's not my birthday."

"Just something to remember me by."

"Remember you..." his gut churned. "Where are you going?" It's true, he thought, she's been.... No, I will not believe this woman is capable of killing."

"I'm not going anywhere," she laughed. "Have you forgotten something called the World Championships?"

"But I will return," he reached out and stroked her face. "Let's see what you got me." He ripped off the paper and opened the box to see a silver Zippo lighter engraved with a rearing horse.

"World class trainers should have a lighter that makes a statement," she said.

Snapping the top shut, he turned it over in his hands. "To my champion, Love, Eugenia," he read the inscription.

"How much longer to you want. Joker and me to wait?" Billie's angry voice broke the spell.

#

Joker stood on the cross ties when Ike and Eugenia walked down the brick aisle. Ike hung back and watched as the colt recognized the woman who always brought him a treat. He arched his neck and took a step forward.

"How you doing, boy?" She smiled and offered him a chunk of carrot. "Feels good to be wanted," she said, "even though I know it's the carrot he wants, not the delivery girl."

He picked up the pair of thirty-foot long lines from the

tack hook and attached the moving pulleys to either side of the bit. Taking hold of the stationery snaps at one end of each long line, he secured them to rings on each side of the bitting rig.

"If you're all set, I got to get ready for my lessons," Billie said.

"We're good."

"Does Ariel come for a lesson today?" Eugenia asked.

"No." Billie snapped back.

Kurwa! He needed to talk to Billie about her attitude around Eugenia. He kept his eyes on the colt, guiding him to the far corner of the ring. He cracked the whip once, and Joker immediately picked up a trot.

At first Joker resisted authority and tried to toss his head in the air but the long lines running through the pulleys encouraged the colt to keep his head arched and his nose dropped. Next he tried to twist his body to the side in order to get away from the pressure on the bit, but the long lines ran the length of his body and kept him in a straight line.

He noticed Benalli join Eugenia at ringside. He picked up on his boss's anger by the way Benalli's head bobbed.

I want to hear this, he thought and discreetly guided his horse closer to where they stood. Benalli picked his head up, stopped talking and handed Eugenia what looked like an envelope. Without another word he turned and walked off. He saw her fold the envelope several times and stuff it in her jeans.

What the hell is going on, he wondered. Joker immediately sensed Ike's attention wandering and made a lunge for the open gate, nearly pulling him off his feet. The web long lines caught in the gate, jerking the bit in the horse's mouth. The horse wheeled at the pain, wrapping the long lines around his legs. Trapped, Joker stood trembling, waiting to be rescued.

"How can I help?" Eugenia called out.

He shook his head, unwilling to break communications again with the horse. After a moment, he dropped the long lines and walked up to the colt. Cautiously, he untangled the horse, picked up the lines, and drove him back into the ring.

Before long, Joker stopped and changed directions smoothly, bending around a line of pylons at his trainer's direction. Ike made the decision to quit on a positive note.

"Long lining is tricky," she said on their way back to the barn.

"It's not as easy as it looks." He drove the horse onto the stable floor. "Can you hand me a halter?"

She took one off the tack hook while he removed the blinker hood and bridle.

"Your colt learned a lot today." He secured the horse on the cross ties and hung up the harness all- the-while trying to come up with a way to question Eugenia. He pulled a couple of towels off the bar and handed one to her.

"I know...no watchers." She laughed.

Damn, he never tired of her laugh. It wasn't squeaky and grating, but soft and womanly, full of the joy of simply being around horses.

"I think he'll be ready to hook for the first time shortly after the World Champions." He rubbed the horse's sweaty face.

"Before winter sets in. Does that mean he'll be ready to pull a sleigh this winter?"

"Probably."

"With bells?" She stopped toweling her horse and laid a hand on Ike's arm. "What's eating at you?"

"Eugenia, you've got to tell me." He moved away and put his towel back on the rack. "Tell me if I'm wrong, but I think we have something going here." He ran a hand across his hair. "Perhaps Lisa made me paranoid, but I think I deserve to understand."

"Understand?"

"Don't interrupt, this isn't easy." It pleased him that Joker stood between them. He didn't want to be tempted to pull her into his arms.

"I've been putting two and two together and I don't like how it's adding up. First," he counted up on his fingers. "Harlan freaked when he saw you and Benalli together and then practically turned inside out trying to deny that seeing you bothered him. Second, there's no doubt in my mind I witnessed hostility in Benalli's body language just now. Third, today was the fourth time I saw Benalli hand you an envelope." He watched her hand go to her jean's pocket.

"Tell me to go to hell, if you want and I'll find you a good horse trainer to finish up Joker. Don't get me wrong. The sex has been great, but I thought we had a lot more going here. Don't keep me in the dark."

Eugenia turned her back on him and hung her towel up.

Kurwa! He studied the rigid set to her shoulders. She's dumping me. He snapped a lead shank to Joker's halter and led the horse back to his stall. He almost hoped she'd be gone when he returned. But no, there she stood waiting for him, twisting a ring around her finger.

"You do deserve to know."

"Let's talk."

"Is Billie apt to come back? I don't think she likes having me around."

"She's finishing up a lesson," Ike glanced at his watch. "We can talk in the tack room." He held the door for her, being careful their bodies did not touch.

"Some years back," Eugenia began, sinking into a canvas director's chair. "Benalli offered me a share in what he'd save in tipping fees if I'd adjust the weigh slips on his toxic waste trucks."

Ike stood in the middle of the room; legs spread, arms folded over his chest. "Go on."

"I was new to the job. Put up with a lot of crap from the old boys who laughed at me. So damn sure a woman would fall on her face as Commissioner of the Department of Environmental Protection." She tucked her legs under her and folded her hands on her lap. "I knew it was wrong. But I loved the feeling of control it gave me over a man like Benalli."

"You accepted kick-backs from Benalli?" He yanked the Camels out of his shirt pocket, realized he couldn't smoke in the tack room and threw the pack on the desk.

"Not really." She twirled a lock of blond hair around a finger. "I never took any money. My stipulation was he had to send a $500 donation to the Environmental Research Education at U Conn for every weigh slip I....altered."

"You're a State Commissioner for chrissake." What

a conniving bitch. With the body of an angel. Maybe devil in disguise.

"I only changed the weigh slips on loads of contaminated soil taken from leaking underground gas and oil tanks. He assured me he'd bury it at the back of his farm. Mix it well with manure and lime."

"That doesn't make it any less against the law." So that's what Harlan is up to at night. And why he's fearful for his life.

"Keep whipping me all you want, Ike." She stood up and shook a finger at him, "but U Conn uses the money to develop better detection and clean-up methods for the really serious toxic waste. Connecticut's Department of Environmental Protection will be more advanced than any other state by the time I leave office."

"Playing a little Robin Hood with toxic waste? If you're not taking money, what's in the envelopes Benalli give you?"

"Receipts for those donations." She jammed a hand in her pocket and pulled out an envelop. "Here." She flung her hand out, shaking the receipt at him.

He snatched it from her, quickly saw it was exactly what she said and handed it back. He grabbed his Camels from the desk, pulled one out and shoved it in his mouth, letting it hang there.

"Ike..." she moved toward him.

He threw up his hands as a barrier. Leave me alone, he thought. "It's a good thing I'm leaving for the World Championships soon. I'll have lots of time to think."

"I wish you hadn't pushed me into telling." She took another step toward him.

"You'd keep going the way we are...were and not tell me?" He folded his arms in front of him. Get away from me, he thought, sickened by her admission. "We'll talk when I get back from Oklahoma. It's obvious now what had Harlan upset. He's actually concerned for his life."

"Don't get carried away. No one's going to kill Harlan."

"Not what he thinks." He walked out of the tack room letting the door slam after him. He hurried toward the lesson barn, hoping she would go away. He found Billie sweeping the floor.

"You got a horse I can ride, Miss?"

"Depends," Billie teased. "Ever been on a horse, Mister? Seriously, what's up? You have another go around with Benalli."

"No." He closed his eyes and pinched the bridge of his nose. "Eugenia told me something very disturbing. How about you and I saddle up a couple of these nags and go for a ride."

"Really? That'd be fun. Who do you want to ride?"

"You choose. One that's not going to fight with me."

She led a rangy black mare out of stall and handed the lead shank to him. "Meet Sugar. She likes everyone."

He nodded, ran a brush across her coat and saddled up. He didn't want to talk and was thankful Billy understood.

"All set?" He swung in the saddle and waited while she mounted before he urged his horse out the back door. He picked up a narrow woods trail that meandered across the back of the farm where it bordered the state forest. The horses walked along eagerly, obviously pleased they didn't have to balance another beginner around and around in circles in the ring.

The trail brought them to a rise above the gravel pit.

"Let's look around." He reined in Sugar and stepped down, taking the single rein over the mare's head and tying it to a sapling.

"What are we looking for?" She tied her horse to a near-by tree.

"Darned if I know." He walked toward the padlocked gate and rattled the chain. The lock held fast. He paced in front of the six-foot chain-link fence. He turned to watch Billie rustling through the underbrush. What's she up to?

When she was almost out of sight, he saw her stop in front of a large tree and put her hands on hips. She reached out and ran her hands along the bark. She turned around, huge smile on her face and hurried toward him, waving something in her hand.

"Bet one of these fit," she said, handing him a key ring with several padlock-type keys.

"How'd you know where to look?" He took the keys from her, squeezing her hand. "You a red-haired Indian or something?"

"Harlan told me. It's how he keeps the spare key to your house. You need a tree with loose bark. He said the shagbark hickory is best. There's a big one alongside the path between the stable and your house."

The padlock opened easily, and he pulled the gate across the stony gravel just wide enough for them to walk through.

"What do you hope to find?"

"I really don't know." He walked along slowly, kicking gravel and small stones as he went. Even though Eugenia just confessed to him, the image of the blond-hair woman curled up on his couch eating Oreos just didn't come across as a woman who would misuse her position as Commissioner. And, a voice whispered, if she'd do that, wouldn't she be capable of killing those ministers, too?

Billie picked up a shovel leaning against the fence and poked it here and there in the ground.

"I learned today that Benalli is burying toxic waste here."

"Geeze, Ike. Thanks for telling me." She tossed her shovel to the ground and ran out the gate, with her hand held over her nose. "Are we all going to get cancer? What about the horses? Will the mares have three-eared colts or something gross?"

He laughed. "Don't go twisting your panties in a knot. It's not stuff from the atomic energy plant."

"How do you know?"

"I know. You think I'd walk in here if there was any chance of it? Eu...I have on good authority that it's just soil contaminated with gas from leaking underground tanks."

"You were going to say 'Eugenia,' weren't you? She told you, didn't she? That's why she and Benny have all those whispered conversations. Underground tanks might be just the beginning." Billie moved cautiously back inside the fence. "Like people who start with marijuana and end up fooling around with crack. They're making money out of dumping toxic waste here, aren't they?"

"Yeah."

"Benny's not dumb. He surely isn't doing this without some major gain. Whatever he makes now he'd probably at least triple with radioactive waste from the Millstone atomic plant. I know he transports that stuff. Think of all he'd save if he didn't have to cart it way out west."

He listened to Billie in fascination. He had no idea she ever thought about anything other than horses. And she made a good observation. He had to admit he liked her slant of playing up Benalli as the bad guy. Not his Eugenia.

CHAPTER NINETEEN

Finally get-away-day. In a moonless pre-dawn Billie helped Ike load Warrior and Annie in their new van. The horses were backed into their stalls, cross ties snapped and chest bars fastened. She adjusted nylon nets stuffed with hay and tried to keep from crying. She didn't want to be left alone on the farm with Ike half way across the country with lots of pretty girls. Eugenia was enough of a problem for her. Together they pushed the ramp back in place and shut the doors.

"Good luck, Horse Trainer." Harlan stepped down from the cab where he had started the big engine.

"Still can't get use to that thing," Ike flinched when the tattooed snake circling Harlan's arm squirmed as they shook hands. "Watch your back, Har."

"I hear you," Harlan nodded.

"Take care of yourself," Billie flung her arms around Ike. "I'll have the weanlings halter-broke by the time you get back." She backed off and swiped at her nose. Thank God he was taking Warrior with him. She didn't think she could face three weeks alone with that rank stallion.

"Thanks for seeing me off, guys." Ike climbed into the driver's seat.

He slammed the door. Warrior let out a shrill whiney.

"That's a long trip for one driver," Harlan raised his cowboy hat and smoothed down his hair.

"Eighteen hundred miles," Billie said as she watched the van purr down the drive. "He planned three layovers."

"How come you're not going?"

"Someone's got to take care of the thirty horses on the farm," Billie said as they walked shoulder-to-shoulder back to the tack room.

"Yeah, but even I can see Ike depends upon you being at his elbow. You don't want him taking up with some pretty thing in Oklahoma." He plunked into a chair and crossed one jeaned leg over the other.

"I don't need that right now, Har." She picked up a napkin and blew her nose. "I'm no more to Ike than a loyal dog. He never *really* looks at me."

"That's not been my observation."

"Besides," Billie continued, ignoring Harlan's remarks, "I've got a good lesson program going. I'd miss that extra income." She poured two cups of coffee, spooning sugar into hers.

"I thought Benalli gave you all the spending money you need."

"Cut it out, Harlan. I am grateful Benalli gave me this great job. Doesn't mean I want to make a career out of showing my appreciation."

"What's so great about being Ike's errand girl?"

"I'm *not* an errand girl." At least that's what I tell myself after hours of currying horses and mucking stalls. She pushed out her chin and recited the mantra that kept her going every day: "I learn how to train colts and run a farm." She sat in a chair, holding the cup between her two hands. "Ike really knows horses. He's teaching me to use psychology, not brute force."

"He can't be easy to work with." Harlan got up and looked out the window.

"That's the truth. But you have to realize where it comes from. There's no way that we're stronger than these Morgans. They weigh up to twelve hundred pounds."

"And you weigh what? A hundred and ten?" He leaned back against the door jamb.

She didn't rise to the bait, simply picked up where she left off. "So, you have to be smarter than horses. Control their minds to the point that they're ready to put their lives in your hands." She sipped her coffee, made a face and got up for more sugar.

"Takes an alpha personality to come across as the leader of the herd," she said. "Means you have to make all the

decisions, not just some. In my opinion that's why horse trainers have such lousy personalities. No compromising." She finished stirring in the sugar and turned to face Harlan. "That's probably what happened to Lisa."

"You're right about that. She didn't much like being second fiddle to a horse." Harlan moved off the wall and set his mug on the counter. "So, with Lisa out of the way, you should be making some progress with Ike. I see him looking at you."

"You're not looking too well or you'd see it's Eugenia that he's been fixating on." Billie drank her coffee. "Maybe he doesn't like redheads. He's never asked me out. You're his roommate. What's the word in the bachelor digs?"

"The word is Ike ought to cool it with Eugenia. Well, I'm off for some shut-eye." He passed a hand over his hair and settled his cowboy hat low over his forehead. "You need help with anything around here with Ike gone, just give me a jingle."

"Thanks. It's good to know you're here." she wished she could get Harlan talking about what really went on behind the chain link fence, but every time she tried to get him talking he brushed her off. Maybe she should have him over for dinner some night before he went to work. She made a mean lasagne. Get a six pack of his favorite beer.

CHAPTER TWENTY

Following a deer trail, Lisa picked her way around stones and over tree roots. One hand held a flashlight, the other a plastic grocery bag of apples, each one injected with a deadly herbicide. She loved this special time between night and dawn when nocturnal animals had settled down after a night's hunting and the earliest-to-rise birds still tucked their heads under their wings.

Ever since Benalli ran her off the farm, she walked this trail, mostly to thumb her nose at him. It brought her up behind the stable and gave her the opportunity to cause undetected damage. Like feeding the horse that Ike was so in love with the poisoned apples. Made the dumb horse sick for a week.

"Never saw that kind of concern in Ike's eyes for me," she groused. All the time the horse was sick, she remembered, either Ike or his "assistant"...trollop if she ever saw one ...stayed with the horse, taking her for a walk if she tried to lay down. She never got the chance to feed her another bag of apples.

But these apples should do the trick. She hoped she wasn't too late. Ike may have left for Oklahoma by now. Christ, it was all that man was capable of talking about. Well, if that fancy horse was gone, she wouldn't let the apples go to waste. Had to be some other horse that would enjoy her treat. Then maybe they'd fire Billie for letting a horse die on her watch.

Lisa didn't understand how that red-headed whore still lived. After everything she heard Ike say about the stallion, Lisa thought it was a sure thing the horse would trample the girl locked in his stall–maybe try to rape her, she smiled, wondering if horses ever tried that with people. Serve her right.

She heard Harlan and his bulldozer long before she

walked up. She usually just stayed in the shadows when the deer trail took her past the gravel pits. She had no issues with Harlan. But recently it occurred to her Benalli might be conducting something illegal behind the chain-link fence. Why else would Harlan work at night? She'd love to go to the police with something juicy on Benalli. Having big bucks didn't give him the right to treat her like dirt.

She pushed her way into a clump of Mountain Laurel, sat on the ground like a Girl Scout around a campfire and settled down for "surveillance." She tested the word softly. Just like she watched on TV.

Not the most exciting way she ever spent a night. At least in the relative cool of night, the blood-sucking deer flies were not the problem they were during hot, sticky days. She watched as Harlan dug deep holes then pulled different...dirt, she thought... into the hole he just dug. Sometimes she caught the scent of ripe manure and reasoned he must be burying the huge amounts of the stuff they hauled daily out the stalls.

Nothing wrong with creating compost. She noted that at times Harlan pulled dirt from different piles into the holes he dug. But this dirt smelled like gas. She squinted and saw it had things in it. Rocks, she thought. Then, when she heard the bulldozer blade scrape metal she guessed it was man-made junk.

Quickly Lisa deducted that Nutmeg Environmental must be burying toxic waste. "Damn," she spoke out loud, "why didn't I bring a camera!" She pulled herself up on her knees and peered into the dark, trying to identify some object she could use against Benalli. She clamped a hand over her opened mouth to keep from screaming. God is good, she thought, watching Harlan dump dirt over a body. A human body.

#

"That's when I saw the body," Lisa told Sgt. John Leary. "A naked corpse."

Leary studied the pretty woman dressed in tank top and shorts. Her heavy brown hair was pulled back off her sweaty face and trailed half way down her back. Lisa Danzig sat on the edge of the padded metal chair on the other side of his gunmetal gray desk.

He listened, took a few notes on a fresh yellow pad. The woman's gleeful attitude at finding a bulldozer burying a body was unsettling. Acted like she brought him the most wonderful present.

"You certain you saw a body? It must have been dark in the woods."

"On my mother's grave, Sargent." She made the sign of the cross.

"And you saw all this on Agosto Benalli's farm?"

"Yes, Sargent." She pulled her hair over her shoulder and picked at the snarls.

"It is a horse farm, Ms. Danzig."

"Your point?"

"Do you think it could have been the body of a horse?"

"You think I'm some imbecile that doesn't know a horse from a man?"

"Accusing anyone of burying a body is a serious accusation." He sat back in his chair, studying the woman's eyes, alight with joy. At finding a corpse? Sick.

"Ms. Danzig, my records indicate the Sheriff served you with a restraining order to never set foot on Agosto Benalli's property." The woman's far-out story didn't ring true. What was she doing in the woods in the middle of the night? He suspected she concocted a tale to get back at Benalli. "I have to question your motive."

"I told you I accidentally came across the body when I was walking my dog in the state forest."

"After dark?"

"Yes. Is that a crime?"

"As a matter of fact, Ms. Danzig, it is. The state forest closes at sundown."

"You don't believe me," She jumped up. "I wonder if the 'Hartford Courant' will feel the same way."

"Allow me to do my job before you lose your mind. I don't believe you'd like to add slander to your wrap sheet."

"Isn't it your job to arrest Benalli?" She demanded as she paced the small office.

"My job, Ms. Danzig, is to investigate the validity of your accusation. I need to remind you that you're behind the eight ball here."

"Me? Is it a crime to for a citizen to step forward and report a body?" She spun around and slammed her hands on his desk glaring down at him. "Most likely a murdered body?"

"Violating a restraining order and trespassing in the state forest after dark are crimes." He stood up and looked down at her. "Nobody saw you this time, but I will arrest you if you step on Benalli's farm. I cannot not do my job."

"How dare you! I know what I saw and if you'd get off your damn ass you'd see it, too." Lisa glared at him, tapping her sneakered toe on the floor. She opened her mouth as though to speak, clamped it shut, snatched her purse off the chair and left.

#

Later that day Leary drove the squad car west out of Tillingly toward the state forest that bordered Agosto Benalli's farm. His Stetson, binoculars and a book of maps to Connecticut's state parks and forests lay on the seat beside him.

Dropping back to 10 mph, he turned off the town road onto a well-maintained gravel road that wound through the woods.

Cresting a hill about a mile into the forest, Leary found a spot where the road widened sufficiently for him to pull his car off the road. He picked up the binoculars, locked the Ford and headed east.

Okay, he said to himself, let's see what has Lisa Danzig so excited. He pushed his way through the wiry Mountain Laurel, stumbled over rocks and squished through soggy areas. In minutes sweat stained his spotless uniform. He battled the vicious biting deer flies that flew in his face. He finally snapped a beech tree twig, swishing it to keep the voracious blood suckers at bay.

He stopped for a moment. Was that heavy machinery he

heard? He changed direction to follow the sound. Before long he caught glimpses of shiny metal through the thicket. He climbed a rise and raised the binoculars.

The deer flies swarmed over him, feasting wherever his skin was exposed. In desperation he jammed small tree branches down the neck of his shirt which brought limited relief. Quickly adjusting the binoculars he observed the scene below.

A backhoe dug into a gravel bank, twisted its bucket and dumped its load into a waiting truck. Nothing unusual about that--as long as Benalli had a permit to extract gravel. He jotted down the truck's license plate number.

Shortly after the loaded dump truck left, he heard another truck lumber toward the gravel pit obviously carrying a heavy load. He raised his binoculars and read Nutmeg Environmental on the door. Toxic waste? He checked for the placard required on all Hazmat trucks and added the information to his notes. Gravel pit permits were one thing, but toxic waste dumping permit? Unlikely so close to the state forest trails and with no visible warnings posted. He would check with the Department of Environmental Protection.

The bulldozer Lisa Danzig talked about sat idle within a chain-link fence enclosure. Scanning the area with the binoculars, he caught sight of something white on the ground. A plastic grocery bag. Not wanting to be seen, Leary moved cautiously toward it. He broke a small branch from a maple tree, tore off the leaves and slipped in through the bag handles. Apples. Flies fed on a bag full of sweet apples.

CHAPTER TWENTY-ONE

Early October mist hung in the valleys as the horse van crept down the twisting country roads leading to the interstate.

The road made a sharp turn and wove through the dense forest of Beaver Brook State Park. Gripping the wheel, he concentrated fully upon giving his horses a smooth ride. He had never handled anything larger than a pick-up truck hauling a two-horse trailer. The power of the truck intimidated him.

Eventually Crowne Stable's green horse van eased onto I-84. Destination: Oklahoma State Fairgrounds. Purpose: to come home with World Championships for Crowne Stable...with horses shown and trained by Ike Cherny.

He leaned back and, one at a time, wiped his sweaty palms on his jeans. He eased the big engine up to 65mph. "Doesn't that beat all," Ike spoke softly, taken with how the rig responded like a sports car. But you've never driven one of those sports cars either, he cautioned himself. Couldn't risk any mistakes with Aristooke Annie and Imperial Warrior onboard. He shoved in the dashboard cigarette lighter and patted the seat trying to locate his Camels.

Life is good, he smiled, taking enjoyment in a long drag, slowly releasing the smoke through his mouth. With the morning fog gone, the sky was brilliant blue. The foliage; crisp golds and reds.

He turned on the XM, radio to a pure country station. He found the strong beat lively and chuckled over the tales of love's ups and downs. Wouldn't a songwriter have a field day with his choice in women? Sure hoped he had more talent in picking out a good horse, or this trip might be a disaster.

With each passing hour, Ike felt more comfortable driving the powerful van. He turned off the radio and called

Harlan's cell phone. Wanted to ask what the square knob on the
dash was for. Only after it rang a half dozen times, did he realize
Harlan was probably sleeping, he hung up and his thoughts
turned immediately to the horses, going over for the uph-teenth
time their chances of coming home a champion.

#

Ike and Billie had worked conscientiously all summer
on sweating Annie's neck till it was as lean and flexible as her
conformation allowed as current trends demanded performing
horses carried their heads perpendicular to the ground. During
the same time, Ike observed and analyzed Annie's attitude after
a work-out. He tried various scenarios to determine how Annie
should spend the fifteen minutes before a class. Attention to the
tiniest detail made the difference between the tri-color ribbon
and an also-shown.
By enhancing the mare's innate presence and motion, he
was counting on the judges overlooking her less...slightly less...
than perfect head set. How was he going to get along without
Billie?
He wished he could just let himself go with his attraction
to Billie. But there were just too many pieces to the equation.
Would it piss off Benalli and cost him his job? Would it ruin
their professional relationship? They had become a perfect team
watching each other's back and really getting horses trained.
And, he had to consider his record with women over the past
year. Lisa. Eugenia. He couldn't picture Billie as having a
thoroughly rotten side like those two. However, when it came
to women, his judgement had not been the best.This is way too
much thinking for now. He turned on the radio. and surfed for a
talk show.

#

Flashing caution lights and orange signs alerted Ike the
traffic would be cut to one lane. He slowed the van and gave his
full concentration to the tricky lane switching. Both lanes of the

interstate were closed. Traffic used the breakdown lane.

He noted the left tank nudged empty, so he followed Harlan's instructions and switched to the full right tank. Keeping the horse van centered between the jersey barriers and the forty foot cliff just beyond the guard rail took his full attention.

"*Kurwa!*" The big engine stuttered. How could he take his eyes off the road long enough to scanned the dials lightening up the dashboard? He heard his horses catch their balance when the van jerked to a stop. Now he saw the fuel gage. Empty.

How can that be? Did I let it get too close to empty before switching? He repeatedly flipped the switch. The right tank was full when he left Crowne Stables.

The horses snuffling, and moving about, came over the intercom.

And then the horns blew– drivers annoyed with the van blocking the road. It started with a few light taps and soon crescendoed into angry blasts from motorists, already annoyed at the construction delay, and now brought to a complete standstill.

He heard the knock on the truck window before he saw the burly, bearded man standing there.

"Hey, man. What's the problem?"

"Out of gas...not really...I don't think. Can't seem to change tanks." He saw the scorn on the man's face.

"Let me take a look," the man said, opening the door, waiting impatiently for Ike to get out. He pulled the hand brake and stepped down. The man slid behind the wheel and didn't waste any time poking around.

"What did On Star say?'

"I forgot the truck had On Star. This is my first..."

"I can see that." He pushed the On Star button and the operator came on immediately.

"Yeah, this guy's going to need a tow but not at all sure how you'll get here with only one lane and no drive-able median."

"Don't leave your vehicle, sir. We'll alert the state troopers of the situation and let you know when help is on its way."

"Thanks." He offered to shake the man's hand as he stepped down from the truck. "I'm Ike Cherny."

"Derek Chambers. Where you headed?"

"Oklahoma City...Fair Grounds."

"I'm going back to my truck. Should be able to catch a few hours sleep."

"Hours?"

"Take a look behind you."

For as far as he could see cars and trucks were at a stand still.

"My guess is the line goes back a good ten miles. No way for a tow truck to reach you."

They'll have to back down from the next exit. That's about 30 miles from here."

Sure enough, On Star called back saying the very same thing, plus reported traffic was backed up an estimated 65 miles. Might as well check the horses, he thought.

"How you doing, my champions?" Annie took a few sips of the water he offered, but Warrior shoved his head up to his eyes in the pail of water, then blew it all over him.

He swiped at the water and hay. "I guess I should take it as a good omen that you're enjoying this trip," he said to the horse and went about adjusting the hay nets so the horses could easily reach their hay.

He left the van door open and stretched out on the truck seat. He thought about calling Billie to pass the time, but knew she'd tell Benalli of his predicament and he didn't want Benalli to know that, hardly a day out, and he was blocking interstate traffic for sixty-five miles. And this time of night Harlan would be working his dozer. Soon he gave himself up to the soothing sounds of horses chewing their hay.

The strident noise of a big truck's back up alarm jarred him awake. A quarter mile in front of the Crown Stable's rig, a big tow truck was backing up the west bound lane of the interstate.

"Sure glad to see you," he said to the man as he climbed down from his rig."It's not switching tanks."

Silently the tow truck driver poked around, thumped on

the right fifty gallon tank agreeing with Ike that it was full.

A state trooper arrived. "Who's the driver of this rig?" Ike produced his driver's license, silently thanking Harlan for insisting he get his Class 2 license. He offered the trooper his notebook of insurance and truck specifics and the documents to prove the horses could travel over state lines.

Satisfied everything was in order, the trooper handed the folder back to Ike and walked over to the tow truck driver.

"Hello, Jack. What's going on?" The trooper turned his attention to the tow truck driver.

"No idea. It won't switch over to the full tank, even though it looks right. We'll have to tow it in."

"Let's not waste any time."

"Wait a minute," Ike said. "You can't tow this rig, the horses....."

"Look behind you mister," Derek bellied up to Ike, eyes glaring, "you've messed up the lives of hundreds of people and you're worried about a couple of nags?"

"It's more important," Ike fought to keep his cool, "not to traumatize these horses than worrying if you're late for dinner." Fists clenched at his side, he hoped Derek would make a move so he could belt him.

"Step back," the trooper intervened. Go back to your truck. And Mr. Cherny, we will tow your rig. The traffic has to move.

"But."

"There is no alternative. You have to accept it."

He agonized over how the horses would ride.

"Relax. I've towed a lot of horse vans. Your horses will travel no differently than if you were driving up a steep hill."

"It's vital they arrive fresh. We're going to the World Championships."

"This ride won't cause any stress. But have you thought about what you're going to do with them once we're at the garage?"

"What do you mean?"

"It's nine o'clock at night. No mechanic will look at your rig till tomorrow morning. You may be spending a day or more in Dolyston. You need to find a barn, right?"

CHAPTER TWENTY-TWO

What luck! Through the horse owner directory, Ike located White Gate, a Morgan farm about twenty miles from where he was stranded at Jackson's Garage in Dolyston, just over the border in eastern Ohio.

"Yeah, I guess we have room," the female voice said. "Our horses left for Oklahoma this morning. I'll get there...when I can."

Now he busied himself unloading the gear needed for a night: pails, grain, blankets. He'd buy a bale of hay from White Gate. Jack was noncommittal about fixing the problem, but he hoped to be back on the road by at least noon the next day.

Before long a truck towing a two-horse pulled up.

"You're a life saver," he said.

The girl slid off the seat and headed for the back of the horse trailer.

"Let's get your horses loaded." She stood on tip toe to reach the tail gate latches and let the ramp bang to the pavement. "You have two, right?"

He nodded. Isn't much for small talk. Annie walked right in. He cross tied her while the girl fastened the rump bar to keep the horse from backing out.

When he led Warrior to the ramp, he trumpeted loudly at the sight of Annie's rump. He couldn't get the stallion's mind into walking up the ramp. He wacked his neck with the stud stick. When the stallion stopped for a second, he quickly led him up the ramp. The girl closed right in securing the rump bar.

The trailer shook as Warrior struck out with his front legs, trying to touch Annie. He crowded against the divider that separated the two horses and bellowed again. Ike snatched the lead shank over his nose and whomped the stallion again. He felt the girl at his elbow, shortening cross ties while Ike kept Warrior's head facing away from the mare he so desperately wanted to get at. They worked together to create a barrier by tying a hay net between the horses.

Satisfied the horse's head was tied as far away from the mare as possible yet loose enough for the stallion to keep his balance as they drove down the road, Ike slipped off the lead shank and the two of them backed out of the handler's small escape door.

Warrior roared his frustration at being kept away from the mare he wanted. The trailer rocked as he threw his weight from one side to the other.

"Let's get moving," he said. Quickly they piled his gear in the back of the truck and headed out of the parking lot.

"Thanks for your help. You're good in a tough spot." He looked across at the girl sitting tall so she could see over the truck's steering wheel. "Not everyone would be so willing to get right in the face of a bellowing stallion."

"Thanks."

This is a chatty one. "I'm Ike Cherny," he tried again.

"Pippa," she said, keeping her eyes on the road. "I'm Pippa Medford." And that was the end of the conversation till they reached White Gates.

Pippa eased the truck and trailer through the white gates.

Quite a spread, he thought looking out at miles of white fencing marching across open, level pastures. In the moonlight he saw a dozen red barns. Pippa slowed to a stop at one of the barns, hopped off the seat and stood at the tailgate.

"Let's get the mare off first," he said, opening the escape door.

#

Warrior's piercing cries jolted Ike awake. He jumped up from the cot Pippa had set out for him in the tack room. Pulling on pants and stuffing bare feet into sneakers, he hurried out of the tack room and down the aisle to the stallion's stall.

Covered with sweat, Warrior paced his stall, alternating between kicking the stall walls and peering out the window. Barely fifty feet away the stallion watched someone working a horse in the ring. He snorted and shook his head.

Ike picked up the stud stick and lead shank before entering the stall.

"You listen to me," he growled, making sure the horse saw the stud stick. Warrior hesitated, stopped pacing and stood while he fastened the lead shank to his halter. The stallion's sides heaved and sweat dripped off his belly.

He led the fractious horse to the wash stall and hosed off every trace of sweat. He poured a glug of Absorbine liniment in a wash pail, added hot water, and sponged it on the horse. He inhaled the strong liniment vapors which, for Ike, were symbolic for a well cared for horse. Warrior relaxed under his administrations. Using a sweat scrape, he squeegeed off the excess water.

"Let's see if we can find a quiet place to dry off," He patted the horse's neck. Together they walked into the sunny morning and Ike led the horse to a grassy area next to the empty indoor arena. Warrior quickly dropped his head and grazed.

"Hey," Pippa said, walking up to Ike.

"Good morning." Ike looked down at the mite of a girl standing before him. In the commotion of getting the horses settled last night, he hadn't gotten a good look at his rescuer. Why, she's pony size. And to think she had no qualms walking right up to Warrior. He wanted to study that delicate heart-shaped face with a trace of golden freckles on a small upturned nose, but the look in her brown eyes offered no invitation to do so. Bits of hay stuck in her light brown hair that was severely pulled into a rubber band-tied pony tail. Her small mouth with a full lower lip didn't have a trace of lipstick.

"The garage called," she said. "They tried your cell. Guess you had it turned off."

"Dead battery. My truck ready?"

"Didn't say. You can use the phone in my trailer when you're finished." She pointed to a small house trailer set off from the red barns. Turning away from Ike, she fidgeted with her pony tail. "I can make you some eggs and coffee."

"Great! I'll be right over."

He watched her stride purposefully toward her trailer, her hair swinging across very straight shoulders.

He sat at her table, a cup of coffee in front of him, mulling over what Jack said about his truck. She set out fried eggs and toast for both of them.

"What's the word on your rig?"

"Not good. Seems as though the gas tanks would switch for one mechanic, but not the other."

"Don't like my coffee?"

"I'm sure it's fine," he smiled and hastily brought the cup to his lips. "It looks like I have to waste another day. Not that the company hasn't been great," he added when he detected hurt in her eyes. "But it's cutting into the days I planned on resting the horses once we got to Oklahoma." *Kurwa*, he thought, noting the irritation in Pippa's brown eyes as she sat down across from him. What did I say wrong now?

"Wish I could be there," she said. He stopped eating to watch her drink coffee. She set the mug back on the table and chewed on her lip.

"They must be counting on you running things here. Looks like you have a lot of horses." Billie had taught Ike a very clear lesson about breakfast etiquette last spring: When a girl makes you breakfast, you make conversation.

"Yeah. But they're mostly all in pasture. Don't require much care. But they did say I could keep working Tippy."

"Mmm," he nodded, his mouth full of jam and toast. Mention of the horse softened her angry look.

"Maybe you'd like to see him go." She looked at Ike straight on, her eyes actually brightening.

"Sure," he said. If working a horse brought a light to those pretty eyes, he could watch.

"They never let me show a horse." she said, her small hands cradling the coffee mug. "Just use me to start them on account of I'm not too heavy for the colts to carry." She ran a finger through the little puddles of spilled coffee. "I thought maybe if I could get him working right smart they let me show him next year. All I need is one chance to show them."

That's exactly what I'm hoping to accomplish at Oklahoma with Annie, Ike thought, drawn to the goal he and Pippa shared: show the world we have what it takes.

But he could see this little slip of a girl had a problem. She was plain–almost unkempt. No one would risk putting out big bucks to have a nondescript mite of a girl show their expensive horse. Most of the big time horse owners want their riders to be....well, show girls. Pippa was definitely not one of those.

He realized one of the reasons Benalli singled him out was because he made a priority of being properly turned out for any occasion.

"Let's see that horse work." He pushed his chair back and brought his dishes to the sink. And for the first time, he saw Pippa smile.

"Then, if it's all right with you, maybe I can get my horses out for a little exercise today."

"Sure. I'll give you a hand."

#

"You have Tippy going good," he said as they unsaddled the gelding together. "Keep working on those canter departures and you'll be hard to beat." The girl really has talent, he thought. He ran the stirrup irons up the leathers, lifted the saddle off Tippy's back and hung it on a tack hook. She rubbed the horse's face with a towel and then ran it over the length of his body. He sat down on a tack trunk and watched her lead the gelding back to his stall.

"We need to talk," he said when she returned. "Come sit with me." He moved to the edge of the trunk and patted a place for her to sit.

"I'm good right here," she said. He saw her back stiffen. Her eyes widened.

"Pippa, you're really good with a horse," he tried to soften his innate commanding horse trainer's voice. "Would you be offended if I told what it's really going to take to get to show good horses?"

"I can handle it."

He definitely had her interest, but she kept her distance. He took a steading breathe and began.

"You have to look at the whole picture here."

"I've been to a lot of shows. I see what it takes to win."

"Yes, winning is a very big part for those who are wealthy enough to keep show horses with a trainer. But that's only the tip of the iceberg. Think about the people who keep horses here at White Gate. What kind of cars do they drive."

"Well the Berghorns drive a Mercedes and the Wilsons come either in a Jaguar or Cadillac Escalade."

"Right. Most people who drive these kind of cars are looking to announce to the world they have the money to belong to the "in" crowd. Chances are they live in mansions and brag about their imported marble bathrooms and mahogany kitchens they don't cook in. Stuff like that."

"So?"

"You're not a jockey racing to get to the finish line first. You're part of the whole picture." He saw Pippa give him her full attention. "Of course they want to win. But then they want a glitzy picture of their show horse, ridden by a show girl to place in the horse magazines and frame for their desk." He watched Pippa smooth her hair and tuck her tee shirt into her jeans.

"And when you're running around the show grounds, they like to point you out as their rider. Make-up, hair style, good clothes make the whole picture."

"Doesn't talent count for anything?"

"Talent is the first prerequisite. It is assumed. But how many plain, big- going horses do you know that became horse champions?"

Pippa hooked her thumbs in her jeans and looked away from Ike.

"I'll bet you clean up pretty good." He smiled gently. "You just have to spend some time on yourself. I hope you're not mad at me."

She shook her head.

"Then how's about you help me with my horses?"

"Okay." He didn't like the defeat in her voice. He hoped he hadn't come on too strong for this girl. But she deserved knowing.

\#

The sun glinted off a silver twelve-horse semi as it inched its way down the drive.

"That must be Paggette Training Stable," Pippa said to Ike as he rode by where she stood on the rail. "They're laying over, too." The rig pulled to stop as they neared the ring. Soon a big Mercedes turned in the white gates, spewing up a dust tail, and came to a stop alongside of the six-horse. Two men got out, talked briefly to the driver of the semi then walked over to Pippa.

"Who's that?" the smaller man asked pointing to Ike.

"Ike Cherny and Aristooke Annie," she said. "Four year old."

"Never heard of them."

"You will."

\#

Annie puffed up at the new arrivals, and Ike couldn't resist showing off a bit. He recognized the tall lean man as Jake Paggette, the horse trainer who stopped by Crowne Stable a while back. Wanted to buy Annie. Rumor had it Paggette had fifty horses in his public training stable. He supposed the other man was the owner of some of the horses on the van.

He crossed the ring and tapped her ever so lightly with his saddle whip. By the time she passed those on the rail, she trotted lightly above level, head high, her expressive eyes glowing with the joy of being alive.

When he looked again, they had left the rail and started up the vehicles. He saw Pippa, her pony tail swinging, leading the way to the stable.

After putting Annie up and looking in on Warrior, he went looking for Pippa. He didn't see her about the farm and then noticed her pickup was not in its usual spot. Good a time as any for a nap, he decided. He wondered where Pippa went. Hope she wasn't avoiding him.

#

"Cherny, here," he spoke into his cell phone, rubbing sleep out of his eyes. Jackson's Garage with nothing good to report.

"Look," he said. "I can't afford to waste another day in Doylston. I'll be in first thing in the morning to pick it up. "Can't afford time to fix a radio, I'll work around it till I get back to Connecticut." He snapped the phone shut, pulled on his shoes and went to feed the horses.

Opening the tack room door, he saw Paggette and the man he was traveling with talking softly in front of Annie's stall. Let's hear what they have to say, he thought, stepping back in the tack room, easing the door shut.

He remembered Pippa had given Annie one of the double-sized foaling stalls with a camera and he had seen the monitor in the tack room. Quietly, he moved across the room and turned on the monitor, adjusting the volume. The camera was angled to see the inside of the stall, but the audio easily picked up the conversation.

"This mare has talent, all right, Mr. Becker. Yes sir...real talent." Ike recognized Paggette's voice.

"Will she be a threat to my junior mare?"

"Possibly. But I think it's safe to say we can out show her. You ever hear of Cherny? Or this Crowne Stables?"

"No."

"Doubt anyone else has either. The kid is wet behind the ears. Won't have good show ring judgement."

Ike gritted his teeth and punched a fist into his hand. "We'll see about that."

"Another thing," he heard Paggette say. "The quality is so deep in Oklahoma that the way that mare carries her head could keep her out of the ribbons."

Grudgingly he had to give Paggette credit for picking up

on Annie's Achilles heel.

"What do you mean?"

" I noticed when she was trotting her best, she had a tendency to let her nose out..not as perpendicular as most winners. The mare's just not hinged well behind her ears."

"Don't know as I've ever seen a mare trot so high."

"That's a fact. But I don't think that alone will be enough to cut it in Oklahoma."

"I'd like to own her." Becker said. Breed her to Highlander Commander."

"Not a chance," Ike spoke softly to the monitor.

"I'd like to see you own her. I tried to buy her for you a while back. She'd be a good choice to breed to your Sargent Denmark," Paggette said. "He's pretty darn good at refining a throat latch so she can carry her head more perpendicular."

"My American Saddlebred? Why the colt would just be another illegal half-bred. Look, Jake, I'm game for an occasional experiment, but I'm not willing to corrupt my entire breeding herd."

Ike fiddled with the volume, but the men must be walking away. He couldn't hear all they said. But it wasn't a new idea. People often tossed around the possibility of adding a little Saddlebred blood to their Morgan breeding program. Thought it would add a little length of neck that would be more flexible. But the operative word here is "talked." The foal resulting from a Morgan/Saddlebred cross would not be allowed in the Morgan Horse Registry.

Suppose, he thought, passing a hand down his face, someone has figured a way to alter the DNA report before it reached the Registry Office? Suppose Luke is right and Annie is sired by the Saddlehorse in Maine?

CHAPTER TWENTY-THREE

Ike turned at the sound of high heels clicking down the aisle. A woman in a skirt that danced about her knees was silhouetted in the stable door. He stood enjoying the sight as she walked purposefully toward him. Oh my God, he thought, a big grin splitting his face. It's Pippa.

"Hey." She smiled, not quite looking at him straight on.

"I'll say, 'hey.' You look great."

"Honest?"

"Let's walk out side where I can get a good look." Did this stern little thing just giggle? He took her calloused hand and led her out of the stable, where he admired her new hairdo and clothes. He raised their hands above her head and twirled her as if square dancing in slow motion. The last few rays of the afternoon sun caste her in a rosy glow as she pirouetted. She actually looked sweet. This event could not go unheralded.

"Would you let me take the lady to dinner?"

"Don't make fun, Ike. You said this get-up is important if I want to get noticed."

"It is. And believe me, you will be noticed. Now, come on. Let me take you someplace nice."

"I guess we could go to Bentley's. It's where they usually take the big- bucks horse buyers. But it's probably way too expensive."

"Let me worry about that." Benalli had given him a credit card and expected Ike to be seen at the best places. "Give me a minute to clean up."

He watched her fairly skip away before heading to wash up in the tack room sink. He dug around in his duffle for a clean shirt. "What the hell," he spoke softly to himself, dug a little deeper and found a tie.

#

A linen tablecloth stretched between them. Silverware gleamed in candlelight. He studied Pippa's transformation. Her newly cropped hair feathered forward framing her oval face. He watched her touch the back of her neck as though searching for the lost pony tail. It looked like her light brown hair had some of that streaking, or whatever it was called, because golden highlights came alive in the candlelight. Looked like smooth, sweet caramel.

"Sir, would you care to choose a wine?" He hadn't noticed the waiter standing by his elbow.

She raised her eyes, her expression like a skittish filly prepared to run. Her dark eyes with their long curled lashes captivated him.

"Yes," he spoke to the waiter but smiled assurance to Pippa. "How about a bottle of Beaujolais?" He chose a light and slightly fruity wine he thought she might enjoy.

"I'm not much of a wine drinker," she said after the waiter left. "I usually get beer when the gang at White Gate goes out."

"Well then, we'll consider this part of stepping into the new era of Pippa Medford. Let's see what Bentley's is offering tonight." He handed her one of the leather-bound menus and almost chuckled out loud when she completely disappeared behind the large opened book.

"I don't understand what half these words mean," She confessed after a few minutes.

"Why don't you tell me what you like, and then I can choose for you."

"Would you?" she closed the menu. "But nothing that's messy to eat."

Rolls and butter arrived while they talked, and the waiter offered Ike a taste of the wine. He nodded his approval and two long-stemmed glasses were filled.

After placing their order, he raised his wine glass. "It's

not medicine," he said, seeing her hesitate. She drew her lower lip between her teeth, then raised her glass.

"To the next world class showman...woman. May her way with horses and her breathtaking presence take her to the top." The crystal glasses clinked approval.

"Not bad," she said after braving a sip. "How'd you learn all this stuff? You told me you're a farm boy."

"Yes, but with a mom who had grand plans for her son." Salads were placed on the gold-rimmed service plates as he spoke. "She went to great lengths to make sure I could move comfortably in all circles. She saved every penny to send me to private school."

"It must have been nice having someone care how you grew up."

"I'm only beginning to realize that. But as a kid it meant she watched me like a hawk. Always use the outside utensil first." He spoke softly, seeing her struggle with deciding which fork to use for the salad.

"Thanks," she said. "So what did your mom think when you decided to be a horse trainer?"

"She died before I chose the horse industry." He told the whole story. How his parents came over from Poland after World War II. Even admitted his real name, Dwight Chernokowski.

"Mom admired General Eisenhower's role in the war, and he became President the day she arrived in the States. Thank God everyone referred to President Eisenhower as Ike. I'd much rather be Ike than Dwight."

"And the winner is Dwight Chernokowski!" She mimicked a horse show announcer. "I can see why you changed it." She giggled. "Ike Cherny is an in-charge man."

He liked this woman. Couldn't remember ever talking so freely about his life. Not sure if it was the wine or not wanting the evening across from a pretty woman to end. He reached out and touched her hand where it lay on the table. She smiled then quickly picked up her coffee cup.

So different from Eugenia. Even though he felt alive being around her, the woman's controlling, manipulating

tendencies raised warning signs. If he'd stop allowing his
testosterone lead him around he'd walk away from Eugenia.
Maybe that's why he understood Warrior so well. Testosterone
was their driving force. He passed his napkin over his face to
mask his chuckle.

On the drive home, he told her that Jackson's Garage
had called while he changed his clothes.

"They found the problem," he said. "Something so
simple as wires to the XM Radio and the extra fuel tank being
crossed. Because of the mix-up, the radio had to be on for the
tanks to switch." He went on to explain that his boss had the
radio and second fuel tank installed at the dealership. It took so
long to discover because the young mechanic who worked on
the truck kept the truck's radio on while he worked, so the tanks
always switched for him. When Jack himself finally took a look,
the older man turned off the blasting radio. Then the problem
became evident.

"I'd like to get an early start tomorrow." He glanced at
her, sitting close to the door, her small hands folded in her lap.
He drove through the white gates to the barn. "Would you drive
me to Jackson's first thing?"

"Sure. Right after I feed."

"I'm going to check the horses, then I'll walk you to your
trailer."

"You don't have to."

"I'd like to. It's only right I see the lady home." They
walked together into the barn, flipping on the aisle lights. She
sat on a tack trunk, while he pulled the hose over to his horses'
stalls, topping off their water buckets and throwing a flake a hay
into each stall.

"How's my *Lakonik* tonight," he spoke softly to Annie
as he slipped into her stall to straighten her blanket. The mare
raised her head from the hay and lightly bumped him.

"See you in the morning." He closed the door and
turned to see Pippa waiting for him, her arms hugging her body
in the chill autumn night.

"You're cold." He put his arm around her shoulders
and felt her tense. In that moment he knew he wanted to hold

her. Protect her. Make love to her. He cradled her face in his
large hands and ever so gently lowered his head to savor the full
lower lip that had tantalized him over dinner. Softly his mouth
held the kiss, afraid that she might bolt if he released her. Soon
he felt her melt into him and hesitantly return his kiss. He placed
his arms around her and held her close.

Her shyness moved him. He didn't want to overpower.
He wanted to move slowly. Savor her new femininity. But
where? He knew if they walked to her trailer, the spell would be
broken. And the cot in the tack room was just that. A cot.

The hayloft came to mind. Would she stay with him up
the stairs? He could take a woolen horse cooler to lay on the
prickly hay. Worth a try.

"Come with me." He stepped back and brought both her
hands to his lips. When she didn't object, he pulled a cooler off
the blanket rack and led her up the stairs.

He spread the cooler on a pile of loose hay and turned
to her. She looked so vulnerable, elbows cupped in her hands,
looking anywhere except at him.

"You don't have to." He offered her his hand.

"I want to." She moved into him and standing on tip
toe, stretched her arms around his neck. Smiling, he bent his
head and kissed those big brown eyes and then moved slowly to
kiss the little hollow in her throat. When he moved back up, her
lips were parted, waiting for him to settle there. He did, moving
his tongue between her teeth, tasting the traces of coffee and
wine.

His hands found the zipper on the back of her dress,
but feeling her tense, he didn't move ahead, yet held her captive
with his kissing. When it felt right, he brought the zipper down
and tugged the dress forward over her shoulders where it
slipped to the floor.

"Very nice," he admired her femininity. In the mellow
light, her saw her blush profusely. He understood no one else
had ever praised her body.

He brought her hands to his mouth, planting little kisses
all the while looking at her directly, smiling, encouraging her
to look at him. Give him permission. When she smiled back,

he guided her hands to his shirt and together they undid
the buttons. She took the initiative and pushed the shirt off
his shoulders and tugged his undershirt over his head. She
explored his chest. He closed his eyes and gave into the rising
sensations.

His eyes flew open. She actually unbuckled his belt.
Even undid the zipper. He moved and his pants fell to the floor.
He heard Pippa inhale sharply. Quickly he toed off his shoes and
stepped out of his pants.

Fearful the spell might break, he wrapped his arms
around her and drifted downward onto the sweet smelling hay.

CHAPTER TWENTY-FOUR

Eugenia stepped off the elevator onto the fourth floor in the State Office Building and walked the corridors to her office. She had replayed her last conversation with Ike again and again. Tossing and tangling alone in her sheets, she cursed having told him about her arrangement with Benalli. She wanted things like they were before.

Then anger erupted over Ike's reaction. Didn't he ever read the papers? He was so wrapped up in his little world of riding around in circles. Government and politics, particularly in Connecticut, were not some McDonald's Playland.

If he'd get off his high horse, he'd see some real good came from her arrangement. If I ever get him back, she thought, I'm sure as hell not going to make the mistake of telling him what else is buried, at Benalli's.

Why can't things be simple? She really liked this guy. First decent thing outside of Bucky that came into her life.

She paused outside the Department of Environmental Protection door and ran her fingers over the lettering, "Eugenia Jordan, Commissioner." She wished she could drag her dad away from the TV to come see it. If just once she could hear him say, "My daughter, the Commissioner." She worked hard for her fame in politics and the horse world.

She understood he missed Serena. God knows she did. The good times they had with their horses. But her father could be proud of his "other" daughter, too.

"Good morning," Brenda, her secretary said when Eugenia walked in. "Phone's been ringing." She handed Eugenia a fist full of pink message slips.

She shuffled through them, grateful to have a lot of calls to make. Perhaps she could forget Ike for a few hours. Brenda placed a manila file in her to-be-filed box. The tab read "Nutmeg Environmental." Eugenia swallowed hard.

"Something I should know about Nutmeg Environmental?" God, did that sound casual enough? Her heart thumped. Her ears rang.

"Nutmeg? It's handled." Brenda waved a manicured hand in dismissal. "Just haven't had time to put the file away." She picked her head up from the keyboard to face Eugenia. "A state trooper asked for any toxic waste dumping information we had on Nutmeg Environmental."

"Is there something about Nutmeg that raised a red flag?" She attempted to steady her shaking hand and casually picked up the file and flipped through it.

"Didn't say. Didn't ask."

Eugenia took the fax cover sheet from the file. Sent to Sgt. John Leary, Tillingly resident trooper. Badge number, Fax number. What was the state trooper on to? She placed the file folder back in the box. How could he have an inkling that Benalli dumped anything on the farm? She turned and walked toward her private office. I suppose it was possible he saw a few loaded trucks turning into Crowne Stable. But that shouldn't cause alarm. It is Nutmeg Environmental's garage.

"Commissioner?"

Eugenia turned around.

"Your messages." Brenda held up the packet of pink slips, her bracelets jingling.

Clutching her messages, she willed herself to walk away slowly. Contained herself till her office door securely shut behind her.

She fished around for the cell phone in her purse, tossed the purse aside and jabbed speed dial 6.

"It's Eugenia. Get ready for company." She told Benalli about the trooper snooping around for permits.

"You need to cool it on dumping." She faced her office window. She couldn't risk Brenda picking up a word of this conversation.

"Dammit, Benny. How the hell do I know? Maybe got tired of handing out speeding tickets." She bent her head and spoke toward the floor. "Maybe he took a drive in the country and what did he see but loaded trucks not only leaving but coming."

She tugged a strand of her hair from the French braid and twisted it around her finger.

"Yes, I know you do most of it after dark. Maybe there's a grouchy neighbor tired of hearing Harlan drowning out the crickets with his bulldozer. Have you noticed any helicopters flying over?"

She paced in a tight circle around her desk as Benalli fumed. She wished she never heard of Agosto Benalli.

"I know you did me a favor. All right. Two. But listen here, Benalli," she pointed her finger, shaking it as though Benalli stood in front of her. "This has been a two-way street. Seems you've made out pretty well on your side." She took the phone away from her ear and walked back to the window while Benalli ranted.

She never should have gotten Benalli involved with the bodies. Why didn't she bury them on her dad's farm? Time was important here. Who the hell knew how fast Resident Trooper Leary moved.

"Quit bitching. Get off your fat ass and let Harlan handle it. With the amount of manure and lime you mix in, there's no need to worry." She snapped her cell phone shut, getting satisfaction from the last word.

#

"Who the hell does that slut think she is?" Benalli snarled at his cell phone. "Someone's got to take her down a peg." He punched a speed dial number on his cell. Thinks Commissioner is another name for God."

"Billie, honey." Benalli schmoozed. "I can't get Harlan to answer his phone. Of course I know it's only ten o'clock. Yes, I heard the dozer most of the night, too."

"Sweetie, this is important. Please find him–wake him up if you have to–and have him come to my office."

#

Harlan walked right in and leaned against the door. A rumpled tee shirt hung over oil-stained jeans. His black cowboy hat sat low on his forehead.

"What's so important you sent Billie to wake me?" he rubbed a hand over thick black stubble.

"Sit down. We have a situation."

"I'm good here."

"No." Harlan said after hearing troopers could be nosing around the sand pits. "No way. My gratitude for you getting me out of jail has been paid in full."

"Glad you brought that up. A phone call and your little girl can visit you in jail. I've already bought a wood chipper. We'll start clearing and chipping that area west of the gravel bank. We'll tell anyone who asks that Crowne Stable needs more pastureland."

"Stick it up yours, Benalli. I'm not going to grind those bodies up."

"You're in this as deeply as I am. How do you explain burying them to the police?"

"Guess I'll have to face whatever is thrown at me. But I will not mutilate those bodes." The snake writhed when Harlan clenched his fists.

"*Merda*, Harlan. There can't be much of them left at this point."

"No." Harlan turned and left.

#

Funny. Joe didn't remember all the people he had taken out over the years. Always men–never women. He had strict principles. Joe pushed his way through the tangle of prickers and Bittersweet vines heading toward Harlan's truck lights in the dark night.

Just a job. If he didn't do it someone else sure as hell would. But these country assignments were the pits. Sure, the odds of being seen were slim, but he hated tramping through the woods. Always messed up a good pair of Italian nappa leather shoes.

Lightning zapped the black night and thunder cracked.

"Shit." The rain pelted the forest drenching Joe in seconds. He snapped the cover shut on his holster where it hung on his belt and pulled his soggy black tee-shirt over it. This was going to cost Benalli big time. Toxic pay.

Joe trudged toward the truck lights. Judged Harlan stood about two hundred feet away.

This time he wished he had the right to decline. Joe squinted, trying to see clearly through the rain. Not that they were best buddies or anything. But Joe thought Harlan was an OK guy. Saw to his responsibilities to his little girl. Didn't want to think who'd be looking after her.

"Ah, Joe. Guess I expected you." Harlan said. He stood alongside the dozer, illuminated in his truck's headlights, emptying out the tool box.

Joe knew his stuff. One clean shot to the head. Harlan hadn't felt a thing, he told himself. He holstered his gun, climbed in Harlan's truck and drove off.

CHAPTER TWENTY-FIVE

Ike's eyes burned. He should have pulled over and slept for a few hours but decided to tough it out and make Oklahoma City that night. He'd been trying to make up for the lost time in Ohio. Several hundred miles ago he had tired of the little stories of love's miseries on the Country Western Station. Then he switched to the strident sounds of heavy rock, but found they just gave him a headache.

He smiled every time he thought about Pippa. Hoped she looked favorably on their night in the hayloft. He suspected a lot of guys didn't give her a second look because of her apparent lack of femininity. She didn't paint her nails or douse herself in perfume. But she more than made up for the plain packaging with an honest sexuality and a delicate woman's body. Add their joint desire to make it in the horse world to the mix and, well, it was great sex.

He had been apprehensive when Pippa drove him to pick up the van the morning after. He hoped she wouldn't want to re-hash everything. Read things into it. Not that it wasn't nice. Even special.

He tried to compare the horsewoman who didn't back off when Warrior threw a testosterone fit while getting him in the horse trailer to the demur young woman uncertain– maybe even in awe of her newly recognized femininity. He hoped her guts and determination to become a show class trainer hadn't dimmed in the process.

The empty interstate stretched on. He missed the changing scenery of the New England roads. The last sign indicated 210 miles to go. He smoked the last of the Camels an hour ago. His body no longer responded to his tricks at keeping awake. He needed to take more drastic steps. He opened the window, changed the seat position and sang loudly into the night.

#

Oklahoma State Fair Grounds! His adrenalin kicked in. No chance of drifting off now. At the Grand National! He pulled the van up to the main stable door and turned off the key.

He bounced through the aisles on the balls of his feet, looking for his stall assignments, noting all the major stables with elaborate set-ups and their horses hidden behind canvas drapes. Mulched flower gardens, water fountains and entire walls of pictures displays. Directors' chairs, color coordinated with the drapes, grouped invitingly around tack rooms. He walked under pastel-colored gauze ceilings that stretched over the aisle of the big stables.

He found Crowne Stable's four stalls in the middle of an aisle in the second-to-last barn. The entire area was shrouded in twelve-foot tall drapes. Ike poked around, checking under tarps to determine which stalls were occupied by a horse. He didn't want to put Warrior in a stall next to a horse where the stallion would spend the entire time trying to get at it and would be worthless when it came time to show.

He made his decision, ripped opened the bagged shavings, spreading them out in two stalls. His remaining two stalls would be a tack room and a ready stall.

One at a time he moved his horses into their stalls. He hung water buckets and found Warrior on his hind legs trying to catch a glimpse of near-by horses. No use getting after him. He had to get it out of his system. He tossed a flake of hay to each horse, set up his cot in the tack room, pulled off his sneakers and collapsed.

He heard Warrior walking his stall, frustrated he couldn't see horses he could smell. I'll have to tie him up if he keeps pacing. He fell asleep listening to the soothing sound of Annie chewing her hay.

#

"Hey!"

Ike tried to focus on the man shaking his cot. "That your stud climbing the walls?" He rubbed his face.

"*Kurwa*!" He heard Warrior kick the wall again and again. He shoved his feet into sneakers and hurried out the tack room and stood in front of the stallion's stall. The horse had churned manure into the shavings and obviously urinated frequently, turning the fresh bedding into a stinking mess which he then rolled his sweat-soaked body in.

"We keep a barrel of warm wash water," the man offered. Ike nodded. He picked up a lead shank and stud stick and entered the stall. Warrior eyed Ike then rose on his hind feet, trying to peer over the stall divider.

"Get off that wall you bastard." He whomped him on the shoulder with the stud stick. The horse dropped to all fours and stood for him to attached the lead shank.

"Hold him and I'll wash him off." The man held a bucket of water with a sponge and sweat scrape.

"Thanks for helping." He snatched the lead shank keeping Warrior still while the man sponged off the sweat and dirty bedding ground into his coat.

"Good looking stud," the man said. "Bet he'd be a happier gelding."

"His owner would never hear of it. Banking on the horse to put his stable on the map."

"I thought he belonged to you." The man ran the sweat scrape over Warrior's body.

"Nope, I'm Ike Cherny. I train for Agosto Benalli at his Crowne Stable.

"Chet Adams." the man stepped around Warrior and reached out a wet hand to Ike. "Seems we're next door neighbors."

"Sorry to get you up in the middle of the night." He looked down at the round-faced man standing before him. "I'll tie him up so we can all get some sleep."

"That won't stop him from kicking. I can let you use a set of kicking chains"

"Worth a try."

Chet hurried away with his bucket. Ike heard him rummaging in a trunk.

"How about these?" He walked toward Ike, holding up a set of heavy chains, a good twelve inches long attached to a cuff of smaller fleece-wraps chains.

"Good." He took Warrior into his stall. "Don't you move," he growled as Chet crouched down next to the stallion's hind legs and attached them.

"I've never used kicking chains on him," he said, releasing the stallion. The two men stood in the door waiting for the horse test the chains.

Warrior kicked out, aiming to strike the stall wall. The chain whipped around, punishing the surprised stallion. He snorted then kicked out with the other hind leg. Instantly the chain delivered its punishment. Dumfounded, he shook his head, but stood quietly.

Satisfied, the two men backed out of the stall.

"Thanks again," Ike said.

"Le'ts get some sleep," Chet smiled, briefly touching him on the shoulder.

CHAPTER TWENTY-SIX

Music from a dozen radios fought for attention. Horses banged impatiently for breakfast. Outside his tack room, Ike heard hoof beats of horses going to and from early morning workouts, their metal show shoes ringing out on the cement aisle.

I'm really here, he thought, pulling on shoes and running a hand over his cropped hair. He pushed through the tack room drape, heart racing, anxious to begin the day. He measured out the morning grain adding supplements and electrolytes, topped off water buckets and hurried along to the work-out ring.

Whips cracked. Trainers whistled and barked commands. Wild-eyed horses careened around the warm-up ring, their pure energy intoxicating those who watched.

A small man stepped into this super-charged circle of people captivated with the horses psyching up for the most important show of the season. He recognized Chet, who helped him out last night, as the man elbowed himself a place on the rail, hooking his elbows on the top rail. Peering over the top, a dirt clod, shooting like a missile from a hoof, smacked him full in the face.

"Shit." He fell back from the rail and swiped at his face.

Ike turned from his spot on the rail and looked down at Chet, sputtering and spitting bloody dirt out of his mouth.

"Chet," he spoke, pulling a rumpled handkerchief from his jean's pocket and handed it to the man. "Wouldn't have minded taking that hit. Came from Jake Paggette's stallion. Maybe a little of his success would rub off on me."

"Yeah, well," Chet swabbed his swollen lip and looked at the bloodied handkerchief. "you can have this split lip."

"Let me find something in my first aid kit."

"Maybe later. Let's watch for awhile. Sometimes this is better than the real classes."

"How does Paggette find the best horses year after year?" Ike asked. "Look at that sucker trot!" The two men stood mesmerized by the red stallion. In his heart he felt Annie could hold her own with competition like this. But was he stable blind?

The horse's ears twitched nervously and foam dripped from the eight inch shank of his bit. Paggette held the thread-like reins in gloved fingers held shoulder high.

Ike pulled a pack of Camels from his shirt pocket and offered one to Chet.

"Naw," he waved them away.

Ike winced when he saw Paggette jerk his horse to a stop. "I've seen enough. Let's get some coffee."

"Hospitality might have some donuts left."

#

No more excuses, Ike chastised himself. His horses were thoroughly groomed, the stalls mucked out and Warrior, exhausted from the night's escapades, lay flat out in his stall, sound asleep.

He stood in the middle of the aisle with his gear– the flowers, harnesses, tack room fittings in a jumble.

Where to begin? He fumbled in the tool trunk, located the staple gun, picked up a heavy green canvas drape and looked around for the step ladder.

He pulled a corner of a drape with him as he climbed to the top rung of the step ladder. "I'd trade mucking ten stalls for a week for setting up one tack room." He mumbled.

"Need a hand?"

He looked down to see Chet's chubby face smiling up at him.

"Sure. I don't think it's right that trainers have to be interior decorators, too."

"There are times I'm sure that's the only reason Tim wants me around," Chet said, holding up the other end of the twelve foot canvas drape.

"You're an interior decorator?" He stapled the edge of the drape to the top of the stall.

"No. Master landscaper." Chet handed up the end of the tarp. "And you've been neglecting your flowers." He picked up the hose and began to water down the containers of Chrysanthemums Ike brought from home. "Are these all you have?"

"This is a horse show. How many flowers do I need?"

"Look around. Tim had me bring the fish pond."

"Fish pond?" From his perch on the ladder, he saw the front of Taber Training Stable's tack room. Sure enough– a fish pond, nestled in a bank of mulch and landscaped with cattails and flowers.

"Tim would be disappointed if his stable didn't win the Tack Room Award."

#

All day Ike looked forward to completing the tack room set up so he could head for the Exhibitors' Lounge, situated on the level above the ring. The ring where Morgan History was made. Everyone needed to be seen in the Lounge, especially young trainers eagerly waiting to make their mark. He climbed the stairs and pushed open the door.

It felt like his first glimpse of what Santa left on Christmas morning. A long narrow room with sweeping views of the main coliseum ring. The entire side adjacent to the ring was open, bringing the show right into the lounge.

He recognized a few faces, but didn't feel comfortable just walking up to them. Then he spotted Chet on a bar stool talking to Tim Taber. He had never met Tim, but had seen him several times today talking to Chet in front of his fish pond tack room.

He started toward them. He ought to introduce himself to Tim. They'd be neighbors for the next week. Half filled drinks sat in front of both men. As he approached he sensed the tension between the two men.

"That's the way things are, Chet." He heard Tim speak.

"You knew before you came that I couldn't take you with me everywhere I go."

"Hey, Chet," He made a quick decision to call out as he approached. "Can I buy you a drink for helping me out today?" Chet looked like a grateful stray pup when he turned his sad eyes toward Ike. Tim, on the other hand, stared at Ike with angry eyes, his mouth in a grim line. The broad-shouldered trainer turned his back to Ike and picked up his drink.

"Sure," Chet said. "Have you met Tim?"

He held out his hand forcing Tim to face him. "Hi. I guess we're neighbors for the week."

"Yeah," Tim said, ignoring Ike's offer to shake hands. "You'll have to excuse me. I'm late for a dinner engagement."

He turned to Chet. "The Bancrofts expect me to take them to Café Marquesa. I'll see you in the morning." Tim threw bills on the bar and left.

"Bad time?" Ike asked as they both watched Tim walk out of the lounge. "If I interrupted..."

"No," Chet said, "You came at exactly the right time."

"Good." He took over Tim's empty stool. "What are you drinking?" He ordered drinks and the two men sat eating nuts and pretzels. He steered the conversation to the horses he'd seen working out, waiting for Chet to relax.

"Thanks for being here," Chet finally said. "I really like Tim, but he can be so unfeeling at times. Especially at horse shows." He heaved a big sigh and wrapped his hands around his nearly finished drink. "I swear all you trainers use up every iota of patience on those damn horses then treat people like shit. He begs me to come along, but then I can't be part of his social life. Says he has to entertain the clients." Chet turned his sad blue eyes toward Ike, "So, I can stay in tack room, clean stalls, create a great tack room for the Taber Training Stable's image, but that's it."

He wasn't sure what to say, but he couldn't leave Chet hanging like that. "Can't you stay in a motel? I've seen at least four grooms with your stable that watch the horses at night."

"Sometimes I get a motel," he said. "Sometimes the horses are more company."

CHAPTER TWENTY-SEVEN

Ike kicked the bedcovers and jerked to a sitting position. His clammy tee shirt stuck to his body, and a film of sweaty gooseflesh coated his arms.

"Today," he spoke out loud in the darkened motel room, "today I show in my first Grand National class." Ike took a deep breath then slowly expelled the air through his mouth. "Today three judges will determine if I'm good enough to make the cut and qualify for the World Championship class on Saturday night."

He swung his legs over the side of the bed and headed for the bathroom. He took it as a good omen that Warrior showed before Annie. It'd give him a feel for showing in the Coliseum before he rode Annie in a class. Meant Warrior would be a guinea pig, but handsome as the stallion was, he didn't think the lazy, testosterone laden horse could turn judges' heads like his Annie.

All I have to do is keep Warrior focused today, he thought, placing a new blade in the razor. He squirted shaving cream from a can and rubbed it on his face. But keeping the young stallion listening to him– could he pull it off?

Back in the bedroom, he pulled a clean tee shirt over head and reached for a blue plaid collared shirt. That's when he noticed the telephone message light blinking for his attention. He picked up the phone, pushed buttons and thrummed his fingers on the night stand while he waited for the hotel operator.

His throat went dry. Billie had called when he was in the shower. She needed him to call immediately. "Extremely urgent," the operator intoned unemotionally. He punched the disconnect button and immediately snapped open his cell.

Kurwa! Why did these cell phones take so long to

connect? Never should have turned it off last night.

Busy! He tried a different number. Busy, too. "Come on Billie, get off the phone." He dialed the first number again– busy. He tossed the phone on the bed.

It can't be! A sour taste filled his mouth as he recalled all the times Harlan hinted Benalli was into something illegal. It couldn't hit the fan now. He patted through the jumble of clothes on the dresser, finally locating a pack of Camels. Maybe I shouldn't answer calls from Connecticut till after Annie shows. He whipped out a cigarette and shoved it in his mouth.

But suppose Harlan's gone missing? He promised Harlan to get that letter to his mom. He couldn't ignore Billie's call.

"Where the hells' my lighter?" Ike yelled, picked up clothes, tossed them on the floor, rifled through papers, knocked the two hundred page show program to the floor.

If Billie called because Benalli's in trouble, he rationalized, it didn't mean he had to quit the show. All I need is five more days.

Turning the pockets of the pants he wore last night inside out, he found the Zippo that Eugenia had given him.

He held the flame to his Camel, took a deep pull on the cigarette, shut his eyes and blew the smoke slowly out of his mouth.

He dove for his jangling cell phone. Billie, he saw from the Caller ID.

#

"Why didn't you keep your cell phone on?"

"What's wrong?" He sat on the edge of the bed.

"Something happened to Harlan."

"What makes you think that?"

I haven't seen him for days. I stopped in at your house several times a day and the same pot of something gross is on the stove. I leave notes for him that he hasn't touched. He doesn't answer his cell. And, Ike?"

"I'm here."

"Someone else is running Harlan's dozer."

"I guess it's time..."

"To come home? I hoped you'd say that."

"No, I can't do that. The show has started. And what would I do if I were there?"

"Just be here."

"Aw, Billie. This is what we've worked for all year. Would you really want me to?"

"Of course not. Annie has to be a World Champion." I'm never going to come before a horse in your life, she kept to herself. "But I don't like being here alone."

"I need you to do something important. Under the TV cabinet in my house is a small drawer. In it is a letter addressed to Harlan's mom. Can I count on you to get it to her?"

"I'll take it today." You depend on me for everything, she thought. Why not add lover to the list? "What's happening?"

"I don't know. Stay away from the gravel pit. Maybe you should go away for a few days."

"Who'd take care of the horses?"

"Is there someone who might stay with you?"

"You're my first choice."

"Now that sounds more like the redhead I know. Be careful, Billie."

#

"You look sharp," Chet reached up and adjusted Ike's tie. "That jacket does good things for your shoulders."

"I appreciate Tim letting you come in the ring and head Warrior for me."

"Doesn't own me," Chet said.

"Let's get him hooked." He picked up the left jog cart shaft and pulled the buggy toward Warrior. Chet took hold of the right side. Together they moved the jog cart into position at the back of the stallion and slipped the shafts through the holders on his harness.

"Got peppermints?" Ike asked as he hooked the trace on his side to the single tree.

"Pocket full," Chet hooked his trace and crinkled the plastic wrapped candies in his pant's pocket. Warrior heard the sound and turned his head looking for a treat.

"Give him one," Ike advised.

Chet stepped out in front of the horse, placed a hand on Warrior's bit raising his head slightly.

"Come up," he spoke to the horse. Warrior immediately took a step forward, aligning his front legs as he had been taught to pose. Chet took a step back, unwrapped a peppermint. The stallion stood, all four feet squarely line up, and stretched out his neck for the treat.

"Well, at least we've got posing down pretty good. He'll look good in the line up if you put him on his feet, give him a peppermint. That way he'll have his ears up looking for another treat when the judges pass by."

They finished buckling the rolled leather lines to the bit and secured the wrap girth around the shafts. Chet went over the horse and two-wheeled jog cart with a clean towel. Warrior's black lacquered hoofs gleamed as sharply as the patent leather trim on his harness.

Together they fluffed out the horse's full black tail. Like a bride's wedding dress train, the excess tail lay almost two feet behind the stallion. Ike picked up the tail and lay it over his arm, braiding the last six inches, and wove in a length of black shoe string. Once braided, he tied the shoe string to the bottom of the buggy, leaving it sufficiently loose to move with the horse, but short enough to avoid catching in the spokes of the bicycle wheels.

He left Chet with Warrior while he stood in front of the tack room mirror and set the gray fedora on his cropped hair. He took black leather gloves off the table and tugged them on his clammy hands as he strode back to the horse.

"Take a deep breath," Chet said, placing an arm around Ike's shoulders.

"I'm still not sure how to warm him up." He chose a six-foot driving whip and placed it in the jog cart's whip holder.

"You made that decision yesterday. Relax. Go with it."

Ike nodded. Chet stood at Warrior's head as Ike stepped

into the jog cart. Chet stepped aside and Warrior walked off like
a gentleman.

Ike and his horse joined sixteen other stallions waiting to
be called into the Pleasure Driving for Four Year Old Stallions.
Chet, and most of the other headers, stood in the middle of
the warm up ring, keeping an eye on their horses. At the end
of the class, they were responsible for keeping their charges
in an orderly line while the judges took a close look at their
conformation.

The bugle announced the class. The gate to the coliseum
opened. Drivers vied for position. Ike wanted to be last to
enter the ring. Sure, the first couple of horses could make an
impressive entrance into the empty ring. Technically those early
horses couldn't be judged until all the horses were in the ring
and the class called to order. But judges could be impressed.
First in the ring was not for Warrior who never had enough
energy for extra trips around the ring before the class came to
order.

Here we go, he thought, guiding Warrior down the
chute into the ring. Warrior hesitated at the bright lights and ring
full of horses trotting smartly in their jog carts.

"Get up in here," he flicked the whip on top of his
rump. Warrior bolted into the coliseum and picked up a good
trot when he landed.

"Class in order," the announcer called out.

He hugged the rail; drove deeply into the first corner
and slowed the horse slightly. Coming out of the corner he
cracked the whip on the inside of his flank. Warrior surged
forward, raising his handsome head and arching his neck. He
risked a glimpse at the judges.

Don't blow it, he prayed. His gloved hands held wide,
were in the hand holds.

So intent upon making a clean pass, he didn't look ahead
to the next corner where five horses and jog carts had slowed
for the corner and created a traffic jam. he jerked his horse to the
inside, narrowly missing plowing into them.

Unnerved by the incident, he floundered for a moment.

"*Kurwa!*" The third judge stood on this side of the ring,

taking it all in. He snatched the lines lightly and touched Warrior
with the whip. The stallion responded and sharpened up just as
a horse came trotting up behind him on the inside. The driver
chirped loudly as he drove by.

Startled, Warrior broke from a trot for a couple of steps
before Ike brought him back to a trot.

The class went from bad to worse. No way could your
horse break from a trot at the Grand National and have any
chance of getting in the ribbons. Well, he couldn't just leave. As
he passed the section of the rail reserved for headers, Chet called
out.

"Don't quit. Others did worse."

Ike snapped out of it. Looked around and made instant
decisions for the remaining class.

"All walk, please," the announcer said.

Warrior did this well. He willingly came back to a walk
and moved down the rail like a gentleman, ears pricked forward,
neck arched, relaxed.

"Reverse please. This is a large class, please use caution.
Reverse on the Ringmaster."

He looked for the red-coated ringmaster and found him
signaling the drivers to conduct their diagonal reverse in front
of him. He planned his approach, allowing for space between
Warrior and the horse in front.

Perfect, he thought. Then he heard the horse behind him
about to pass. The driver disparately attempted to restrict his
horse to a walk, but he jigged and jingled the bit. They came so
close it could cause a problem

Warrior lost it. He bellowed at the other stallion
impinging on his space. The stallion struck out and whipped his
tail side to side, threatening the challenger.

But the tail was tied to the jog cart! Warrior, convinced
the other stallion stepped on his tail, viciously kicked the jog
cart, his hoofs stirring the air above Ike's head. When Warrior
landed, his rear legs were straddled over the left shaft. Furious
and hurting, he took off at a gallop.

Seasoned drivers pulled their horses into the center.
Headers and horsemen on the rail leapt into the ring. Warrior

tore to the rail, mad and in pain. The jog cart slammed into the rail, smashed to pieces leaving Ike on the ground. His hands, held captive in hand holds, jerked violently before they came loose.

Free of Ike and the jog cart that cause so much pain, Warrior careened around the ring at a full-out gallop.

CHAPTER TWENTY-EIGHT

Ike slumped in the director's chair in front of his tack room. Towel-wrapped bags of ice numbed the pain in his injured hands, but the novocaine the emergency room doctor injected in his face in order to stitch the gash under his right eye was wearing off.

"He won't need kicking chains tonight, " Chet said, backing out of Warrior's stall and latched the door. "He's hurting. The vet pulled out splinters around his testicles and put sixteen stitches in his flank. Anything I can get you?" He hovered over Ike, pulling up a corner of the towel and peeking at the ice.

"A cigarette and Jack Daniels."

"You can't hold a cigarette in those hands," he placed a hand on Ike's shoulder. "but I'll get you a straw for your JD."

"How am I going to ride Annie the day after tomorrow?"

"Look," Chet pulled up a chair and sat facing him so that their knees touched. "Life doesn't always hand you the cards you'd prefer to play. I'll keep your hands iced like the doctor said. And I'll make sure you have your medication. We've got two full days to pull it off."

"Annie can't sit in her stall for two days and be ready."

"I'm not much of a rider–that what Tim keeps telling me anyway–but I can hand walk her every day. Several times a day if you think that'd be good."

"She needs daily grooming..."

"Don't you get it you dumb Polock? I'm here for you."

"What about Tim?"

"That's for me to worry about. Let's go get you that

drink."

"At the Lounge? I thought you'd bring it here."

"So you can sit and feel sorry for yourself? Come on. Everyone will want to hear about your accident. See for themselves you're still alive."

"Hear about what? That the professional trainer couldn't control his horse?"

"I can put up with a lot, but not your gloominess. I'm going."

"Chet?" Ike called out as he walked away.

"I got to take a leak."

"So?"

"I not going to yell it through the whole barn." He waited till Chet retraced his steps. "I can't zip my pants–or anything else"

Chet clapped a hand over his mouth stifling a raunchy laugh.

#

Tonight the Exhibitors Lounge had two distinct groups of people. Ike watched the smiling group standing at the bar, buying drinks for everyone. Easy to see their horses won. Ear to ear smiles, great claps on the backs, women getting hugged. Alcohol sloshed in glasses raised for toasting.

Off the in the corner farthest from the ring the other group sat at tables hunched over their drinks, those with hats wore them down over their eyes. No doubt these were the day's losers. Occasionally a burst of raucous laughter caused the losers to turn their heads toward the bar. Ike walked in the direction of the losers' tables.

"Don't you dare sit with them."

"I don't exactly feel like celebrating," he mumbled but followed Chet as he pushed his way through the revelers to reach the bar.

"Double Jack Daniels on the rocks," Chet ordered. "And a straw."

"Straw?" The bartender cocked his head.

"You heard right," Chet growled. He stepped back and made room for Ike to stand at the bar. He sidled up and eased his arms over the rail, gently laying his ice-wrapped hands on the bar. Chet leaned over and placed the JD between Ike's two hands. He pulled the paper from the straw and placed it in the glass.

"I'd like to buy you a drink." A man spoke. "I saw what happened in the ring today. Cherny, isn't it?"

"Ike Cherny," he nodded and turned to look at the man.

"Hugh Becker." The man held out his hand. "Christ, I'm sorry." He pulled it back and laid it on the bar. "Are they as bad as they look?"

"Couple of bones broken," he said. "Nothing that won't heal. You look familiar."

"We both laid over at White Gates in Ohio."

"Sure. Jake Paggette's your trainer." he nodded. "Did a nice job for you in the In-Hand Class."

"Thanks. I think that stallion's going to make Morgan history. And a lot of money for me while he's at it."

Let's just hope he's all Morgan, Ike thought, recalling the extremely long neck Becker's young stallion had. And, from the conversation he eavesdropped on back in Ohio, he learned Becker also owned Saddlebreds...and intimated they illegally mixed the blood.

"Tough break to get banged up so early on. Shame you won't be able to show."

"Ike may be down, but he's not out," Chet chimed in.

"Really?"

"Well, the stud is finished. Sixteen stitches and hurting pretty bad."

Becker clucked in sympathy.

"We're not quitting. Ike's going to ride his mare in the Park Saddle later this week." Chet patted Ike on the back.

Becker looked at Ike's hands and studied his swollen eye.

"Think you'll be ready?"

"Do my best."

"So you plan to ride the little mare I saw you work in

Ohio."

"Aristooke Annie." He stood up a little straighter.

"Nice kind of horse. Ever think of selling her, let me know." He placed his business card on the bar. "Hope you heal." Becker dropped bills on the bar and left.

"Guess I ought to go," Ike said, suddenly terribly weary. He needed more pain medication. His right eye had swollen shut. But where could he go? Sure as hell couldn't drive back to the motel.

"I'll take you back to the motel," Chet said as Ike turned to leave.

Ike spun around glaring at Chet hoping no one thought they were a couple.

"Don't look at me like that. I promise not to seduce you."

The bar room babble halted. Eyes snuck looks at them. Some over the rims of glasses, some discreetly over their shoulders. Other eyes boldly studied the two men.

Ike's face burned, his pulse thumped in his temples. "I'm leaving. Do not follow me," he growled between clenched teeth.

What do I do now, he thought, gingerly making his way back to the tack room. Here he was at the proving grounds of his chosen industry and so far he showed everyone he couldn't control his horse and his only friend was gay.

Chet's been a real friend. And right now he couldn't even use the john without him. But for him to come out and say something like that in front of everyone....

Easing himself down on a director's chair in front of Crowne Stable tack room, he looked at the flowers and corn stalks Chet had arranged for him. The new green and gold stable banner looked good. The way things played out today, he was thankful Benalli stayed home. Would not have been pleased with his trainer's performance. *I pay good money...* Benalli's familiar refrain came to mind.

He hadn't told Benalli what happened to Warrior. He'll be furious the stallion never got in the ribbons–didn't even complete a class.

"Tough class today."

"I've had better." If I hear that one more time, he gritted

his teeth at the female voice loaded with pity.

A woman, her brown hair piled on top of her head stood before him, her slim silhouette in a bright blue pantsuit. A white frilly ruffle spilled out of the jacket collar.

"Like some company?"

Not really. For once in his life, he didn't much care how pretty the woman standing in front of him was, he was not going to stand up. He nodded toward an empty director's chair.

"I saw the whole thing. You're lucky to be alive."

"So they say."

"I'm Veronica Rouseau."

"Ike Cherny. You have horses here?"

"No. I work for the American Morgan Horse Association in the Registry Department." She settled in the chair and crossed her legs. "AMHA sent me here to help out in their booth. I've enjoyed seeing all the faces behind the voices I talk to in the Vermont office."

He nodded and shifted in his chair. Go away, he thought.

"Can I get you something? Coke, coffee? How about a sandwich? Geeze that was insensitive," Veronica said looking at his broken hands. "How can you handle food?"

"Don't worry about it." His cell rang. He couldn't even answer the phone.

"Let me." Veronica stood up and reached toward his shirt pocket and the ringing cell. She flipped it open and stuck it in his hand then helped him raise his hand to his ear. He watched her stroll away, looking at the picture displays along the aisle.

"Ike," Billie said, her voice as panicky as the morning he found her locked in Warrior's stall. "The police just left. Asked a million questions about Harlan and the gravel pit. They trashed your house. What are they looking for? I'm scared."

"Take a deep breath," he said and did the same. How much more can go wrong?

"And dogs," she kept on. "Cadaver dogs roaming the gravel pit. They only bring them in to find bodies, right?"

"I think so." Jesus, Christ Almighty, he prayed. Please

don't let it be Harlan. "What does Benalli say?"

"They took him away for questioning this afternoon. I haven't seen him since. What should I do.?"

"There's nothing for you to worry about." He spoke with a confidence at odds with roiling gut. "Don't talk to anyone but the police."

"Oh, God. Do I need a lawyer?"

"Get a hold of yourself. You haven't done anything wrong."

"Wish you were here." The fright was still clear in her voice, but she sounded more like herself. "You better win. We need something good to happen."

"I'll call first thing in the morning," he assured her. He fumbled with the phone. It slipped from his injured hands and fell onto the cement floor and the battery popped out.

A flash of bright blue signaled the arrival of Veronica, who picked up the pieces.

"Good as new." She snapped the battery back in place and placed it in his shirt pocket.

Chet walked toward them. Ike watched the man take in what looked like a cozy scene with Veronica. He paused, raised his head, thrust out his chin and strode down the aisle, flashing Ike a hurt look.

With his nose in the air, he watered the horses then checked on Warrior's injuries. Ike watched him measure out the stallion's night meds, mix them with a little grain and sliced apple.

"That your groom?" Veronica asked.

"No, that's a friend," he admitted and watched her raise her eyebrows and cock her head.

"Not that kind of friend. Chet," he called. He walked over with a real attitude. He had to make amends for treating him so badly in the Lounge.

"Veronica, I'd like you to meet my friend, Chet Adams. He's here to take me back to the motel." He was gratified to see Chet smile and stand a little taller.

CHAPTER TWENTY-NINE

Sgt. John Leary eyed the woman sitting on the other side of his metal desk. He pulled a fresh yellow pad in front of him, straightened his sharp-shooter's trophy so the inscription faced the woman, and selected a pencil. He tapped his finger on the point, testing its sharpness.

"How can I help you today, Mrs. Burke?"

"Something terrible has happened to my son." The woman pulled a rumpled envelope from her vinyl purse and set it on the desk. "A young woman brought this to me yesterday. Harlan is a good son. And father. He brings me money every week since his wife died." She laid her raw-knuckled hands on the desk.

Leary pulled out several sheets of plain paper from the envelope. The letter, written in splotchy blue ink, covered the page. A number of fiercely scratched out words almost broke through the paper.

"I, Harlan Burke, of sound mind and fearing for my life, am writing this letter to be turned over to the police if something should happen to me. Seven years ago on August 8th, my wife Caroline Burke, was killed while I attempted to rob a convenience store in Hartford. The clerk pulled a gun and shot at me but missed. Instead he shot Caroline, who had no idea what I was doing. I'll never know why she followed me into the store.

The morning after I was formally charged, Agosto Benalli bought me. He told me he'd make all the charges go away if I would work for him on the farm. His only rule was 'No questions asked.' I've been operating Benalli's bulldozer ever since.

Mom, please get this letter to the police ASAP. They need to test right away because I know for a fact I've been burying loads of toxic waste in a section of the gravel pit on Benalli's farm.

Benalli owns Nutmeg Environmental Clean-Up and every so often his trucks, loaded with contaminated soil, mostly from gas station leaking tanks, dump their loads. My job has been to churn it in with the gravel and manure and store it in a certain area. I know after a while, Benalli sells that contaminated soil.

I've kept quiet all these years because I want to provide for my daughter, Jane Burke, and not have her grow up thinking her dad's a jail bird.

But a month ago all that changed. Benalli ordered me to bury a body. I don't have any idea who it is. All I know is it was a naked man wrapped in a ratty horse blanket. Have the police look to the northwest area of the pit.

I've been freaked-out ever since. Really leaning toward going to the police, but Benalli is threatening to send me to jail if I talk. I'm can't sleep trying to figure what to do. I want to be able to watch Jane grow up and maybe even get to be a grandfather but I know the right thing to do is call the cops to put Benalli away. But if I do, it sure as hell means jail for me.

And, Mom, I can never thank you enough to taking your granddaughter in. If you're reading this, chances are I'm gone. Go see Mr. Biedermeyer at the bank and he'll tell you about the investment fund I got for you and Jane."

The letter was signed by Harlan Burke. Leary turned the letter this way and that as though more information might be lurking. Lots of secrets on that horse farm. He was getting the feeling there was more going on that they hadn't begun to hear about. He brought his attention back to Mrs. Burke.

"The girl that gave it to me said Mr. Cherny asked her to bring it because he's away. Think she said Oklahoma."

"I need to keep this letter, Mrs. Burke. Leary stood up and placed the letter in the copy machine, "I'll make a copy for you."

"You going to arrest that blackmailer? My God, he's a murderer, too."

"We'll certainly investigate it. I'll turn it over to the Crime Unit Investigators today." He handed her the copy and watched as she stuffed it back in her purse. "Here's my card. If you think of anything else we should know, I'd like to hear from you." Leary kept standing, hoping Mrs. Burke would take the hint. "Thank you for coming in."

"Don't mean to keep you. Sure you got other things to do."

"Nothing more important than looking into this."

CHAPTER THIRTY

"So, you'll pick me up in the morning?" Out of habit, Ike attempted to reach for his Camels. He winced at the pain running from his crippled fingers clear to his shoulders.

"One good thing is coming out of your accident." Chet said, pulling his rental car up to Ike's motel door.

"Two days before my first saddle class at the World Championships on a horse that has never been in this ring is not the day to lecture me about smoking. This withdrawal crap is real."

"This show might end up a wash-out for you, but if you quit that filthy habit you'll add ten years to your life."

"Look, Chet. I appreciate your help. But I need a friend here, not a mother."

"Fine. When would you like your chauffeur in the morning. And do you need help undressing?

"I have all night to handle it. Probably be up anyway looking for a cigarette."

"You shouldn't be alone tonight. Let me stay with you."

Ike froze. He couldn't keep pushing his only friend away. But he just couldn't see himself spending the night with a gay man.

"Look at you," Chet said. "How do you plan to even open the door? This is just a friend thing. My principles will not allow me seduce a wounded man.

"Will you help me get a few puffs on a cigarette?" Who was he fooling? He couldn't do anything for myself. But he sure as hell didn't want anyone to see them go into the room together.

"I guess under the circumstances," Chet sighed, "we need to consider smoking medicinal."

"Won't Tim be jealous if you stay with me?"

"I know you're hurting, but it doesn't give you the right to say things intended to hurt me. You know very well Tim hardly knows I exist when we're at a show. My purpose for being, as far as he is concerned, is to win the tack room award."

"Sorry. I need someone to share my pain."

"Come on, let's get you to bed." Chet smiled, his blue eyes twinkling. He pulled the key from the ignition and went to open Ike's door.

"I'm in no mood for your double entendres."

"Lighten up. Where's your room card?"

"In my wallet. Back pocket."

Chet slipped his hand in Ike's pant's pocket just as a car pulled in. Ike was mortified seeing the occupants of the car stare at them.

"Should we give them something to talk about?

"Quit it."

"Afraid the horse world will think you're one of us?"

"Look, I sincerely appreciate all your help, but when it looks like...."

"I get it. It's dirty to be gay, right?" Chet pulled back, placing his hands on his hips.

"That's not it." How was he going to get out of this? "I don't have a problem with you being gay, but is not what I am."

"God forbid someone might think you're one of us."

The two men stood in front of the motel door facing off.

"I'm on so much medicine I don't know what I'm saying and I want to fight with someone. Unfortunately you're the only one around."

"I'll take that as an apology. Now, let's get inside."

#

The next morning, Chet helped Ike feed the horses and medicate Warrior.

"I'd better check in with Tim," Chet said, "then I'll come clean your stalls and sweep down the aisle."

"Thanks." He picked up the hose and attempted to water

his chrysanthemums.

A simple, every day job and he could hardly get by the pain. He still had a day and a half till Annie's saddle class. Would it be enough time to heal? It would have to be.

The force of the water knocked over the pots. The hose took on a life of its own, squirting water everywhere while Ike struggled to turn off the flow with his injured hands The horses snorted as it sprayed against the canvas drapes covering their stalls.

Ignoring the pain in his hands, he managed to turn the hose away from the horses.

The water shot forward, perfectly aimed at a horse and young rider obviously turned-out for an early morning class. Luckily the rider's coach snatched the terrified horse's bridle before he could bolt.

"Hey!" The instructor screamed over her shoulder. "Turn that damn hose off." She stood like a barrier in front of the horse, her hands on both sides of the bridle.

Gritting his teeth, he gave the valve one more twist and cut the flow. He gabbed towels and headed for the horse.

"I'm so sorry. It was an accident. These hands..." He looked up at the young rider. The force of the water had washed her derby away. Couldn't have been more than thirteen. So close to tears. Strands of wet hair hung in the girl's face. Make-up and mascara ran down her face onto her starched white shirt. Her gloved hands still gripped the reins.

"Claire, you'd better get down." The instructor said.

"But they're calling my class," Claire whimpered.

"Hurry up, then. We got a minute to put you back together."

The girl stepped down and the instructor handed the horse to Ike flashing him looks that spoke every swear word in the book. She took the towels from him and turned her back on him.

He breathed deeply, willing himself to bypass the pain and hold onto the horse.

"Hey," she called out to a passer-by. "We're in a pickle here. Please run up to the ring and get a hold on this class."

"Sure." the man headed toward the ring at a jog. "What class?" he called over his shoulder.

"Saddleseat Equitation 13 and Under."

That's the frosting on the cake. In the Equitation Division, the rider's turnout carried a lot of weight in the placing. Neat, clean, dry saddlesuits. He sure ruined this kid's chances.

The instructor knelt in front of Claire, dabbing at the girl's make-up with a corner of a towel. From a small red pail, she picked up a comb and bobby pins and got her hair back in place.

Good instructor, he thought, watching her keep her cool, instilling confidence in the young rider.

She painted a fresh red mouth on the girl and straightened her tie. Looking around, she located the derby, sitting in a puddle of water and muck. Using a horse brush and the towel, she cleaned off what she could. With a big smile, as though they had all the time in the world, she placed it just so on Claire's head.

"Okay. Let me give you a leg up."

"I'm not finished with you," she glared at Ike when she took the horse away from him.

He watched them hurry away. His hands throbbed from the few minutes of everyday day work. I'll never be able to ride Annie tomorrow. He sat down in front of his tack room in a full-blown funk.

Angry voices from TKB Stables broke into his consciousness. He recognized Chet's voice and the harsher shouting of a second man. Next he heard the sharp ringing sound of iron-shod hoofs on cement. Not the rhythmic click of a horse walking. This horse was out of control. Voices rose above the noise. He heard people running, probably to help.

Other horses called out, fear over unseen trauma to one of their own, in their whinnies. Then came a loud splash as though a muck bucket full of water had been thrown about.

By the time he reached TKB Stable area, he saw Chet on his knees; his colorful Koi fish flopped on the aisle. His prized fish pond in shambles.

"Get this mess picked up." Tim ordered. "My customers

pay top dollar for TKB Stables to present a good image." He turned his back on Chet and walked off to where a groom held a horse for him to mount.

Ike wished he had his hose now.

"Come on," he said to those standing around. "Let's get these fish back in water. Who has a bucket?" He went over to Chet and placed a hand on his shoulder. "We got water buckets coming."

"He did this on purpose." Chet said. Even though he kept his head down, he knew his friend was crying. "He let his horse trample through everything I did."

Buckets arrived and people worked at picking up the slippery fish.

"Will they be okay?" someone asked.

Chet nodded. "Probably. Thanks everyone."

"Come on," Ike said when they were alone. "Let's see what Hospitality has for coffee and doughnuts."

"I can't leave," Chet shook his head. "I've got to put this tack room back together."

"Or?"

"You're looking at the results of Tim's displeasure of knowing I was with you."

"You didn't tell him..."

"No, I did not." Chet raised his head and thrust out his chin, but the hurt still shined in his eyes. He walked away into the supply stall.

Ike didn't back off. He waited for Chet to return. He wanted an answer.

"Okay, I guess you should know." He sprinkled fish food on the two pails of Koi. "One of his customers saw us going into the room together."

"*Kurwa*," he shook his head and turned away. This will be a fresh piece of gossip for the whole show grounds. It took all his will power not to blast something hurtful.

"Don't you come down on me, too. I can't take anymore."

"Me neither. I never want another day to start like this for the rest of my life. Let's get coffee. Tell the grooms to pick

everything up. Have them sweep the water away. You can't
plan a winning tack room on an empty stomach. Wait till you
hear what I did to an equitation rider just before your fish got
loose."

Chet moved the pails of fish into the tack room and went
to find the grooms.

"Ready for coffee and a fresh start?" he said when he
returned. "By the way. What's this 'Kurwa' you keep saying. Is it
something bad?"

"Polish swear word." He waved his hand in dismissal.

"That's a relief. Thought it might be a new hurtful term
for gays."

CHAPTER THIRTY-ONE

Ike sat off by himself in the coliseum and watched the remaining classes in the morning session. The quality and finish of the horses in the ring amazed him. He fretted that his mare would not cut the mustard. As he gimped his way back to his stalls, he decided to find Chet and buy him lunch. He deserved that much after what Tim put him through.

When he reached the Crowne Stable area, he saw Warrior's stall door open. Empty. No Chet around either.

He hobbled towards the veterinarian's stalls, but no one was about. Had Chet forgotten to latch the door and Warrior escaped? He headed for the nearest door. His banged-up left knee complained at every step in spite of huge doses of Vicodan. He made his way around the perimeter of the barns where horses were exercising.

Trudging along, he searched among a dozen or more horses being hand walked. No sign of his stallion. Then he caught a glimpse of a horse in the distance. He recognized the bay stallion ambling along side of Chet, stopping now and then to grab a mouthful of grass. He couldn't believe the little man had the macho to take Warrior for a walk.

Ike stood with his weight on his right leg, watching for any signs of Warrior's typical unruliness, but he had to admit the stallion behaved like a puppy dog in Chet's hands. He headed back to his stalls, going straight to the tack room where he hung Annie's bridle on a hook.

He picked up the reins and stepped back creating tension on them. Carefully, he inserted his fingers through the reins and held them as he would have to when he rode tomorrow. He clamped his tongue between his teeth and willed his fingers to work the reins. The caliber of a performing Park Horse required a finesse in the signals sent to the horse, not unlike the skillfulness require to play a Stradivarius Violin.

He glanced at his bruised hands and broken fingers. He had refused casts till after the show. Even so, no way would his leather gloves fit over the mangled mess.

"Practicing?" Veronica poked her head into the tack room

"Yeah."

"Painful?" She stepped inside and watched him maneuver his fingers. He nodded, concentrating on working his fingers independently of one another.

"I've never ridden with more than one rein. Does a horse really understand all those signals?"

"If he doesn't, he doesn't belong at the World Championships. Watch." He sniffed discreetly, enjoying Veronica's fresh-from-the-shower scent. "When I wiggle my pinkies, the signal travels along the reins to the curb bit. Because of previous work in bitting rigs, this clues the horse to respond by tucking his chin towards his neck.

"The thicker rein is attached to the snaffle bit. A wiggle on that rein encouraged a horse to raise its head. If you over-do the signal, your horse may stick his nose out."

"Way over my head. I'm happy if my horse goes the direction I want and stops when I want." Veronica laughed and her danglely ear-rings danced. "My turn to man the AMHA booth. Drop by if you get a chance." She picked up her purse and walked off. He stepped out of the tack room and watched her walk away. He liked the way the gray slacks caressed her derriere. Kind of both sexy and lady-like.

She stopped to talk to Chet as he led Warrior back. The horse looked a little gimpy, like a warrior coming home from battle. Unfortunately not the conquering warrior. Damn horse sure messed up his aspirations. Probably crazy of him to even think about riding tomorrow.

Ike had refused to let the emergency room doctor attempt to put his fingers in casts, or restrain them in any way. His fingers would be his main line of communication to Annie via the reins. But he did accept pain pills. Lots.

"Hey, Chet, how about lunch?" He called out. "I'm buying."

CHAPTER THIRTY-TWO

Sgt Leary, with Mrs. Burke's letter in hand, took the steps two at a time to the Criminal Investigation Unit located on the second floor of the barracks. He had already passed on all the bits of information that kept coming his way to his buddy Detective Joe Tearsall who went for a search warrant. He'd want to add this letter to his arsenal.

"Joe?" He knocked on the open door and walked in.

"Not here," a voice from across the hall said.

He changed directions and headed toward the voice.

"Joe got his search warrant and left for that horse farm in Hampton. He's meeting the cadaver dog unit there."

"Thanks." He hurried back down stairs, checked out on the board and left the barracks. He strapped himself in the squad car and zipped along to Benalli's gravel pit. Cadaver dogs, he thought. They must be taking seriously Lisa Dansig's claim of sighting a body. Now the Burke woman's letter confirmed a body on the farm.

He eased the Crowne Vic down the road to the gravel pit. Constant dump truck traffic resulted in an unusually smooth dirt road. Even so, the bull briars waved from the sides, reaching out for his shiny car. As he rounded the final bend he saw the Crime Scene Unit's vans.

When he was last here, the wood lot to the left of the gravel bank had been filled with a healthy growth of hardwoods. Not a standing tree left. Just a crop of raw stumps clinging to the ground. Huge piles of newly chipped wood dotted the naked land. A pile of massacred forty-foot trees lay about. Several troupers worked their cadaver dogs near the chipper.

He walked directly to Tearsall who stood next to the

bulldozer within the chain linked fence. Someone dusted the bulldozer for prints.

"Hey, Leary." Tearsall greeted him. "Couldn't keep away?"

"I see you got your search warrant," he said.

"Pressure's on to find out what's happening to the clergymen. All clues are to be given top priority. We've subpoenaed Benalli's phone records. What do you make of the Commissioner of DEP being his most frequent call? And usually to her cell phone?"

"Has to be a connection to dumping stuff here."

"Something's not right. Find anything? He called out to the agent dusting the bulldozer. The man shook his head negatively.

"The men haven't been able to pick up one print from either the bulldozer or the wood chipper."

"I'm probably to blame for that," Leary stood at parade rest and locked his hands behind his back. "Hind-sight and all that."

Tearsall turned to face him.

"After Lisa Danzig came to me about seeing a body here, I came down to look around and when I noted loaded Nutmeg Environmental trucks coming in and dumping, I made a call to DEP requesting everything they had on Nutmeg." He looked unfaltering at Tearsall. "I found it hard to believe they had a hazmat dumping permit with no visible perimeter signs. If Commissioner Jordan is in cahoots with Benalli, I sure gave them a heads-up."

"Don't blame yourself. It's always a hard call. Our guys have never handled the combination of what they're finding in the soil."

Leary followed Tearsall as he walked toward a group of agents sifting through the soil.

"Finding anything useful?" Tearsall asked.

"Horse manure and lime are doing a great job of masking whatever else is here. It's mixed in as thoroughly as though someone was baking a cake."

"Have you questioned Benalli about the calls?" Leary

asked.

"Yes." Tearsall bent down and ruffled through a patch of old leaves. "Benalli said the Commissioner has a horse here and he calls her about its progress. The red-haired girl that runs the barn..." he stood up and flipped a few pages on his notepad and read "... Wilhelmina Jones, she goes by Billie, confirms she keeps a horse here to be trained by..." He consulted the notepad and, "Dwight Chernokowski, professionally known, the redhead said, as Ike Cherny. She let slip that the Commissioner and Cherny are an item. Then she clammed right up and started mucking out those stinking stalls."

"What's with all the downed trees? When I was here checking out Danzig's story, this was all standing timber."

"That's what I'd like to know. Benalli said they're being cleared to create more pasture. I don't believe him for a minute."

"I've got something here that should help," he reached in a pocket for the letter Mrs. Burke gave him and handed it to the Detective. "It's a letter Harlan Burke left for his mom to bring to the police if he should disappear. Mrs. Burke brought it in this morning. She indicated your Wilhelmina Jones, the redhead, brought it to her because Burke hadn't been around for a number of days.

"How does Harlan Burke figure in?" Tearsall pulled a copy of the handwritten letter from the envelope.

"Letter spells it out. Burke appeared to fear for his life. And now he's gone missing. The lab is going over the original for prints."

Just then a flurry of activity came from the cadaver dogs. Their human partners dropped to their knees and sifted through the gravel. Out came collection bags. One investigator placed a marker in the ground.

"We've got body parts." the CSI agent shouted. "Minute parts." He and Tearsall hurried over.

CHAPTER THIRTY-THREE

"Ike!" Veronica called out.

Ike turned from where he stood in Annie's open stall door watching Chet groom the mare. He enjoyed watching the lithe woman swing down the isle, a big smile lighting her face.

"I found you a horse to ride." She bounced on her toes. "Come on," she reached to take his hand then snatched hers away. "Oh God, I'm sorry. I'm so excited I almost grabbed your hand."

"Horse to ride?"

"So you can practice with all those reins."

"No body's going to give me a horse they paid thousands to transport to Oklahoma to practice on. These are show horses...."

"Stop preaching. This is an equitation horse that's finished showing. He didn't do well enough in the qualifier to make the cut. Come on– they're waiting for you."

Reluctantly Ike fell into step with her.

"Hugh Becker stopped by the AMHA booth," Veronica explained as they made their way to the prestigious stalls in the high profile barn next to the coliseum. "Everyone was talking about your accident."

"Great. Exactly how I want to be remembered."

"Stop feeling sorry for yourself. I told them to look for you in a Park Saddle class tomorrow and how you were practicing with the reins. Well, Hugh said you could use his daughter's equitation horse now. Jake Paggette has all Hugh's horses in his stable. So that's where we're going."

They arrived at the Paggette Training Stable area with its lavish blue and gold drapes. Ike eyed a line– a long line–of displayed blue ribbons.

"Hello, doll," a parrot greeted them from his perch in a golden cage. "Trot, please."

A groom stood patiently holding a horse, one hand looped through its reins.

"Hello, Ms. Rouseau," he said. "Do you want a mounting block?" he asked Ike.

"No!–thank you." His pride hurt far more than his hands. Big time horse trainer needing a mounting block to get on a kid's horse. He wanted to bolt in the worse way, but knew it would make him look like a jerk. To Veronica.

"As you say," the groom steadied the saddle and placed a restraining hand on the horse's nose.

He managed to gather the four narrow strips of reins in his left fist and then reached for the stirrup with the other. But the twisted left knee would not bend to reach the stirrup. He gritted his teeth and tried again. He sensed someone behind him and saw Veronica out of the corner of his eye, moving the mounting block into place. Without a word, he got on and carefully arranged the reins.

"Thank you," he nodded to the groom and urged the horse to walk off. Veronica followed him out of the barn.

He chose a quiet spot. Sure as hell did not want an audience. His left knee hurt like the devil and he was only walking. How could he trot and canter? It crossed his mind he might pass out. Great exhibitors' lounge gossip that'd be. *Macho horse trainer faints while riding a kid's horse.*

"Get over it." He hollered at his pain and asked the horse for a trot. "Focus," he demanded of his body. First he needed to concentrate on finding a comfortable position for his knee. Good thing he was on a laid-back horse.

Soon he turned his attention to positioning his hands, raising them well above the horse and slowly spreading them two feet apart.

So far, so good. Then he worked his fingers on the reins. It took tremendous will power to make them do his biding, but was gratified to see the patient horse respond as he should. He kept trotting till he felt he could handle a real class.

"Whoa," he spoke quietly and the horse obediently came

back to a walk and then stopped. He looked around and saw Veronica sitting crossed-legged under a tree, smiling broadly. She clapped her hands.

He grinned and walked the horse back to the Paggette Training Stable.

"Good job." Veronica said walking alongside. "I knew you could do it."

The same groom met him. He steadied the horse so Ike could dismount.

"Thank you." He tugged his wallet out of a back pocket and offered the groom some bills.

"Thanks, man." he took the horse's reins and walked away. "Good luck tomorrow," he called over his shoulder.

"I think you could use a drink." Veronica said.

"Or two. Thanks for arranging this."

His cell rang as they walked toward the Exhibitors' Lounge.

"I need to take this," he said, noting Billie's name pop up on the LED screen.

#

"Ike! Terrible things have happened." Billie paced around and around the little table in her apartment kitchen.

"Take a deep breath. Tell me everything."

"There's bodies all over the farm. They arrested Benny." It took both of her hands to steady the phone next to her ear. "Please come home."

"Billie," he shouted. "I can't understand what you're saying. Slow down and talk about one thing at a time. What bodies–where?"

"Harlan's, she sobbed. No longer trusting her legs, she pulled out a chair and sat down. "Who would do that to him?"

"Do exactly what?"

She swallowed hard and closed her eyes before answering. "The cadaver dogs found pieces of him– *tiny pieces*– scattered around the gravel pit." She hiccuped through her tears. "Some sick pervert put his body through a wood chipper. They must think Benny had something to do with it."

"Holy Christ in Heaven," he prayed. He broke out in a sweat. His hand shook trying to hold the phone to his ear.

Billie heard a woman's voice ask: "Are you okay?" Great, Billie thought. Gone just a week and he has women trailing him.

"Ike?" She screamed into the phone. Would he ever take her problems seriously? And dammit...she was telling him that their friend was brutally murdered.

"I'm here. Harlan's been murdered?"

"Yes," she whispered. "And they found teeth they matched up with the two missing ministers. Ground up with Harlan. That's when they arrested Benny."

#

Ike knew in an instant that this is what gnawed at Harlan all summer. He brought his attention back to Billie. Turned out the poor girl had a right to be terrified.

"I don't know what to do. I'm all alone with these horses. Mrs. Benalli left, too, so I don't have any money to run the farm. The grain man wants $800. This place is too scary. All my lessons students have quit so I don't even have that cash coming in."

Veronica placed a styrofoam cup of water in his hands. He nodded his thanks and drained it.

"Ike?"

"Yeah." His head spun, trying to make sense of her ghoulish story. His phone slipped out of his hand. Veronica caught it before it fell to the cement floor.

"Ike! Ike?" He heard Billie's screams.

Veronica wrapped his fingers around the phone and he raised it to his ear.

"Sorry. I dropped the phone."

"What am I to do?"

"I don't know. Call Luke and see if he'll stay with you." He doubted anyone could get at Billie with the burly blacksmith by her side. Even so, he didn't like the picture of Luke spending the night with Billie. Doubt he'd stay on the couch.

"I hated dumping all this on you before your class but I didn't know who else to turn to."

"You did right, but I haven't been much help."

"When do you show Annie?"

"Tomorrow. Stay safe, Billie."

"Don't drop the trophy."

#

"I can't help but notice that call really upset you. Would it help to talk about it?" Veronica asked. They sat at a table at the far end of the Exhibitors' Lounge.

"I can't believe what Billy told me." He arranged his broken hands around the high ball glass, the icy-cold easing the pain. "I'm completely stupefied. But it must be true." He took a long swallow of Jack Daniels.

"My roommate's been murdered. His body put through a wood chipper along with the bodies of two ministers that went missing this summer."

She covered her mouth and turned away.

"That's bad enough, but this all happened on my farm–Benalli's farm." He raised his eyes to see the horror reflected in Veronica's eyes. "They've arrested my boss. His wife left. Sure as hell can't blame her. She must think he's guilty." Using both hands, he raised his glass and drank. "That leaves Billie with no money to run the farm with thirty horses to feed."

"My, God, Ike. I can only guess what you're going through. What will you do? You can't go back to Connecticut."

"I don't have any right to stay here. And, let's face, what kind of chance do I really have at placing well in tomorrow's class with these hands."

"Don't you dare be a quitter. What possible difference could one more day make?"

"What do you mean, 'one more day'?" It's a four-day drive home and I doubt I could grip the steering wheel with my crippled hands either."

"Ride your class tomorrow and qualify for the World

Championship. Then fly home to do what you can for Billie. Just make sure you get back in time to win."

CHAPTER THIRTY-FOUR

Ike tapped his fingers on the table, loosening them up. They were awkward, but didn't hurt nearly as bad as yesterday. Good thing. Today's the day he devoted his life to.

Three and a half years ago he caught his first glimpse of Annie trotting across the field in Maine. Driving home from the Aristooke Breeding Farm, he started planning her career. Their career. Their combined talents would determine one another's success. But after this accident, Annie would have to do more than her part win the World Champion Park Saddle title for her and a World Class Trainer's title for him.

"You should eat a good breakfast today," Chet broke into his thoughts when the waitress set plates down.

"You're right." He picked up his fork and moved the Western Omelette around. He didn't sleep well last night worrying about what Billie was going through and then every time he turned over he ended up squishing his hands.

"Your hands look good today," Chet said, pouring syrup on pancakes.

"The new medication works well." he stabbed a home fry. "Swelling is way down and I don't feel all doped up. I think my gloves will fit."

"You're going to make it."

"I owe you a lot, Chet." He concentrated on slipping two fingers through the coffee mug's handle.

"You owe me a winning class this afternoon."

#

"First call," the PA system blared, "for class 204, Four Year Old Park Saddle Mares."

Count down! Twenty-five minutes to show time. Annie stood on cross ties in the ready stall. Chet sprayed clear lacquer over the mare's freshly blacked hoofs.

"Did I get it all?" He stood back to study each hoof.

"They're like patent leather." Veronica said. "What can I do?"

"Pick her tail out." Ike said. The tail was done up in two freshly shampooed braids, each folded over and wrapped in masking tape. She ripped off the tape and undid each braid.

"That's just the start," he said. "Now you have to separate each tail hair so it doesn't look like it was up in curlers.

Chet picked up a clean towel and wiped every inch of Annie's body. Next he placed the saddle on her back, loosely attaching the white patent leather girth.

"Get dressed." he ordered, and chose a woolen cooler and covered the horse's body from ears to tail, securing it at the neck with a spring clamp.

Obediently Ike went to the tack room and took his red stripped tie off the clothes hook and wrapped it around his neck. I can't do this, he thought. Well, if you can't knot your tie, he lectured himself, you sure as hell can't ride a horse. He looked in the mirror and concentrated on the job. Next he buttoned his navy saddlesuit jacket and settled his fedora on his head. Quickly he located his favorite saddle whip and hurried back to the ready stall.

"How do you do the curb chain?" Chet asked, settling the bridle on Annie's head and tucking her foretop under the patent leather browband.

"Drop two links on both sides. I want to get on when they give the second call."

Ike felt Veronica's hands on his back and knew she was securing his number to his jacket.

"Thanks," he said.

"I'm not done. Turn around." She pinned a red carnation to his lapel.

Meanwhile Chet had applied baby oil to the horse's muzzle, around her eyes, and inside her ears. "Enough oil?" he asked.

"Good to go," Ike said.

"She wears more make-up than me," Veronica laughed. "The oil makes her eyes look huge."

Chet slid the cooler off and snugged the girth.

"Second call..." came over the mike. Ike's stomach lurched. The mare started to paw.

"Let's get out of here." Ike said.

Ike and Annie joined the procession of fourteen four-year old mares and their support teams heading for the warm-up ring. Out of this qualifying class, only four would make the cut and be eligible for a shot at the World Champion Park Saddle title. Chet and Veronica followed with a bucket of emergency supplies: brush, towel, jackknife, shoe string and black electrical tape.

"Forgive me for this afternoon." he spoke out loud to his mare. "You're going to have to do more than your share." He heard the applause for the winner of previous class. This is it. His mouth went dry.

The Ringmaster, blew a rousing fanfare to call the class. His adrenalin pumped all out.

"OK, *Lijkonik*. Our turn." This time he vied with the other horses to be first into the ring. He knew Aristooke Annie would be breathtaking if she had the coliseum all to herself for a few seconds.

CHAPTER THIRTY-FIVE

Eugenia haltered her horse and led him out of his stall. "You're my personal version of comfort food, Bucky," she said, wrapping her arms around the gelding's head. "I couldn't stay another minute in my office. Let's go for a trail ride." She picked up a brush and went over his golden coat.

Maybe a ride in the state forest would help her see things more clearly, she thought, hefting the heavy western saddle on his back and taking up the cinch. The horse dropped his head so the silver-trimmed bridle slipped easily over his ears. She mounted and urged her horse out of the barn into the early morning sun.

Why did I let myself get into this tangle, she thought. She pointed the gelding toward the forest trail and let him have his head. Her arrangement with Benalli didn't hurt anything and did add considerably to the environmental research fund at U Conn. Bucky moved into a comfortable jog and chose the left branch in the trail. The one that led to the river.

I never let him dump seriously contaminated waste, she thought, trying to prove just cause for her illegal arrangement with Benalli. She came to her favorite evergreen-lined trail and signaled Bucky to lope. She gave in to the rocking sensation. Enjoying the wind in her face, she closed her eyes, trusting her horse to keep to the trail.

Minutes later she pulled him back to a walk. "Good boy," she said and patted his neck.

There's the other thing they sure as hell are going to hang me on. Literally. She shook her head at her choice of words. But she did not kill those ministers. The shadowy evergreens gave way to a meadow and she let her horse graze as she thought.

    The world without those perverts was a better place. Still, things would be different if she hadn't gone poking in that pile of old horse blankets. Sure wouldn't be in this pickle. One was bad, but why did she allow herself to be talked into sending the second one to Benalli?

    But she would not tell the police who killed both preachers. Branded them, too. Way to go, girl. She only did what I didn't have the courage to do.

    And see–the one time she decided to take out a minister, he got away. Another Eugenia Jordan scheme gone sour. And wouldn't you know that minister led the police right to the farm.

    "Are you ashamed of me, Serena?" She wondered if her sister knew what was going on down here with the ministers. She pulled Bucky's head up and they moved on down the trail. My sister's gone, my lover despises me, my father hardly knows I existed and the police are bound to blame me for the missing preachers. She couldn't come up with one good reason to perpetuate the Jordan family.

    It became clear what she had to do. One simple act would solve all problems. Riding her horse always led to solving her problems. And the investment fund she started for the rescue horses would see Bucky through his retirement.

    At the river, she dismounted and found a treat for her gelding in the saddle bags. She stoked his coat then buried her face in his neck, inhaling the salty, sweaty horse scent that always brought her happiest memories to mind.

    "You're a great horse," she crooned. "A champion and my best, un-judge-mental friend. Thank you for being here for me." She looped his reins around the saddle horn and turned him toward home.

    "Go on." She slapped him on the rump. He snorted and looked at her. "Go on–get back to the barn."

    Bucky started off slowly, stopping once to make sure he got it right.

    "Get out of here," she yelled and clapped her hands loudly. Bucky jogged towards home, the stirrup leathers slapping his sides at every stride.

Fame and Deceit

She waited until she no longer heard her horse. Then she turned toward the river bank, looking twenty feet down to the fast moving water. She closed her eyes and jumped, glad she never learned to swim.

CHAPTER THIRTY-SIX

Ike aimed Annie down the long chute that led to the coliseum. He heard a horse coming up on his left, challenging him for the privilege of being first in the ring. He moved his horse over, deftly blocking any chance of his competition being first.

Aristooke Annie stepped into the ring as a gracious lady. Within a few strides she became a showgirl. He knew his mare well enough to know when to leave her alone. She didn't let him down. She raised her lovely head high and waved her legs in the best Rockette tradition.

Taking it all in, the little mare took command of the ring. All three judges stared at her, ignoring the other horses as they made their entrances. The photographer knew a good shot, too. Ike saw him take a series of pictures, the flash working overtime. Only four years old and she knew how to work a crowd!

Now that the first impression had been made, he brought Annie back a hair, saving her best performance till the class was officially in order. He looked around, trying to locate an open space on the rail. When he made his passes he wanted the judges' full attention. Finding one, he cut across the ring as the gate closed.

"Trot, please." Judging began.

He swished his whip and the mare moved into the bit, arching her neck and tucking her chin so her head was virtually perpendicular to the ground. This was not her favorite position and he knew if he demanded it of her for too long, she'd sour, pin her ears and give a second rate performance.

So much to concentrate on! After years of training for this day, he knew Annie turned heads when encouraged to trot free and bright, but at a lady -like pace. Above all, he had to keep her enjoying every minute in spite of the crude signals issued from his injured hands.

As he prepared to make a pass before the judge, he heard a fast trotting horse charging up behind him. Damn! The horse drew up alongside and hid Annie from the judge's view. The mare nervously swished her tail and twitched her ears at the intruder. Not a winning pass!

He noticed the photographer about to take a shot of the speeding horse. The flash popped. The horse jumped away from the light and rammed broadside into him, smashing his twisted left knee.

Pain blazed through his body. He lost control of his reins, jerking Annie's bit. He couldn't focus. The little mare faltered, breaking her stride. Somehow he managed to pull the horse together and continued trotting down the rail. It felt like slivers of iron jabbed his knee at every step.

Annie lost her bloom. It wasn't fun anymore. Just a chore.

"All walk, please." The announcer called out over the PA system.

Both Ike and Annie needed this break, but he knew a stylish walk carried a lot of weight. Not a time to mope. He encouraged his horse to show off, trying to get by the excruciating pain in his knee as he bounced to her prance.

The command to canter came and with it came the first relief since his knee was rammed. He sat easily to her comfortable canter, rested his knee and planned the second half of the class.

"Reverse and strike a trot." He opted to cut across the ring, staying out of the judges' lines of vision as much as possible. The crowd whooped and hollered for their favorites. He caught a glimpse of Chet and Veronica jumping up and down, waving towels. Annie saw them, too, and came to life.

He felt the mare raise her head, pick up a high trot and claim the ring. Leave her do her thing, he lectured himself. He resisted the urge to tickled the curb bit so she'd keep her chin tucked. Had to keep her liking this job. That would make her a winner. She responded by breezing the second half of the class and when the announcer called to line-up, the little mare pranced to the center, still fresh and sassy.

After the three judges walked down the line of fourteen young mares, the horses retired at the out gate end of the ring waiting to learn the judges' decision.

The waiting was nerve-racking. He'd be happy with fourth. That would make him eligible for the World Championship class. He snuck looks at the horses milling around, waiting. They were all beautiful. Not a second-rate horse among them.

Finally the announcer named the first place horse. Not Annie. That's okay. Then second place was called, the horse happily trotted off to pick up the red ribbon. Ike sweated profusely. Not much wiggle room left. It looked like the tally for his first Grand National would be one driving accident and one also-ran.

"Hey, man, they're calling your number."

"You sure?" He jerked back from feeling sorry for himself.

"Aren't you 314?"

A thrill ran through his body. He was definitely number 314! He swished his whip and Annie trotted gaily off. He guided her to the Ringmaster.

"Good show," the Ringmaster said.

"Thanks. Wait till you see us in the championship." With her third-place yellow ribbon fluttering on her bridle, the mare paraded out of the ring.

Veronica and Chet met him at the out gate, grinning like fools. Chet rubbed the sweat running down Annie's face with a towel. He snapped a carrot and offered her a small piece.

"Keep moving," the gate man ordered. "Let the horses out."

He urged Annie on. Chet walked along one side, towel tossed over his shoulder, stroking the mare's neck. Veronica walked on the Annie's other side.

"You looked wonderful," she babbled, her bright eyes smiling up at him. She squeezed his good leg. "Everyone around us wondered who she was, where she came from."

"Wait till Sunday night. They'll never wonder who Aristooke Annie is again." Or the man who trained her.

"Nice kind of mare," a man said, catching up to them. "Plan on showing back?"

"You bet."

Chet steadied the horse while he dismounted, being careful to land on his good leg. Veronica threw her arms around him.

"All that for third place?" he teased. "What comes with World Champion?"

"What would you like?" She cocked her head and raised an eyebrow.

"Are we forgetting our horse?" Chet cleared his throat. "I think she deserves a good Absorbine wash and rub down."

"Yes, sir." Ike saluted and clicked his heels together. "Then we're off to the Exhibitors' Lounge. He took his fedora off and wiped his face on Chet's towel. "I'm buying. Let me get out of my saddle suit and I'll give you a hand." He headed for the tack room and Chet led the horse away to the ready stall.

Veronica and Chet unsaddled Annie, hanging the sweaty tack on a hook. "It's amazing how a good ribbon makes everyone smile," he said, pouring a good-sized glug of Absorbine into a pail of warm water. The menthol laced liniment filled the air, mixing with the smell of a sweating horse. To a horseman, smelling the pungent mix was like smelling a rose bush in full bloom.

"And when the horse loses?"

"Everyone looks for an excuse to kick the dog." He plunged a sponge in the spicy water and sloshed it on the horse. "And at TKB Stable that's usually me."

#

They found a table in the Exhibitors' Lounge. As they waited for drinks, Ike kept clenching his fists, noting how much more limber they felt.

"Are they hurting?" Veronica ran her hand across his

knuckles.

"Hardly at all. Riding must have loosened them up. Can't tell you guys how much I appreciate your support. If I go home with nothing more than getting to know you two, the trip has been more than worth it." He still rode the high of his good ribbon. Celebrating with his new friends was a damn sight better than a night with only Jack Daniels for company.

"Nice ride, Mr. Cherny." A woman with a drink in her hand touched him on the shoulder and kept on her way.

"Look at you grin because a pretty woman called you by name." Veronica said.

"There were a lot of good horses in my class. I find it hard to believe people who saw the class actually recognized me. It was only a third place."

"Stop putting yourself down! Making the cut for the championship is not 'just a third place.'"

"That man," the waitress interrupted, "in the suede jacket bought this round for you." She set down drinks and hurried off.

"That's Hugh Becker," Veronica said.

"Let's have him join us." Ike waved him over. He reached for his Jack Daniels and, for the first time since the accident, he picked it up with one hand.

"That's one talented mare you rode today." Becker said, settling in the chair Chet dragged from another table. His steel gray hair had a precise part on the left side. But his shaggy white mustache needed a good trim.

"Yes, sir. She is that."

"Beat the pants off my bay mare. We didn't even make the cut."

"Sorry to hear that." Ike said. "It's a long trip not to get a shot at the World Championship."

"You're right. My mare was undefeated till this afternoon."

"Ouch! That hurts. Takes a show like this to get a good horse beat."

"Enough of my mare. We're here to celebrate Aristooke Annie's great class." Becker raised his glass.

"To Annie." Ike and Chet called out.

"To Ike." Veronica said softly, looking at him over the rim of her glass.

"Don't suppose I could talk you into parting with her? She the talented type mare I'd like in my breeding program."

"I'm flattered, Mr. Becker. You're raising some good Morgans. But Annie has just started. Mr. Benalli and I plan on promoting her to her full potential."

"Understandable." He nodded and drained his drink. "Is Mr. Benalli flying out for the World Championship? I'd like to meet him."

"Doubt it. He's in the middle of some serious — negotiations — back in Connecticut."

"Good luck, Ike." Becker stood up. "I'm meeting Jake at Molly Murphys for dinner. Your hands look a damn sight more comfortable."

"They are." He raised them and wiggled the fingers. "Thanks for the drinks. And even more, thanks for loaning me that equitation horse. It really helped."

They watched Becker move away, swallowed up in the crowd of winners celebrating at the bar.

"Nice guy." Ike said.

"Don't you dare sell Annie to him," Chet said.

"What do you know that I don't?"

"Jake Paggette is his trainer."

"I know that. And a good one. Granted he's a little rough on a horse, but he does get results."

"There's a lot of talk that Jake is encouraging the breeders he trains for to get a little Saddlehorse blood in their breeding programs.

"That's just sore-loser talk." He shook his head. But the conversation Ike overheard between Becker and his trainer Pagette back at White Gate farm came to mind. Pagette definitely promoted breeding his Annie to a Saddlebred.

"You think so? There's a growing group of young horses he's training that don't look or perform anything like the parents their registration papers say they are."

"But DNA and blood-typing weeds them out." Ike

observed Veronica eyes widen before she dropped them to intently stir her drink with a swizzle stick. He couldn't understand why, but she looked decidedly uncomfortable when the conversation turned to Becker's breeding program.

"That's the mystery. Listen more closely to the grooms' scuttlebut. They'll have you believing the possibility. They say the colts are outstanding."

"I have to go." Veronica looked at her watch and picked up her purse.

"Wait a minute," he took hold of her wrist. "I've decided to take your advice and fly home."

"But your class?" Chet said.

"I owe it to Billie to give her some support. She's going through hell now and doesn't have anyone to lean on. She needs money to run the barn. Things seem to be going from bad to worse."

"Like?" Chet asked.

"Buried bodies on the farm. My boss in jail. I worry about Billie handling everything on her own."

"Buried bodies?" Chet shook off a rain of shivers. "What kind of a ghoulish farm do you work on? Is it safe for you to go back? Suppose you have to stay?"

"Nothing," he looked directly at Chet, "could possibly keep me from the Sunday night championship. Thing is, could I count on you two to look after Annie and Warrior?"

"You bet." Chet sat a little taller. Squared his shoulders.

"I'll be Chet's assistant." Veronica smiled.

CHAPTER THIRTY-SEVEN

"Billie?"

"Oh my God!" Billie's voice carried from the far end of the barn. "Ike!" She bolted from a stall and raced toward him, pitchfork in one hand.

"I'm so glad you're here." She crashed into Ike, throwing her arms around him. "It's been a nightmare."

He held her for a minute before untangling her arms and stepping back. Puffy black shadows ringed her tearful eyes. He picked bits of hay out of her red hair.

"What happened to you?" She looked with horror at his battered hands. "And your face." She touched the line of stitches below his eye. "Were you in a fight?"

"Long story." He held his hands out between them. The bruising had turned an ugly yellow-green and some of the fingers were shaped peculiarly. "Guess I'm lucky to be here to tell about it. I got doughnuts in the car. I'll meet you in the tack room and we'll trade stories."

#

"Who's looking after Annie and Warrior?" she asked, pouring coffee.

"A couple of nice people who have been helping me out."

She bit her lip so she wouldn't ask if the "nice people" were female.

"I'm getting the seven am flight tomorrow morning. The championship is at night.

"You can ride with those hands? You can hardly hold

the coffee mug." He looked terrible. Sort of like he had a run-in with...a wood chipper. She shivered and hugged her arms close to her body.

"Already did—and can you believe Annie qualified for the big championship? Look, I brought pictures. A couple of good ones of Warrior, too– before the accident."

"Accident?"

"That's what did my hands in. Probably my fault. I must have tied his tail to the buggy too tightly. When he got rattled at another stallion coming too close, Warrior challenged him." Ike stirred sugar in his coffee and picked out a powdered jelly doughnut.

"He kicked out, got a leg over the shaft and took off. We smashed into the railing but my hands didn't come out of the hand holds right away. Vet sewed him up. Jog cart is kindling." He sunk his teeth into the doughnut making sure it included the raspberry jam.

"I'd have done his tail right if I were there." She leaned against the counter and sipped her coffee."

"That's the truth!"

Kind of nice to hear she was needed. Even if it was after the fact. She opened the manila envelope and looked at the colored pictures. "These are terrific. "That's my Annie." She held one up to the light. "Let's get this one framed."

"I did play a role in making the cut, too."

"Here we go." She rolled her eyes and grinned. "Big shot trainer attitude." She slipped the pictures back in the envelope and chose a chocolate-glazed doughnut.

"Well, it didn't come easy. And before you can say anymore, I am well aware your dedication to getting Annie trained played a role as well."

"Thanks. It's nice to be appreciated."

"The only reason I left the show was to help you. What's going on? Did they really take Benalli away?"

"I don't know where to begin." She plunked down on a tack trunk and stared at the floor.

"The Criminal Investigation Unit spent days down at the sand pit. Just like on TV." She licked the sugar off her fingers.

"They made me feel like a suspect with all the questions. First it was a trooper, Sargent Leary. Several days later Detective Tearsall asked the same questions."

"Like what?"

"Did I ever see loaded trucks coming *in*. I told them trucks come and go all day. I have thirty horses here to keep me busy without wondering what truck is hauling what where. And when did I last see Harlan. I couldn't pinpoint the day. They must of felt I knew a more than I said because they both kept asking how I knew about the letter Harlan wrote to his mom."

"You really don't know when Harlan went missing?"

"Isn't that what I just said? Damn it, Ike. I've had it with being asked the same question a zillion times."

"Hey, I'm on your side, remember? I know you've been through a lot and I am sorry I haven't been here."

She glared at him through her tears. He looked sincere as he drank his coffee and waited patiently for her to continue.

"All I remember is Harlan didn't stop by for coffee one morning then freaking out seeing the new guys Benny hired wandering around the farm." She got up and poked through the doughnut box.

"They made my skin crawl, the way they looked at me. I asked Benny where Harlan was and he said he didn't know, just didn't show up for work and that's when the weirdos came."

"Is that all they wanted to know?"

"No. Detective Tearsall showed up one morning while I was feeding and showed me a picture of Eugenia. Asked if I knew her. I told them you're training her horse so she comes by several times a week."

"Well, I better get going if I'm going to see both Eugenia and Benalli today." He got up and set his mug on the counter. "We have to find out how to keep the farm operating while he's in jail."

"Will you stay with me tonight?" She rinsed out their coffee mugs turning them upside down on the edge of the sink. "Your house is off limits. It's wrapped up in yellow tape."

"My house?"

"Harlan lived there, too. I know in the pit of my stomach

Benny's not getting out which means I have to find another job."

"I'm proud of you, Billie, for sticking it out. A lesser person would have high-tailed it out of here."

"I have thirty horses depending on me," She said. "But I'm scared silly most of the time. Too many dead bodies. I want to cooperate with the police, but I sure don't want to end up in the gravel pit if the killer thinks I'm talking too much."

"Don't you worry, we'll come through this. Will you be okay if I leave now?"

"You just got here."

"I'm not leaving Connecticut till tomorrow morning. And I'm not leaving before I talk to both Eugenia and Benalli. I can be pretty sure Benalli isn't leaving the Montville Prison any time soon, but I called Eugenia at the DEP office and they said she hasn't been in for two days and she's not answering her home phone. So, I thought I'd see if I can catch her at the barn when she keeps her Cutting horse."

"Didn't you dump her before you left for Oklahoma? Have to admit I can't figure why. She's pretty, can talk horse till the cows come home and she really likes you." Come on, Ike, she silently prayed, say something like you prefer redheads. Throw me some crumbs.

"I didn't dump her. But you know my reasons for wanting to cool it. She knows things about Benalli that may help us understand our future a little better.

"So, will you stay here tonight?" 'Our' future, she savored that word. That was definitely a step in the right direction.

"You bet." Ike pulled her to her feet and held her close.

Billie buried her face in his neck. Thank you, God, she prayed for no longer having Ike think the sun rises and sets with Eugenia. Maybe there is a chance for me.

#

Good. She's here, Ike thought, seeing Eugenia's SUV parked under the trees when he pulled up to the barn where she kept her horses. Away from all distractions, he might get the

whole truth from her. He ground out his cigarette in the ashtray
and headed for the barn.

A saddled horse stood on the crossties. He recognized it
as Eugenia's gelding, Bucky. A black-haired woman, hands on
hips, stood looking at it.

"Good morning," He called out as he entered the barn.

"Can I help you?" The woman looked up and dropped
her hands to her side.

"I'm looking for Eugenia. That's her horse, isn't it."

"And you'd be?"

"Ike Cherny."

"Sure." The edge in her voice turned cheerful. "Eugenia
talks a lot about you." She took a step forward and offered her
hand to Ike. I'm Paula Stilton. I run this barn for my mom."

"Is Eugenia here?" He shook her hand. "That is Bucky,
isn't it?" He moved to the other side of the buckskin and stroked
his neck. The horse was cool to his touch and appeared relaxed.

"Yeah. But I don't have the foggiest where Eugenia is."
She stroked her arched nose. "I got here a half hour ago for
morning chores. I saw her car and noticed her horse was out
of his stall so I figured they went for a ride. A little later Bucky
walks into the barn, calm as can be. But no Eugenia. I've been
calling her cell phone every few minutes but it goes to voice mail
on the first ring."

"I can't believe she fell off." He took a closer look at the
horse. No scrapes or other signs of distress.

"If she did, Bucky would never leave her. She taught
him to ground tie."

"To ground tie, she would have to drop a rein to the
ground," he said. "And look here, the reins are tied around the
saddle horn."

"That's really strange. She would never ride like that."

"I agree. She must have tied the reins to the saddle for
some other purpose."

"So she must have wanted him to go home. Oh my god!
Do you think she's hurt and sent him home for help? But why
wouldn't she call me? She always carries her cell phone."

"I'm going to go look." He unsnapped the cross ties and

untied the reins.

"What's your number." He took his cell phone from a holster on his belt. "I'll call if I find something out." He punched Paula's number into his quick dial, then swung up in the western saddle and urged the horse out the door.

"Try the trail to the river. That's Eugenia's favorite."

He prompted Bucky into an easy-going lope and picked up the trail Paula suggested. Once he got in the forest, he pulled the horse back to a walk and searched along each side. Part of him hoped he'd find her with a broken arm or leg from falling off her horse, although he doubted that would be the case as countless years of pine needles cushioned the forest floor and Bucky simply was not the kind of horse to dislodge a good rider like Eugenia.

He shied away from thinking about the alternative. Benalli certainly had a great motive to make sure she never ratted on him.

Perhaps she might be calling for help. He reined the horse to a stop and listened intently. Not a whisper of a breeze stirred the towering pines. An occasional blue jay and nut hatch flitting through the shadowy forest broke the quiet. In the distance, sun reflected off patches of the silent Quinnebaug River. He nudged Bucky into a walk and headed toward the river. As the trail neared the river, the evergreens opened onto a meadow.

Not knowing what else to do, he stepped down when he reached the river bank and dropped a rein, signaling Bucky to stand still. The sun in the cloudless sky quickly warmed the October day, so he tugged his sweat shirt over his head and stuffed it in the saddle bag.

He peered over the river bank, judging it to be about twenty feet above the swift-flowing river. He pulled a Camel from the pack in his shirt pocket and tapped in on the back of his hand before fishing his lighter out of his pant's pocket.

"Jeannie," he spoke quietly, "where are you?" He had been so angry at her the last time they were together, but he sure as hell didn't wish her any harm. He looked at the detailed carving of a rearing horse on the lighter, remembering how he couldn't get enough of her the day she gave it to him. He raised the little flame to his cigarette, drawing in a lung-full of smoke.

Slipping the Zippo back in his pocket, he walked slowly along the crest of the riverbank. Crayon-bright leaves fluttered onto the river and swiftly bobbed downstream. He sat on a boulder and smoked as he looked across the sixty feet of black water at the eastern bank of the Quinnebaug.

On the far bank, two turtles caught his attention as they made their way down the hill and slipped into the water where a partially beached log was caught in a tangle of low-hanging branches. He watched the turtles set the log in motion, as they attempted to climb on it and, he assumed, warm themselves in the autumn sun. Suddenly he realized it could not be a log by the way the turtles made it undulate. Actually, he thought, it looked like the turtles were feeding on it.

Curious, he stood up for a better look.

"*Kurwa,*" he cried out. The turtles were feeding on a body. He lowered himself down the steep bank, grabbing branches and vines to keep from catapulting into the river. Once on the shore he took a closer look. No doubt now. A body–looked like a woman's–dressed in jeans floated face down on the other shore. He threw stones at the turtles who pulled in their heads, but stood their ground.

He yanked off his shoes and dove in the water, immediately surprised at the strong current. With every stroke he fought the to cross the river and not be carried down stream, finally coming ashore about twenty feet down from the body. He picked up a handful of stones to pepper the turtles as he made his way toward the body.

"God in Heaven," he prayed out loud, seeing long, pale-blond hair stream out in the water, "please no." He struggled to turn the body over, bracing himself to confront what he feared he'd find.

"Ah, Jeannie!" He moaned, holding the sodden body to his chest. "Who did this to you?" He pulled her up onto the river bank. Gently he drew long strands of golden hair off her face and recoiled at the sight. He let her fall from his grasp and turned away, trying to come to terms with her ravaged face. Chunks of

flesh had been torn from her nose and lips.
Tears flowed down his face. "Why?" he cried out. "Why
did I leave her thinking I hated her?" He sat down on the wet
sand and pulled her onto his lap. Stroking her hair, he berated
himself for not being there for her and vowed he'd find her
killer. And he knew a very good place to start. Sure Benalli was
in jail, but that wouldn't stop him from hiring someone to do his
dirty work.
Look what happened to Harlan.
Gently, he laid her back on the sand and stood up. He
should call 911. His injured hands, numbed from the cold water,
worked at retrieving his cell phone secured in the waterproof
holster at his waist. After alerting the authorities, he made a
second call.
"Paula? This is Ike."
"I was just about to saddle a horse and come looking for
you. You've been gone a long time."
"Look, my phone is beginning to beep, so I have to be
quick." He swallowed hard and pinched the bridge of his nose.
"I found her. In the river. She's dead." He choked on the last
word.
"Oh my God! This can't be happening."
"Paula, listen up." He had to cut through her wailing.
"There's no time for the whole story right now. I've called 911.
Send them down to the river when they get to your farm."
"But Ike..."
He snapped the phone shut. No way could he talk about
this. He sat back down next to Eugenia and held her hand.

#

The constant clicking of a CSI's camera drove him crazy.
He sat off by himself, a lighted cigarette in his hand, watching
agents crawl over the area like ants. Detective Tearsall told him
not to leave–as if he'd leave Eugenia in the hands of strangers.
Several dinghies, powered by small outboards, came
around the bend. One beached near her...body.
That cold, lifeless word used for his vibrant Eugenia set

his heart pumping.

Idly, he watched an agent step out of the boat with something draped over his arm. He dropped it on the ground next to Eugenia and spread it out. Several other agents joined him.

He jumped to his feet and turned the other way. He couldn't watch Eugenia being zipped into the black body bag. Even so, from where he stood, he heard the zipper.

"Mr. Cherny?"

He startled at the voice and turned to see Detective Tearsall.

"One of the men can take you back to your car. Ms. Stilton took Jordan's horse back to the barn some time ago. You ought to get out of those wet clothes."

"No big deal. They're almost dry now anyway."

"Well, we're wrapping things up here."

He saw the crime scene yellow tape swaddling the area.

"Is there another number besides your cell phone where we can reach you?"

Ike gave him the stable number. "Remember I leave tomorrow morning for Oklahoma."

"But you'll be back in Connecticut by next Wednesday?" Tearsall jotted down the number on a small note pad.

"Yes, sir, barring any problems on the road."

"Good," he nodded. "There's more we need to know about Eugenia Jordan and her ties with Agosto Benalli."

"You know where to find Benalli." Something told Ike not to tell the detective that he was on his way to see his boss. And what good would it do to sully Eugenia's reputation at this point by telling them about her arrangement with Bennali? He was still going to keep a lid on that.

"Yes. And we have enough to keep him there for awhile."

#

At the Montville Correctional Center, Ike underwent a quick body search before proceeding. He emptied his pockets,

taking a moment to rub his thumb over the etching on the Zippo
Eugenia had given him. After getting his driver's license scanned
and signing in, he followed a guard through locked doors and
down the hall. By the time he reached the visitation room,
Benalli already sat at a table, his arms folded over his chest.

"Didn't think you'd be home till next week."

"I made a quick trip after hearing everything that's been
going on." Not even a hello, he thought, understanding his boss
was embarrassed to be seen in jail. Had to admit it surprised him
to see the orange jumpsuit. It brought home the reality of the
situation even more than the body search. He sat across the table
from the older man.

"Were you in a fight?"

"A little horse and buggy accident." He ran a finger over
the line of stitches under his eye then rested his hands on the
table.

"And your hands?" Benalli leaned forward, frowning at
the sight.

"Same accident." He looked at them. Kind of look like
they may have had a run in with your new wood chipper? He
wanted badly to say this out loud. Instead he took the time to
explain about the accident and ended with Annie making the
cut.

"So, turns out you were right about your little hillbilly
mare." Benalli pushed his chair back on its rear legs, his eyes
darting from Ike's eye to his hands.

"I'm flying back tomorrow morning. I'm here to
understand the future of Crowne Stable." It sickened him to do
business with this man.

"They're planning on fining me up the kazoo for
dumping. My assets have been frozen."

"Let's be honest with each other," he said. "Dumping
toxic waste seems to be the least of your problems. What about
the ground-up ministers and Harlan?" He leaned forward
spiting out things he hoped didn't carry to the other orange
jump-suits and their visitors. "And did you have a hand in
drowning Eugenia?"

"What?" Benalli bounced his chair back to all four legs.

The guard at the door stood a little straighter.

"Don't play innocent." What a cold bastard this man is. "You really think I'd believe you know nothing about her body floating in the Quinnebaug?"

Benalli slumped forward supporting his head in his hands.

He scrutinized his boss' reaction to the drowning. It appeared Benalli was genuinely surprised about Eugenia. But if not him—who? He couldn't accept the picture of her jumping in the river on purpose. Then he recalled the abusive childhood she had told him about. Probably left her more scarred. More fragile than she outwardly appeared.

"She told me, you know. All about your donations to U Conn."

Benalli snapped to attention. It did Ike good to see he struck a nerve.

"This is the first I heard about Eugenia. *Merda*, Ike, I've been stuck in this god-awful place for a week. How could I drown her?"

"Oh, I don't know. Maybe the same way you silenced Harlan. You sure had reasons to want to."

He held Benalli's murderous stare. Felt good standing up to his boss.

"I'm shutting down the stable operations," Benalli broke eye contact. "Arrange a liquidation sale as soon as possible. These legal proceeding will take all my resources. Probably for several years."

"We need money today. The horses have to eat till they're sold. It costs money to get home from Oklahoma. And Billie needs to survive until she can find another job." The end of Crowne Stable, he thought with a twinge of sadness. "It'll take a couple of months to put together a sale."

"Submit bills to my attorney, and he'll see you're paid. The court will release money. They won't let horses starve on their watch."

"Fine." He stood and walked to the door. He learned what he came for. He didn't need to stay another minute.

"Detective Tearsall would like to talk to you." The guard

said as they walked down the hall.

Did the man follow him here?

The guard opened the door to a small room. Tearsall stood up as he entered.

"I didn't know you intended to be here, Mr. Cherny."

"Benalli is still my boss. I do need to check in with him." He didn't want more of the detective's interrogations. He needed to think about the steps he'd have to take to close the farm. He couldn't lose Annie. But he'd never be able to afford to buy out Benalli's share.

"Take a seat. Please."

He pulled out a folding chair and sat opposite the man. Tearsall sat back in his chair making Ike feel like he settled down for a long chat. His thick white hair contrasted sharply with a deeply tanned face. Droopy bags under his eyes made his face appear long. He studied Ike's hands.

"Is horse showing a physically dangerous sport?"

"Horses are big animals." He touched the stitches under his eye. "During the tension of competition, anything can happen."

He leaned forward and glanced at a rumpled yellow-lined pad. "How well did you know Eugenia Jordan?"

"You must have a short memory. You asked me this just a few hours ago. My answer has not changed in that time. Eugenia was a customer on the farm." What is he thinking, Ike wondered. "Bought a colt from Benalli last spring. Left it there for me to train."

"Don't you usually get a commission when you sell one of the farm's horses?"

"Usually. But not in this sale. I always suspected Benalli gave her the horse because, well because of her position with DEP."

"Are you suggesting bribery?"

"I've always made a point of staying out of his Nutmeg Environmental business." Back off, Ike thought, shoving his palms toward the detective as a barrier. "I trained his horses. Period" He met Tearsall stare full-on daring him to question that.

"Did you know Eugenia Jordan other than training her horse?"

"I dated her for a time this past summer." Till he learned about her arrangement with Benalli.

"I see." He tapped a pen on the table. "And you just so happen to take her horse for a ride when you have, what, twenty-thirty horses of your own to ride?

"What is this? The third time I've told you I went to her barn hoping to see her?"

"Humor me. I have a bad memory."

"I was looking for her.

"Because?"

"We had–some words just before I left for Oklahoma. I felt badly I left on a bad note." Try all you want, Ike thought, but I will not tell you that I wanted her to tell me what she knew. And what if she jumped into the river on purpose because I blew her off. "You think she committed suicide?"

"Do you?" the detective shot back.

"I know she was sexually abused by her family's minister. But things were going good for her now. Great high-profile job." He passed a hand down his face. "I find it hard to believe she'd throw it all away now."

"How do you know that she was abused by a minister?" Tearsall stopped tapping his pen on the table. Ike saw he didn't know this about Eugenia's past.

"She told me."

"So you must have known her pretty well." The detective stood up and paced the room. Do you know anything else that may have been troubling her?"

His mouth went dry. He sure did. But it seemed to bother him more than Eugenia. Her arrangement with Benalli should have made her uneasy. But she was kind of proud of it. Justified it because of the donations to U Conn. He swallowed several times while he decided how to answer.

"No." He knows I'm lying, he thought, trying to meet the Detective's penetrating look. He hadn't thought he'd be interrogated like this. He needed time to think about the ramifications of admitting Eugenia told him about the toxic waste scheme and why he didn't come forward sooner. Wouldn't that make him some kind of accessory?

"You had no idea she was pregnant?"

"What?" He brought his attention back to Tearsall. Eugenia was pregnant! His? "No, sir. I did not." His head reeled.

"How did you find that out so quickly?"

"Easiest test in the book. What will take awhile is the results of your DNA test."

He nodded, trance-like, and followed the Detective out the door. Eugenia carried his baby?

CHAPTER THIRTY-EIGHT

On his return from prison, Ike found Billie in the stable.
"All right if I turn in?" he asked?

"Sure. I'll sleep better knowing you're here."

"I thought you'd get Luke to stay."

"I asked, but this is the week he goes to Maine to shoe. I have to do the night check, then I'll be right in. Pillows and blankets are in the bathroom closet"

Ike watched her move away. She lost all her sparkle since he left for Oklahoma. Got to be scary for her. Bodies dug up on the farm. Eugenia drowned. Boss in jail. And he's half way across the country. Wouldn't have blamed her if she had bolted.

He went inside Billie's stable apartment for the first time ever. He'd never hear the end of it if he had passed through the door when Lisa lived with him. That and feeling strongly Billie somehow "belonged" to their boss made him dig his heels in at the door step no matter how many times Billie invited him in.

Even when Billie invited him to a going-away steak dinner before he left for Oklahoma, he wouldn't do it. When she insisted, he agreed to having her make dinner at his house...and ask Harlan. He chuckled at the thought of Harlan playing the role of chaperone.

It surprised him to see her homemaking skills. Nothing fancy, but colorful scatter rugs on the old linoleum floor. Lots of pillows on the couch and recliner. And horse pictures and drawings pinned to the wood paneled walls. The galley kitchen didn't have a dirty dish in it. Very inviting. He used the fresh-scrubbed bathroom noting the wild horse scene on the shower curtain and towels. Everything in her apartment spoke of Billie's commitment.

He knew from the beginning how seriously she took her responsibility to the animals and students in her care. Seeing how she lived really brought home that fact that she was a hundred percent a "horse girl." How would he tell her Benalli wants them all gone by years' end?

He shook out a blanket, threw a pillow on the couch and settled in, lying on his back with a hand behind his head. Two magazine lay on the coffee table shaped like a blacksmith's bellows: the latest "Morgan Horse" and "Equus." None of those women's magazines that Lisa read all day.

He made the decision not to tell her about the sale and the closing of Crowne Stable. He knew she'd feel like her children were being auctioned off. There was a good chance once he got the word out at Oklahoma that someone would hire Billie. Conscientious stable personnel who could give lessons were hard to come by. He owed it to her to find her a good job in the horse industry.

That was the easy decision. He didn't have a clue on how to resolve all the other issues careening about his head demanding attention.

Like Eugenia. He could not accept she purposefully took her life. And the life of his child. Would he have married her if she told him about her situation? She probably asked herself the same question. His opinion of her the last time they spoke, when she told him of her arrangement with Benalli, must of come across loud and clear. She had to know he had lost all respect for her. That was hardly a sound foundation for a lasting marriage. So, she may have felt jumping was the best solution.

On the other hand, there was every reason to think Benalli ordered her death. She knew enough to send him away for a long time. But, she was hardly squeaky-clean, playing Robin Hood with toxic waste.

And what about the ministers' bodies? Hard to imagine Benalli ordered them killed. But he did know one person with a very vivid hatred of the clergy, he thought, remembering the day Eugenia told him about her sister's rape and murder and her repeated abuse in the hands of a minister.

He had to force himself to stay with the thought of

Eugenia as the minister murderer. It seemed even more logical when he added the fact that their bodies were found on the farm of the man she was already in cahoots with for disposing toxic waste. How much longer could he delay going to the police with what he knew?

Woven throughout the whole mess was the threat of losing Annie. He could never afford to buy Benalli's share and be the mare's full owner. Could he find someone willing to buy Annie with the contingency that he remained her trainer? Unlikely. As nice as it was that people recognized him after the class, that was just one class out of hundreds. Unless he won the World Championship, he'd be forgotten by the new year.

"Horses are fine," Billie said, walking in. She kicked her shoes off at the door and headed for the frig. "Soda? Beer?"

"Beer sounds good." He tossed the blanket aside and sat up. "I need your advice on something."

"Pointers on how to show Annie?" She handed him a beer and sat on the corner of the coffee table so their knees touched.

"Have to admit I miss having you on the rail offering advice when I ride." He took a swallow, holding the icy can in both hands. "This isn't about horses. It's about Eugenia."

"You find her this morning?"

"I found her." Ike pinched the bridge of his nose and squeezed his eyes shut. "I found her floating in the Quinnebaug. Dead."

#

"Oh my God." Billie wailed and sprung to her feet. "Another death. Where is this going? Who wants so many people dead?" She paced about her kitchen table, throwing her hands about with each question she asked. Sure she wanted Eugenia out of Ike's life, but not like this.

"You found her? That must have been terrible. How did you know to look there?"

"Are you one of them?"

"One of who?" She came to an abrupt stop and faced Ike.

"What are you talking about?"

"I'm sorry to be so gruff. It's just that the police asked the same question–how I knew where to look." He got up and held her close. "You know I went looking for her hoping she could shed some light on what Benalli's been up to.

"I can't believe she'd kill herself."

"Neither can I." He moved away from Billie and sat on a stool at the breakfast counter. "After the CSI guys...took her away, I went to the prison to see Benalli. Detective Tearsall found me there and told me she was pregnant."

"Oh my God! Your baby?"

"I'd like to think I was the only one she was sleeping with."

"I'm sure of that, Ike. She really liked you."

"That makes it even worse. Suppose she found out she was pregnant after she knew I pretty much lost all respect for her?"

"This is the twenty-first century, Ike." She reached out and stroked the back of his hand. "There's lots easier ways to terminate a pregnancy than jumping in a river."

"You already know about Benalli and Eugenia's arrangement for burying toxic waste."

She nodded.

"I know something else about Eugenia. She believed her sister was raped and killed by a minister. The same minister that molested her till she left for college."

"That's terrible, but how does it fit in." Billie sat on a stool next to him.

"Think, Billie. What did they find buried down at the gravel pit?" He patted his shirt pocket.

"The missing ministers' bodies. Don't you dare light up a cigarette in here."

"And who can you think of that's nursing a vendetta against clergymen?" He dropped his hand to his side.

"If I were Eugenia, I'd certainly hate ministers." She rummaged in the cupboard, pulling out a can of nuts. "Want some?"

"No thanks. Concentrate, Billie, don't you think it's kind

of convenient to have Benalli both so indebted to you and also the owner of an out-of-the-way farm for a burial site?"

"Eugenia's was a murderer?" She whispered.

"Very good possibility."

She tried to sort through the disturbing events, her fingers tapping on the soda can.

"I told Tearsall about Eugenia's childhood this afternoon. I should think he'll put two and two together."

"But with Eugenia gone, how can they prove she killed the ministers?"

"I hope they never do. I don't want to believe she was capable of that."

"It must be creepy thinking you might have slept with a murderess."

"Hey, Billie! I really didn't need that."

"Sorry. "But I bet I only said what you've been thinking."

"Let's drop it." He went back to the couch and stretched out, pulling the blanket up to his chin. "I need to be out of here by four tomorrow morning to make my flight out of Hartford." He gave his pillow a couple of punches. "I'll be home with the horses in less than a week then we'll make a plan for the future."

"The future won't be at Crowne Stable, will it?" She sat back on the coffee table in front of Ike.

"Try not to think about it. I gave you enough money for expenses. Try to keep to your routines and..."

"Yeah. I know. Stay away from the gravel pit."

"These are bad time, Billie. Stay safe."

"I wish I could watch you win tomorrow." She drained the soda and headed for her bedroom."Good night."

CHAPTER THIRTY-NINE

"Thanks for stopping by." Tearsall welcomed Leary into his cubicle of an office. "I'd like to hash this Agosto Benalli mess out with you one more time. Coffee?"

"No" Leary sat on the cracked vinyl chair and removed his Stetson, trying to find a spot for it on Tearsall's littered desk and finally set it on the floor. "Your coffee tastes like tar."

"Coffee for real men." He poured mud-black brew in a stained mug and dumped in sugar. "Concentrated caffeine keeps me sharp. So," he said, returning to his desk, "big news of the day is Benalli finally gave us something to chew on. I don't believe for a minute he's told us everything, but hopefully it's enough for us to add some piece to the puzzle."

"What do you have?"

"Benalli said Jordan agreed to alter his weigh slips from underground fuel tank removals but, now get this, she didn't want any payback."

"She have the hots for that toad or something?" What did a good looking woman like that see in Benalli that she'd be willing to risk her career for?"

"Purest case of altruism ever to come across my desk. If you can believe it. She demanded he make a large donation to U Conn's environmental studies program every time she helped him out."

"Come, on Joe." He got up and looked out through the glass door into the main office where detectives sat at desks, talked on phones and shot the bull with one another. "You brought me in here to listen to this crap. I thought you had something we could sink our teeth into."

"Truth." Tearsall raised his right hand as though

swearing on a bible. "Checks out. Dozens of donations to U
Conn from Nutmeg Environmental. Tax deductible donations."
"Go figure."
"I've been figuring it plenty and I'm putting my badge
on the fact that she got off on the power of holding something
big over the man. I'm pretty comfortable that part of the saga is
how it went."
"What about the bodies?"
"That's where I'm stymied." Tearsall got up and
went to the dry-marker board where he uncapped a blue pen.
"Dental records gave us the most reliable evidence. Other body
fragments were so chewed up and dosed with manure and lime
they were sketchy." He scrawled on the board as he spoke:
"Rev. Calvin Wilkins from Coventry reported missing by
his wife on May 2nd.
Rev. John Gibbens from Mansfield reported missing by
his wife on June 4th.
And Harlan Burke, reported missing by his mother and
Whilemenia Jones on October 11th.
But," Tearsall grabbed a red marker and drew a line
between Gibbens and Burke and inserted Rev. Daniel Riker's
name. "On August 13th, Riker was chased into the river and he
reported it to you the next day."
"And, Riker and I," Leary continued the time line,
"located where the horse that chased him was stabled and that's
when I learned of the Stilton family."
"Shortly after that the Danzig woman came to see you
about seeing a body on the Benalli farm. Right?"
"Correct." Leary sat back down.
"As of last night," Tearsall sat down and chewed his
shaggy mustache, "Benalli still played dumb about Burke. But
he was emphatic that Jordan forced him into burying bodies
because of what she held over him. Claims he had no idea who
they were. Thought it was best he didn't know."
"Do you suppose the wood chipper was Jordan's idea?"
Leary moved uncomfortably in his seat trying to avoid the
jagged tear.
"That's where your inquiry into Nutmeg's records at

DEP came into play. Someone, probably Jordan's secretary, must have alerted her you were snooping around and she must have told Benalli to expect a visit from the police."

"I only spoke by phone to the office for a minute. Asked the secretary to fax pertinent information."

"Just enough of a catalyst to get things moving." Tearsall sat back down and raised both feet on his desk. "I located the store where Benalli bought the wood chipper. They supplied the delivery date. Turns out to be the day after DEP faxed you info on Nutmeg Environmental."

"Benalli has good motives to want to see Jordan gone. Being in jail's a good alibi, but my money's on a hired killer for her and Burke."

"ME's report says Jordan drowned." Tearsall sat up and riffled through papers. "Here." He handed the form to Leary.

"Death by drowning?" Leary scanned the paper. "Suicide?"

"And wait till you hear this. She was two months pregnant."

"You think she jumped because of that? There's a lot less drastic ways to terminate a pregnancy."

"It'll be another week or so before DNA confirms parenthood. My money's on Cherny. Guess we shouldn't rule out Benalli, though."

"Cherny would back up what the redhead said about them. The ME's report said there's absolutely no sign of struggling or bruising. If she were pushed, there'd have to be some signs of a struggle."

"How about if she knew her killer well and they were in the middle of a romantic embrace on the river's edge when whoops?"

"Possible scenario." Tearsall nodded."Her SUV was at the stable."

"At the stable of the golden horses. Too bad we can't take their testimony." Leary had heard all this before, but knew going over the facts one more time often brought some overlooked item to light. "Paul Stilton." He rolled the name around his mouth. "We've been overlooking her.

"What do you mean."

"We've been leaning toward the Jordan woman since the horse trainer told you she was sexually abused by a minister."

"We only have his word for it. But her father thinks she was just a kid spinning yarn. I need more coffee." Tearsall got up and poured the dregs of the Mr. Coffee into his mug.

"Something like this simmers for years till you have to find revenge or explode."

"What's your point. Sounds like Jordan. How does this Stilton figure?"

"Stilton's brother spent jail time for raping a girl. A crime that a minister eventually confessed to on his death bed. The kid, Peter Stilton, became in imbecile in jail."

"Worth looking into but doesn't solve how Jordan got in the river." Tearsall sat back down.

"Try this on. We know the women knew each other. We know they both rode horses. We know they kept them in the same barn. We know they were both male gold horses, one of which was used to run down Riker. We know they both have good reason to hate ministers."

"They worked together!"

"Maybe." Leary sat forward and laid his arms on the desk. "Maybe Jordan's part was disposing the bodies because of her ties with Benalli.

"And Stilton killed the clergymen."

"Then when we picked up Benalli, Stilton worried Jordan might implement her in order to save her own hide. So they went for a ride. Probably did that all the time anyway. But Jordan went swimming." Leary picked his Stetson up off the floor.

"How about going for a ride?"

"See a woman about a horse? Man, I wish I could. I'm chained to this desk today. That's why I asked you to come over here. Let me know what you find out."

#

Sgt. Leary found a boy forking stinking manure into a wheelbarrow when he arrived at the barn.

"Paula Stilton here today?"

"Naw." The kid leaned on his pitchfork and tossed his hair off his face. "She's at the cemetery. The one off Route 21 in Dayville.

CHAPTER FORTY

Ike walked down the stable aisles headed for his stalls. He bum knee felt tight but he knew the cramped plane trip made it stiffen. By the time he reached the back barns, the joint had loosened. Even felt good to stretch his legs.

As Championship Night was the last of the show, some stables that didn't have horses preparing for the World Championships had begun the packing-up process. Others with horses showing tonight, were quiet with drapes drawn and flowers freshly watered and in-your-face displays of ribbons and trophies claiming they were among the winners.

He finally reached Crowne Stable's tack room with its lone yellow ribbon. Chet sat on a step stool in front of a tack hook, vigorously rubbing metal polish on Annie's bits.

"Hey! I'm glad to see you. Had all sorts of visions of you missing your plane."

"Not a chance! Everything okay?

"Think so. Annie had a thorough grooming, and I washed her tail again. But maybe you should look at this." He slipped off the ladder and threw his towel on the hook. "I was going to touch up her feet but then I remembered they'll measure the champion's hoofs in the class so I decided to check."

"They should be fine."

"They are not a hair shorter than five and three-quarters inches."

"They don't have to be."

"They could get measured a hair over." Chet put a halter on Annie and led her out of the stall. She snuffled a greeting to Ike and bumped him in the chest.

"I missed you too," Ike said, pulling her foretop out of her eyes.

"See what you get," Chet pulled a six-inch rule from his shirt pocket and handed it to him.

He crouched down next to her left forefoot and placed the short edge of the ruler flat on the cement floor, laying it up the front of her hoof to the where the hair grew on her coronary band.

"It's right on the line."

"I think you're taking a chance on getting measured over. After all you've been through you wouldn't want to be measured over and have to hand back your championship ribbon."

"That'd hurt a damn sight more than these hands did at their worse. But I could risk messing up her motion if I get her re-shod. She's going just perfect with these shoes at this length and angle. She'd only have hours to get comfortable in new shoes."

Ike walked the mare over to the blacksmith shop.

"We're a hair over."

"You and half the horses on the grounds." The blacksmith took his rule from a pocket on his leather shoeing chaps. "Steady, mare." Annie nuzzled his back when he leaned over. He moved the ruler to several locations. "Right here you're fine. But over here you're a quarter-inch over."

"Too risky. You'd better fix her."

"Don't be so hasty. I haven't been shoeing these Morgans for twenty years without some tricks up my sleeve." He picked up Annie's left forefoot, set it on his hoof stand and chose a rasp from the tool box. "I'll take off a an eighth of an inch."

Ike stood at the mare's head as he fixed all four shoes.

"She still could be considered over." Ike said, measuring the hoof again.

"One more trick." He started removing the back two nails from each shoe.

"I thought you weren't going to re-shoe her."

"I'm not," the blacksmith said through a mouth full of

nails.

Ike could see he enjoyed tormenting him.

"Okay," he said, placing the last foot back on the ground. Here's what I did. I replaced the nails with ones that have larger heads. That will roll the shoe forward over the rounded toe gaining another eighth inch. Measure her. I guarantee she's a quarter inch shorter." He wrapped an arm around the mare's barrel and leaned on her.

"She's legal," Ike exclaimed. "What do I owe you?" He reached for his wallet.

"Nothing. How about a couple of round of drinks tonight? After you win."

"You're on." He walked Annie back to her stall, pleased one problem had been handled. He found Chet relaxing in a chair outside the tack room.

"Since everything is ship-shape here, I think I'll get a nap and a shower. Annie's class probably won't go till 9:30. Have you seen Veronica today?"

"She's working the AMHA booth. You plan on asking her to go in the ring with us tonight to strip?"

"I hadn't thought about it. Most everyone will have two people to pull the saddle, clean up the horse and get it posing well. Sure. If you're OK with it. How does Tim feeling about you helping me instead of him?"

"He hasn't asked me to help and I'm not at all sure I'd do it anyway after what he did to my fish. Unless there was a way I could sabotage it."

"No revenge, Chet. It'll come back to bite you."

CHAPTER FORTY-ONE

Stake Night at the Grand National!
An open Landau Coach pulled by a matched pair of
Morgans stood in the warm-up ring waiting to transport the five
judges into the ring.

Judge Jacquelyn
Jacquelyn Turick gave the red-coated Ringmaster her
hand as he helped her step up. Did he feel her jitters? Looking
back she wished she never accepted this invitation to judge
the most prestigious show on the circuit. She didn't have the
experience to be under the gun for six days. When she learned
her duties included judging the park saddle division, she
experienced numerous flutters of doubt. She spent the summer
studying the Judging Standards Manual. Knew the class specs
practically by heart.

But she had enjoyed one of the perks of being a chosen
World Championship judge. Made her feel like one of the elite
all summer. Everyone was nice to her. And the ribbons she
won! Unbelievable. Grand National judges experienced a better
than usual summer show season because the judges of those
early shows were hoping to be looked favorably upon when
they exhibited at the Grand National in October. But she was
determined not to let it sway her thinking.

Even so, she had screwed up really bad in one of the
qualifying classes. The other two judges were united in choosing
first a horse that she didn't even place in the ribbons. She had
raced away from the show grounds the minute the session
ended. Ran to the motel. Stood in the shower going over and
over the class. What had impressed her colleagues so much

about that horse that she didn't even see? She imagined what the entire show grounds said about her. Neophyte. Can't tell a good horse from a bad. Tonight she carried her Judging Standards Manual.

She chose tonight's evening gown to exude self-assurance. At least with her looks. A slinky royal blue evening dress sparkling with sequins. Finger-tip sleeves. It encircled her delicate neck in soft turtle neck folds. But when she turned around, it was backless all the way down to the two little dimples below her waist. It took a bold confident woman to wear the dress when she knew she'd be scrutinized by hundreds during the night.

It crossed her mind she may have been chosen because the show committee knew she would dress up the ring. Maybe they thought she'd go along with the seasoned judges. Maybe she didn't have what it took to be a good judge.

Judge Clint
"Mighty pretty, ma'am," the next judge said as he sat next to her." He doffed his cowboy hat. "You're so dazzling us men won't want to look at the horses." Clint Nour wore a proper satin-stripped formal and snake skin cowboy boots.

Judge Phyllis
The springs groaned and listed to the side as Phyllis Warner took her seat, wedging her flowing maroon chiffon bulk next to Clint.

"Good evening, all. Sure good to see the last night finally here. I don't think my feet could stand up to another day." She pushed her sneakered feet forward. "Goodness, Jackie. Can't believe you'd punish yours by wearing those high heels."

Judge Todd
Todd Greenly stepped up, nodding to each of the sitting judges.

"Your hair looks...bright, tonight, Todd.

"Don't be coy, Phyllis, it doesn't become you. Yes, I did

have it highlighted this afternoon. The exhibitors take pains to look their best. I think we owe it to them to do the same." He thought Clint's cowboys hat and boots degraded the formal night, but knew those showing in the Western Division like him dressing like one of them.

He sat on the rear-facing seat across from Jacquelyn, observing how she clutched her Judging Standards Manual and kept crossing and uncrossing her ankles. She's worried, he thought. I'd be too if I had made such a mess in that class. Can't imagine she actually left a former world champion completely out of the ribbons. That horse had paid its dues. He deserved to at least make the cut. You can't make enemies so early on in your career, girly. Or pretty quick you won't have one.

Judge Horton

Horton Phelps waited patiently at the end of the line. After a week of standing on his feet hour after hour, he knew his decision to retire at the end of this show was the correct one. Yet he didn't foresee it affecting him like this. He stood back and took off his glasses pretending to wipe something off them. Fifty years of judging. Had to be some kind of record. His last Grand National Championship night. Wondered if they'd give him something. Not a watch, he hoped. Not much need to keep track of time after tonight.

"One more session, Horton," the Ringmaster said. "We've seen a bunch of history made in that ring over the years, you and I."

"That we have, Paul, that we have. He leaned heavily on the hand his old buddy offered and realized he'd have to sit next to – but not too close – to Todd. Good thing he was getting out of this game. He could not accept his kind and he hated the inroads they had gained into the industry. They still had to do a damn sight better than normal exhibitors for him to tie them, though. It fought with his conscience all the time.

He was well aware nothing in the Judging Standards allowed him to make it harder for gays to win. But he didn't much look at that bible of the show ring anymore. After all these years he ought to be able to recognize a good Morgan Horse, but a gay in the saddle messed everything up.

Paul latched the carriage door and took his place as the footman on the step provided at the back of the carriage.

"All set." The driver picked up his lash whip and spoke to the team. They swung around the warm-up ring, picked up a bold trot down the chute, their patent leather and brass harnesses gleamed and jangled into the bright ring light. The pair trotted smartly around the ring while the announcer introduced the judges to the spectators.

The Landau slowed and pulled up alongside of the judges' gazebo, banked by flowers and ornamental grasses and placed exactly in the middle of the ring. It held chairs for all the officials, plus coffee, soda and snacks. Polite applause greeted the them as they stepped down and chose a seat for opening ceremonies.

CHAPTER FORTY-TWO

Ike arrived back on the show ground dressed in his winged shirt, red bow tie and matching cummerbund. He wore his new formal jodphur pants with a satin stripe that matched the satin lapel on the formal saddlesuit jacket.

"You look the part." Chet said. They stood in front of the refreshment stand waiting for their order. "Stage fright?"

"No–yes. Have you heard how many will be in my class?"

"Just eight."

"I thought there'd be more." Ike picked up his hot dog and loaded it with sauerkraut.

"Too many trainers rather not show if they don't feel they can be champion or reserve."

"That's too bad, because when Annie wins tonight I'd like there to be at least twenty horses that she beat." Ike bragged. "Have you heard who's showing?"

"Steffi Vicari is showing her gelding back."

"The ladies' horse?"

"Yes," Chet said around a mouth-full of hot dog. "Don't make the mistake of dismissing her. He's the one who *won* the Ladies Park Saddle class."

"He won't have the fire for the open championship." He took a long swallow of beer. "He goes too much like a machine."

"A very-big trotting machine. You've got sauerkraut on your mustache. Steffi's a good trainer with a number of horses to choose from. I doubt she chose Cadet on a whim."

"I heard Jake Paggette entered Redmann."

"You can bet he'll pull out all the stops. Remember Redmann has won this championship twice before. Win it tonight and he'll retire the challenge trophy." Chet popped the last of his hot dog in his mouth and tossed the napkin in the trash.

"What's Tim riding?" Ike wasn't sure he really needed to hear about all the horses that would be hard to beat. Someday, he hoped, at some future horse show, exhibitors would worry if they could beat Ike Cherny and Aristooke Annie. If he didn't have to sell her.

"Delaney's black mare, Green Meadow Bewitched."

"She is elegant, but doesn't trot nearly as high as Annie." Ike said. They ambled back to their barn. Too much time on their hands to fret about the class.

"Most likely she'll get the full fifty percent allotted to type and conformation. Hard to fault her standing still. And she won her qualifier with the same judges where performance was the prime prerequisite.

"Are you sure you wouldn't rather be stripping for Tim? Seeing that you feel his horse is better qualified than Annie?"

"Of course not. But you have to go in there knowing what you're against. Most of the other horses are stallions who will be trotting full bore. A lot of spectators are here to choose the stud they'll breed their mares to next year. They'll be studying this class carefully."

"Reporting for duty," Veronica said, standing by the tack room dressed in crisp black slacks and a snug red vest buttoned over a white long sleeved shirt. Why the long face?"

"Chet's been telling me who I will be showing against. I got one third in a junior horse class and I think I have a chance with these mature winners. They all have so much more finish than Annie."

"You're a new face." She touched his arm. "Judges have been known to brag about being the judge who gave a great horse its first win. And none of the horses in tonight's championship have ever shown against Annie. So how do you know you can't beat them?

"I want you on my team." He liked the way she always smelled like she just came from the shower. He wondered how many she took a day.

"First call," the PA system interrupted, "for the Park Saddle World Championship. First call."

"I am on your team. Now don't we have a horse to get ready?"

A bolt ran down Ike's spine.

"Ike Cherny." came over the PA system. "Message for you in the Secretary's office. Ike Cherny, phone message."

"Mother Mary in Heaven," he prayed. "Something happened to Billie."

"How do you know?" Chet asked.

"What else could it be?" He jogged to the secretary's office located next to the warm-up ring.

"Excuse me. I'm just picking up a message." He elbowed his way to the front of the line of exhibitors waiting to make post entries or scratch horses from the night session. "Message for Ike Cherny?" A woman with a pen stuck in her hair, stopped counting money and handed him a pink slip.

He scanned the message: Attorney Mendocini. He recognized the name of Benalli's lawyer who gave him expense money yesterday. Urgent, he read. Please call.

He glanced at the time. The second call for his class should come anytime now. He wanted to be in the saddle when it did. He hurried back the his stalls, placing the call to the attorney as he walked.

"This is Ike Cherny. You called?"

#

"Are you all right?" Veronica asked when Ike returned. "Sit down. I'll get you some water." He slumped in the director's chair she dragged over.

"What happened?" Chet laid a hand on his shoulder.

"I'm out of a job." The words echoed in his head.

"Drink this." Veronica wrapped his hand around a paper cup of ice tea. "You don't look good."

"The phone message was from Benalli's attorney. Someone made an offer to buy all the horses. Benalli accepted."

"Even Annie?" Chet asked

Ike nodded.

"They can't do that." Chet kicked the wall. "It stinks worse than....sorry Veronica. How can they? You're a part owner." He paced, snapping the towel he carried.

"Ten percent. Gets me zip."

"What does the contract say?" Chet, hands on hips, stood in front of him.

"We never put anything in writing. Just Benalli's word."

"Maybe they'll ask you to train." Veronica offered.

"Fat chance." The men said in unison.

"Someone with the big bucks to buy an entire herd," Ike explained, "is sure to have his own trainer."

"Maybe not. I know it's hard, but put this out of your mind for now. You're going to miss the championship." She tugged on Chet's elbow.

"She's right. We better get moving. Bring you saddle," he said over his shoulder as he hurried back to Annie. Veronica went straight to her tail, picking out the tangles.

"Doesn't she look real good?" She said when Ike arrived with the saddle. He set it on the mare's back, reached under her belly for the white patent-leather girth and buckled it in place. "Look at the shine on her coat. Isn't her color called liver chestnut?"

"Yes, she's a liver chestnut." He knew what lay behind Veronica's cheery attempts at conversation. But he and Chet didn't rise to the bait. They felt the impending loss of Annie too keenly.

It disappointed him that she didn't feel the pain of losing his mare to a stranger. He watched her loop a rubber band on the bottom-most tail hairs and fasten the bouffant tail to a strand at the top so it wouldn't trail on the ground on the way to the ring. Her indifference didn't make her a bad person. Simply not a real horse person. He wondered what did get Veronica fired up.

"Did I get it right?"

"Like a pro." He pulled gently on the mare's ear.

"Leave her be." Chet growled. "I just oiled her face. You'll get it all over your suit."

"I wish I knew who bought her."

"Why is that so important?" Veronica asked.

"I swear I'll take her and run if it's someone that doesn't treat their horses right."

"Oh, come on." She straightened his bow tie. "Do you really think someone who can afford to buy an entire herd would be so foolish as to abuse them?"

CHAPTER FORTY-THREE

Paula Stilton kept one hand on her mom's elbow and the other held a wadded up tissue to her eyes.

Old Mr. Wilson was doing an okay job of coming up with something nice to say about Peter before they stuck him in the ground. Mr. Wilson had Peter in his third-year European History class. Back when her brother was handsome and cocky and liked by just about everyone. He understood why she and her mom just couldn't stomach having a minister recite nonsense at his grave. It was a relief to be able to turn it over to Mr. Wilson.

If the truth were known, having Peter gone was probably the best thing to happen to her and her mom. She'd never know if it was really an accident.

#

Paula had found her mom sloshed to the gills that night, asleep at the kitchen table with a piece of Peter's tee shirt and an empty vodka bottle. She went to check on Peter and found him face down at the fireplace, blood everywhere. Couldn't get a pulse. Called 911 and made her mom drink a pot of coffee. Thank God her story stayed consistent for the police or they'd probably have her locked up by now for the murder of her son. Harriet Stilton said she was moving Peter around by tugging on his shirt as she often did, when a piece tore off in her hands and her son went smashing into the brick fireplace. End of story. End of Peter Stilton's sorry life.

#

That minister's lies all those years ago ruined her

mother's life as well as her twin's. Clergymen save souls. Yeah. Right. Look what they did to her family. And Eugenia's. How can she continue to live with all the years of hatred and deceit? Her best friend and her twin don't need her any longer. Her mom will start a new life with her sister far from Connecticut.

She needed to get it all out or she wouldn't be any better than the minister that kept the truth bottled up till his death bed. But it'd probably mean the death penalty.

If confessing would give me the opportunity to tell the world what scum men of the cloth can be, I'd be doing the right thing for the next generation of young people putting their trust in ministers. I could do it.

Paula handed her mom over to Aunt Noreen who had come to take Harriet home with here.

"You okay to drive home?"

Paula startled at the voice breaking into her thoughts. She turned to see Sgt. Leary, sharp in his crisp uniform, compassion in his gray eyes.

"My Aunt Noreen is driving us." She pointed to the woman walking with her mom. "She's going to take mom back to live with her in Maryland after she closes up the house."

"That's good to get away from all this."

"Yeah. First day of the rest of her life and all that."

"What about you?"

"Well." She kicked a loose stone about. "I've just about made the decision you and I should have a talk." She looked back at her twin's fresh grave. "Guess it was fate you came by. I might not feel so strongly by tomorrow morning." Paula pressed her mouth together and looked up at Sgt. Leary. "Different place, different time, we might have had something." She gave him a shaky smile.

"Paula." Aunt Noreen called. "You coming? Your mom's getting cold."

"Go ahead," Sgt. Leary waved them off. "I'll see Ms. Stilton gets home."

"Thanks. If I put this off, I might get chicken. Well, here's the thing."

Sgt. Leary stood at parade rest and hooked his hands

behind him. Paula looked down at his spit-shined shoes.

"I hear the talk. Read the papers. I don't like what they infer about Eugenia. Everyone seems to think she killed the ministers."

"There's a lot of circumstantial evidence pointing that way."

"Eugenia was my best friend. Clergymen ruined both of our lives and we both turned to horses to keep sane." Her soggy tissue couldn't begin to mop the flow of tears. "But I know," she looked the trooper in the eye, "as much as she was pleased they died, she did not kill those ministers."

"How can you say that with such certainty?"

"Because I did. You better arrest me." Paula jutted out her chin and shoved her shaking hands out to Sgt. Leary."

CHAPTER FORTY-FOUR

"Second call." the PA strident sounds interrupted. "Second call for the World Championship for Park Saddle Morgans. The class before you has just reversed."

"Let's get you up." Veronica flicked a strand of hay of his saddlesuit jacket and set down the groom kit that had a flat top. Against Ike's arguments, his support team demanded (his pride be damned) he stepped up on it to pamper his knee while mounting. "Annie will get you smiling again."

Chet led Annie out of the stall to the mounting block. Ike picked up his reins and settled into the saddle in one fluid movement.

"You're really improving." She tugged on the bottom of his jodphur pants and ran the elastic under the heel of his patent leather boot. She wiped dust off the boot before moving to the other side.

"You've got to get moving." Chet said. "Where's your saddle whip?"

"I'll get it." She hurried to the tack room and caught up to Ike as he made his way to the warm-up ring.

"You forgot the ring bucket." Chet barked orders. "And get two towels. We need one to lay the saddle on in the ring."

Veronica ran back to the tack room again to pick up the supplies.

Annie blew softly through her nose when she saw her competition warming up. She began to prance, eager to join the group. The horse succeeded in jostling Ike out of his despair.

"*Lajkonik*," he vowed. "If we win I guarantee your new owner won't separate us." She trotted once around the ring before the winners of the previous class were announced. Steffi charged by on Cadet. Powerful animal. Damn, look at him trot, just about bumping his nose with his knee.

"Last call. All horses must be in the warm-up ring."

He flexed his fingers and guided Annie to the middle and stopped.

"Great attitude," Chet said rushing up to run a towel over her as Veronica untied her tail. "But I think she could use a little more ginger," he whispered.

"If you can do it discreetly."

Chet cocked his head and raised an eyebrow. He moved toward her tail and ran the towel over her rump. When the mare humped her back, Ike knew Chet had inserted the tingley ginger paste.

"Have fun." He felt Veronica pat his leg.

"Cause it will all end after this class?" He reached down and took his girth up a notch.

"Knock it off." Chet said. "Get in there and kick butt."

"Ladies and Gentlemen. Let's welcome the last class of this Grand National for Morgan Horses. Eight of the world's finest park Morgans have returned. Only one will be crowned the World Champion of the Park Saddle Division."

The Ringmaster blew a fanfare. A tingle ran down Ike's arms through his fingers, telegraphing the excitement to Annie. She carried her head so high, he could barely see over her ears down the darkened chute and into the blazing light of the ring.

Ike sensed he couldn't improve on the performance. With his body still stiff and aching from the accident, he concentrated on interfering as little as possible. He guided her to the rail with the lightest touch on the reins. A quick glance at judges told him what he wanted to know. Annie had the undivided attention of all three. Even the one in the sparkling blue dress.

By the time he reached the far corner, he heard a horse storming up behind him. He resisted the urge to let her move on. He didn't want to be suckered into a fast trot. The other horse flashed by. Hilltop Redmann– with Jake Paggette in the saddle. Paggette clucked loudly to his stallion as he passed.

Annie jumped at the sound. Afraid she would break stride, Ike's clumsy hands snatched her back. Damn, he couldn't

be so crude. The mare shook her head at the rough treatment.
She trotted on, but not with her eye-catching light heartedness.

Get control, he demanded of himself. Only eight horses
in the big ring. No reason I can't keep her by herself. Casting a
brief look around, he spotted an open spot across the way.

He cut out from the rail and aimed toward it. Just what
the mare needed to get her mind off the jerk on her curb bit. She
trotted gaily where he guided her.

"Class in order." The announcer said. "Trot, please."

Ike overcame his jitters. He kept his weight back in
the saddle, freeing up the mare's front end. She responded by
waving her legs well over level-high.

#

Judge Horton believed in judging just one side of the
ring. He felt exhibitors had a right to depend on him not to look
when they were on the back side of the ring. Gave them a chance
to rest–get after their horses. Besides, if the truth were known,
even with his new glasses, he really couldn't see the whole ring
well if he stood by the in-gate.

Could see this horse real well, though. Steffi on her
white-faced gelding barreled down the rail in front of him.
Horton wrote her number down. Couldn't help but like it when
these good-looking women flashed him a smile as they trotted
by. He liked the powerful horse, too. Had good Morgan breed
type. He added a plus, just as an elegant black mare took his eye.

Beautiful, he thought, then noticed Tim Bartlett in the
saddle. I will not let one of them be a World Champion. Not
during my watch. He wrote the mare's number down in second
column and drew a line through it. He looked back up as a liver
chestnut mare approached. Look at that little thing move, he
thought, his rheumy eyes glued to the mare, noting the mare was
a natural show horse. Couldn't remember ever seeing the man
in the saddle. Decent horseman, but scared shit-less. Deserves
a second look. Horton place a check next to the new-comer's
number.

\#

For *Jacquelyn*, it was Steffi's gelding. The horse never took a mis-step. Didn't hold his head very high. But well trained and talented. She really liked the total picture of Steffi sitting effortlessly in the saddle, a smile plastered on her face and her turquoise formal jacket contrasting nicely with her horse's chocolate coat. No one could fault her on choosing Steffi. Jacquelyn circled the gelding's number just as he stormed pass another high trotting horse. My god, she thought, the little mare held her head way higher than Steffi's horse. Look at her motion! Doing her own thing, not being conned into racing. She circled the liver chestnut mare's number.

\#

Todd kept his eye on Redmann. The finish and ring-savy of the red stallion was outstanding. Jake Paggette knew the handsome horse well enough to keep him right on the edge. One hot pepper, looking like he might come apart at the seam. But never did. The attitude of a genuine open Park Horse. He wrote Redmann's number down and scribbled a star next to it.

That's an interesting little number, Todd thought, giving the liver chestnut mare his full attention. He liked the way her rider let her do her own thing. Damn fine performance. I may be witnessing a new star being born right before my eyes. Todd placed two exclamation points next to her number.

\#

By the time the announcer called for the reverse, Ike felt elated with his mare's performance. Most of the class executed the reverse by boldly trotting through the infield, going close to a judge they wanted to impress.

He took a chance of changing directions right on the rail, loosening contact on the bits for a second, giving the mare a chance to freshen. Then he raised his hands shoulder high and wiggled the bits, telegraphing Annie to come together. At the same time squeezed with both legs and swished his whip in the air. He'd knew she'd be offended if he actually hit her with it.

His ploy worked. They had a large section of the ring to themselves and his mare knew how to take advantage of that.

Spectators filled the ring with resounding whoops and hollers. Annie knew they cheered for her. She sashayed down the rail. A real show girl. Head up, eyes bright, waving her legs high in true park horse fashion. Ike feared she may not have been as collected as rigidly as the more seasoned competition, but he didn't have the heart to interfere.

When the call came to walk, she did, just as they were about to come into a corner. He could almost feel her disappointment that the show was over. Unlike a lot of high-trotting Morgans, Annie picked up the correct lead easily and had a rocking-horse canter. So, Ike started to think about the position he should choose for the line up. The biggest mistake of his career.

#

Disaster waiting to happen, Judge Todd thought watching the group of horses gathering behind the liver chestnut mare with the newbie in the saddle. He knew these were the horses that didn't pick up the correct lead well, so they lollygagged at the corner where it was easier for their riders to force the correct lead. Eight horses in the entire class and five of them clustered just inches apart from one another. Talk about broadcasting their horses' inability to canter correctly.

#

They should all be disqualified, Judge Jacquelyn thought, looking at the pile-up in the corner. Who did they think they were coming to the Grand National with horses that didn't canter properly? It was the downfall of a lot of high-trotting horses, but damn it, the class specs called for three gaits. And they were going to have to do it properly or she would not give them a good ribbon.

#

"Canter, please," came over the PA. "All canter. "

Ike was coming out of the corner at this point. He gave her the cue to canter. As she quietly lifted up into the third gait, the riders behind chirped to their horses and smacked them with whips. These horses burst into canters scaring the living be-jesus out of Annie who snorted and leapt through the air to get away from the herd.

An audible "oohh," came from the spectators, arcing in unison with the mare's leap. He kept his seat, taking the full brunt of the jump in his injured knee. Briefing he thought that if the judges didn't actually see the incident, they sure as hell heard it.

He blew it. Rack it up to lesson learned. But why did it have to be with the best horse he'd probably ever sit on?

"Line-up, please." The announcer gave the command. "Head to tail, facing the Ringmaster."

Several horse raced to be first in line, nearly colliding. Ike slumped in the saddle and guided Annie toward the end of the line.

"Grooms in. Saddles off," came the order.

Ike stepped down and went to Annie's head. He slipped the curb rein over her head, leaving the snaffle rein laying on her withers.

The pack of grooms jogged toward their charges, tack boxes and pails in hand and towels fluttering from their shoulders.

Vernonica lay a towel on the ground a little distance from Ike.

"Tough break," Chet said running the stirrup leathers up and unbuckling the girth. He lifted it off her back and set it on the towel.

"My fault. I didn't think. She canters so well I never gave it a thought to my position or the other horses."

"Stop the gloomies. You didn't get to see the fiasco behind you. At least when you cantered it was on the correct lead." Chet toweled the sweat off Annie's face, rubbing her itchy spots.

"What do I do now?" Veronica asked.

"Run a clean towel over every inch of her body. I'll do the same on this side." They worked quietly, being careful to run the towel in the direction her hair lay.

"Where are the judges?" Chet asked.

Ike turned around to look. "Three horses away."

Chet went to the mare's head and took the reins from Ike.

"Step back,." Chet said. "And turn around so the judges can see your number. Veronica," he barked. "Pick up the pails and get out of the way." He took over the horse, positioning her so her rear legs were even.

"Come up," he said, raising her head. She took two small steps with her front feet so they, too were even. He pulled some cellophane-wrapped peppermints out of his pocket and rustled the paper. Annie perked up, leaning forward for the treat, just as all three judges came to assess her Morgan breed type and conformation which counted for fifty percent of the judging.

#

Pretty correct, Judge Horton thought, walking around the horse, noting her straight legs. Her forearms and cannon bones attaching to the middle of the knee and fetlock joints. But her eyes cinched it for him.

#

Nice specimen of a Morgan mare, Judge Todd observed. Feminine. Well proportioned head that screams Morgan and expressive dark eyes. But something about her neck bothered him. Good length. Surely carried it high. He looked more closely at how the neck hinged to her head. That was it! She wasn't hinged terribly well. And the reason why she carried it slightly out when she performed. Her conformation made it uncomfortable to carry her head more perpendicular. Had to give it to her wet-behind-the ears trainer not to force it and make the mare miserable. Let her be free to do her thing and her attitude really shined.

#

Such a plain little thing, Judge Jacquelyn thought. She really preferred horses trimmed with white. She did like the mare's lines, flowing smoothly from her little ears, down her back, across her nice Morgan-y croup to the top of her tail.

#

"Saddles on. Riders up. All riders turn to your right when mounted."

Chet handed the reins back to Ike and picked up the saddle.

"She looked wonderful." Veronica said.

"Yes. Chet did a good job."

"Thanks." He smiled. "And thank you, sweet girl." He kissed the mare on the tip of her muzzle then went to hold the stirrup while Ike mounted. Veronica quickly placed the groom kit/mounting block in place."No matter how it's tied, you did a great job."

"Thanks, guys." Ike said to their backs as they walked out of the ring with the other grooms.

"There will be a work-out. As I call out the numbers, please take the rail to the left."

A hush fell over the audience, making bargains with God that their favorite would be chosen.

"Number 139." Whistles and cheers shrieked through the audience as Steffi's popular gelding exploded from the line-up at a furious trot.

"Number 760," the announcer continued when relative quiet returned. Spectators banged their chairs and applauded the choice of the black mare, Bewitched. Ike watched Tim spur his horse to life, trotting small circles till the horse collected herself.

"And number 314." A jolt of adrenalin shot through

Ike. Annie didn't have the following of the other campaigners, so only a smattering of cheers approved of the judges' choice. What luck! Chosen for a work-out meant he was back on even footing with the other two. Like a brand new class. With Steffi and Tim as his competition, he knew it had to be for the top ribbons. But what about Jake and Redmann?

Steffi had Cadet charging around the ring. Even a quick glance told Ike speed didn't cover the gelding's fatigue. He struck the ground heavily as though it was a chore to lift his feet. Steffi smiled brilliantly.

Tim kept after his mare, jabbing his spurs into her sides at every step. Her eyes looked wild, but he could tell not from good spirits.

Not Annie! A thrill of pride raced through his body, feeling the little mare, respond to the roar of the crowd. She hadn't begun to tire. He kept himself well back in the saddle, nicked her curb bit lightly a couple of times to encourage the horse to tuck her chin.

"Just a hair, *Lajkonik*, please just a hair." He came out of the far corner and freed her up as a thunderous banging of seats began. The noise carried her over the top. She raised her tail. Ike felt it spike to the sky. Whistling and shouts rang through the coliseum. Gave Ike goose bumps. They cheered for him. For Annie.

Once around and the three followed the command to reverse and strike a trot. Each of them chose to blast through the infield.

He guided her close to the judges, showing off his mare's tireless attitude. His competitors took the route behind the gazebo, a blatant ploy to churn up their tired horses out of the judges' line of vision.

Some how the tide changed along the way. Ike sensed the spectators had changed their allegiances. They wanted Annie to win. He hazarded a glance into the grandstands. Sweet jesus! Some stood and waved their arms.

"Let's give them a show, *Lajkonik*! Ike whispered to his mare and his show girl responded by trotting light and airy as though on springs.

He was slightly disappointed when the call came to line up.

Some of those who didn't make the work-out, spoke to Ike when he returned to the line-up:

"Good show."

"Did you feel her flag her tail?"

"Nice ride."

He smiled and nodded his thanks.

The judges handed their cards to the Ringmaster and the eight contenders retired to the out-gate end of the ring.

"314," he prayed. "Please 314." He concentrated on his number to the point that he averted his eyes from accidently catching sight of someone else's number.

"Ladies and Gentlemen, we're proud to announce the World Champion Park Saddle Horse is number 529. Hilltop Redmann. Owned by Hugh Becker with Jake Paggette in the saddle.

"Redmann?" Then it dawned on Ike the stallion was kept out of the work-out because all three judges had decided he'd be champion. So, the three of us worked off for reserve, third and fourth. He turned in the saddle to watch the three-foot blue, red and yellow ribbon hooked to Redmann's bridle. Then the Ringmaster placed the blanket of roses across the horse's withers.

Photographers danced about the winner, clicking frame after frame. Jake rode out of the ring to get measured.

"Reserve World Champion goes tonight to number 314. Aristooke Annie."

Ike almost jumped out of the saddle. He hugged his mare around the neck. The crowd burst into applause. He spun Annie around and headed for the Ringmaster who held the red, yellow and white ribbon up in the air.

The announcer waited for the din to settle before continuing. "Aristooke Annie, trained and shown by Ike Cherny. Our champion was owned until the other day by Agosto Benalli of Crowne Stables in Connecticut. We're pleased to be the first to announce that this lovely mare has just been purchased by Hugh Becker for his Beckmere Farm."

"Congratulations. You worked hard for that."

"Thanks." Ike couldn't concentrate. Hugh Becker? Bought Annie? All the joy wicked away. Jake Paggette trained for Becker. He would never have a place in her life again.

"Son," The Ringmaster touched him on the leg. "You have to get measured."

"Yeah. Sure." He picked up his reins and moved in a trance out of the ring to where the steward measured the length of hoofs. Chet waited for him, grinning from ear to ear. Veronica bounced up and down.

Veronica. He knew in an instant. She sold my horse. She's responsible for putting my Annie in the hands of a cruel trainer. A cold hate spread through his body. She was friendly with Becker. Must have told him Benalli had to sell.

"Get away from me." He spoke quietly, a hate so acute, his hands shook.

She stepped back, shoving her hands in her pockets, then turned and pushed her way through the crowd.

"Ike!" Chet's voice pushed into his consciousness. "Come on." He took a hold of Annie's bridle and led her onto the board where a front foot would be measured.

Angry voices came from people surrounding Jake and Redmann. Ike couldn't make out what they said, but their attitude upset his horse. She danced around and tried to pull away from Chet.

"Hold her steady." The steward said. The grayed hair woman pushed the glasses back up her nose.

"What has Jake in a tizzy?" Chet asked. "You'd think he'd be on a cloud after his win."

"That's the fly in the ointment," the steward squatted and held a six-inch rule down the front of Annie's hoof. "I just measured him out."

"What?!"

"Pure and simple. Remann's hoof length is more than the rules allow. But you're good to go." she looked up at Ike. "On the line, but legal. And," she patted the horse. "Congratulations. You just became Champion."

Jake sprung from his saddle, threw his reins at his

groom and strode toward the steward, smacking his saddle whip on his thigh as he walked.

"My horse is legal. You have no right..."

"I have every right, Mr. Paggette. Your horse is a good quarter-inch over-length.

"Everyone will laugh at you giving the championship to this nothing mare."

"I didn't *give* the championship to any horse, Mr. Paggette. The judges gave you the championship and you chose to thumb your nose at the rules. Have your groom remove the blanket of roses and ribbon."

"They put this show in jeopardy by hiring people like you. Women. Can't trust them to get it right. I've got connections, bitch. You can bet you'll never steward this show again."

"And you, Mr. Paggette, can bet I'll will bring you up on charges of harassing officials. Now, send the ribbon and blanket over here or I'll call security."

"Sure thing." he tipped his hat, glaring down at her.

"Don't you understand what happened?" Chet shook the reins to get Ike's attention. "You're champion!"

Ike nodded, trying to push Veronica out of his mind.

The blanket of roses was pulled off Redmann's withers amid wicked laughter.

"Whoa."

"Whoa there." several of the stallion's contingent yelled. The confused horse jumped around as the blanket fell to the ground. Ike saw Jake strike him under the belly with a whip. *Kurwa*, Jake would have the right to do that to Annie after tonight. Over my dead body.

"Hold him still," Jake ordered, a smirk on his face. Jittery and scared, the horse churned the blanket into the dirt.

Chet pushed his way into the foray and snatched the blanket off the ground. "I believe this is ours." he said. Chin in air, he walked back to Ike and draped it over Annie. The steward followed and secured the crumbled ribbon on her bridle.

Jeers and cat calls came from those surrounding Jake.

"Get them out of here," the steward directed the security

guard. "And you," she looked up at Ike. "You're holding the show up. Time for your victory pass. You know what to do?"

"Never done it before, ma'am. But I bet we can figure it out."

Every light in the ring went out. Several big spot lights swirled around the ceiling. Ladies and gentlemen, let's welcome back our World Champion Park Saddle Morgan."

"Such sweet, sweet words, *Lajkonik.*" Ike squeezed his legs against her barrel and she came to life. The double ring gates swung open.

Annie stepped cautiously into the dark ring.

"Aristooke Annie and Ike Cherny!" Then a startling hush as the spectators struggled with understanding what might have happened to Redmann.

In a second the applause began and rose with the mare's every step. Ike felt her quiver as first one spot and then the other captured her and danced with her down the rail.

Hundreds of feet stamped. Seats banged. Spectators whooped and whistled their approval.

Ike came out of the far corner, hands held shoulder high. He nicked her ever so lightly to tuck her chin then turned her loose as he felt her flag her tail. As he passed the gazebo, he placed all the reins in one hand and doffed his hat with the other.

The audience roared and rose to their feet. Aristooke Annie trotted into Morgan history.

#

It took longer than usual to thread their way through well-wishers on the way back to their stalls. Everyone wanted to touch his horse.

"Give us some room now," Chet said when they reached the stalls. "The mare deserves to relax." The crowd stepped back as Ike dismounted. "I think the After Glow party is starting. Hear the music?" Chet smiled at their fans. "We'll see you there after we put the horse up for the night."

"Not *just a horse*, that one." someone said and others murmured assent.

"Real Champion."

"Congratulations."

Ike nodded and the three walked into the ready stall, shutting the drape behind them.

"Okay," Chet said, plunking his hands on his hips. "Now that we're alone, what's bee's up your ass to make you piss off your fans like that?"

"Didn't you hear?"

"That you won?"

"That Benalli sold Annie to Hugh Becker."

"What are you going to do?" Chet dropped his hands. "We can't let Jake abuse her."

"I don't know, Chet. Not many options open to me." Ike squeezed his eyes shut and passed a hand down his face

"We could take her and disappear."

"Crossed my mind. But we'd never be able to show her again. And she was born to show, Chet." He thought briefly about what Eugenia said about her gelding. Once in a lifetime horse. That was Annie for him. The mare put him on the map and now he had to turn his back on her. Leave her with a trainer known to be heavy-handed with the whip.

"Come on, we have to get her washed off. He picked up the Absorbine, pouring it into a pail of warm wash water. Both men paused to inhale the pungent fumes. Chet rubbed the sweat off the mare's face while Ike sloshed her with a big sponge.

"You should change out of your saddle suit."

"Why? God know when I'll use it again." He picked up the sweat scrape and squeegeed off the excess water.

"It's not the end of the world." He picked up two large towels and tossed one to Ike.

"I'll have to start all over again."

"Not really. A lot of people saw you perform tonight. You know how word gets around in the horse world. I bet you'll have at least one offer to train by the time the After Glow is finished.

"I'm not going to any party." He stooped to dry the little

pockets above each heel that collected puddles of sweat.

"You don't have a choice. You're a Champion. Everyone will want to talk to you. Touch you." I'll throw Annie and Warrior some hay, then I'll be ready. Straighten your tie." He unsnapped the crossties and led Annie out onto the aisle.

"Wait."

Ike cracked a carrot and fed her the pieces. He pulled her foretop out of her eyes as she crunched.

"Where did Veronica disappear to?"

"She better not show her traitoress face here." Ike shoved his hands in his pockets. "It had to be her, you know. It all adds up. She knows Becker and she knew why I had to make a quick trip back to Connecticut."

"Did it ever cross your thick Pollock head that just maybe she was trying to find a good home for the horses?"

Ike chewed on that awhile. "If it was something so simple, why didn't she tell me?"

"Probably did not want to spoil your night."

"My night? No, she didn't spoil my night. Just my life. And doesn't she see how rough Jake is with horses? How could she wish that on Annie? Something else is behind this."

"Like?"

"Don't know. But I suspect she knows more than she's telling."

They followed the noise past the warm-up ring and down the chute into the coliseum ring and stopped at the sight before them.

"My God," Chet said. "Look at that spread. If you don't mind, I'm going to get a plate full before the best is gone."

"Knock yourself out."

The After Glow committee transformed the ring into a noisy party land. Spotlights whirled colored lights. Two tables, almost the entire length, set up on either side. One groaned with shrimp, sandwiches and salads, slices of prime rib and ham and entire turkeys. The other offered elaborate sweet confections dripping with chocolate and mounded with whipped cream. Two huge silver punch bowls held additional whipped cream.

They better have Jack Daniels, Ike thought, heading for

the out-gate end of the ring, where a life-sized ice sculpture of a Morgan head and neck reigned behind a twenty-foot bar. Lines of people kibitzed while waiting for the attention of one of ten bar tenders.

Like Ike, most of those who showed saddle horses earlier in the evening shed their satin lapeled jackets and came in tucked shirts, bow ties and cummerbunds. Cuff links twinkled when glasses were raised.

Women who showed in park harness and pleasure driving classes decorated the party with their shimmering gowns. Some really attractive. Some really rich who wore heavy gold jewelry and screwed gems in their ears.

"Hi." Ike turned to see a woman in formal jods. She raised a glass to her lips. Her tucked shirt had several buttons open and her face had an abundance of sweaty make-up. "You had a great class tonight."

"Thanks." Can't you see I'm not interested, Ike tried to convey. I've had it with women.

"You don't recognize me..."

"Sorry." Ike shook his head.

"You practically squirted my eq rider off her horse the other morning."

"Oh, yeah. Hey I'm really sorry about that." He held up his hands. "These hands..."

"I heard. I wanted you to know I was ready to give you a real bad time, but turned out my rider did better than we hoped. Won her age division."

"Congratulations." Ike raise his glass and she met it with her in a salute.

"Have a good trip home." She smiled and walked off.

Ike raised the iced bourbon to his lips, anticipating its woody undertones. "Home," he thought. Where was that going to be anyway? He swirled the bourbon around his mouth, closing his eyes as it flowed down his throat.

He opened them to find Veronica observing him from forty feet away. She had on the bright blue pants suit that she wore the first time they met. Just as he expected, she was part of a small group that included Hugh Becker. She didn't smile.

Her eyes were sad, apologetic–as though seeking permission to approach.

He connected to her stare, letting his eyes grow cold and his mouth compress in a mean line, clearly conveying his opinion of her. Didn't have to work at it. He felt it to the marrow of his bones. She knows full well why. Traitor. He stayed till she broke eye contact, then he turned and walked slowly to the food table.

The band, eight-foot speakers blaring, set up next to the gazebo. There was much gesturing and drinking as the noise prohibited all but the most cursory of conversation.

Hard-working grooms let loose on the portable dance floor spread out in front of the band. After a week of polishing horses and harnesses, sleeping on cots in tack rooms and putting up with foul tempers when their employers didn't win, they laughed and swung with the music.

Plate in hand, Ike walked the length of the tables overloaded with food. With the knot in his stomach, nothing looked appetizing. But since he fully intended to have several more JDs, he plunked shrimp, roast beef and potato salad on his plate and looked around for someplace to eat where he could think.

He by-passed a number of the little bistro tables set about the ring and headed toward the solid ring railing. He placed his plate on the flat top and drank deeply. He wanted a cigarette something fierce, but smoking was prohibited in the coliseum and all the barns. Too far to walk outside.

"Ike?"

Leave me alone whomever you are, he thought, clenching his jaw. He turned to see Hugh Becker looking smart in his tux.

CHAPTER FORTY-FIVE

Sgt. Leary couldn't remember when a confession had affected him so profoundly. But Paula Stilton's story tested his professional objectivity to the hilt.

They rode in silence to Tearsall's office. Occasionally he stole a glance at Paula in the rearview mirror. She looked out the window, no emotion played on her face. Once seated in the office, he took off the handcuffs. Tearsall gave her a cup of thick coffee. The detective snapped on the tape recorder and Paula told her story. He sensed relief in her outpouring.

The bitterness Paula and her mom lived with over Peter's fate was compounded when her best friend, Eugenia, told her what happened to her sister in the hands of yet another minister.

"We had a special bond," Paula said. "We learned early on that preachers are despicable. And do you know the terrible thing about it was that most parents encourage their kids to believe in preachers and Santa Clause – all in the same breath? If we were to breathe a word of this in this great country of free speech, we'd be booted out as heretics."

He hated it when people in positions of trust abused young people. And it was happening in rural Connecticut as frequently as in the big cities. Just not spoken about as loudly.

"The scummy ministers Eugenia and I were exposed to tore our familes apart. And our families took their sides. Thank God we both escaped to our horses. And I do thank God for sending us horses to keep us sane." She looked at both lawmen. "I doubt He was very pleased with those perverted clergy pretending to spread the Word."

"So," Tearsall interrupted. "this preacher hatred festered

till you women devised a plan to take them out."

"Never happened like that. The first one was an accident. "That scumbag came on to me and I thought I'd have some fun with him. Let him feel some real terror. Yeah, I chased him on my horse, but he fell and cracked his head open on a rock. I didn't set out to kill him. But I didn't cry any either."

"So, how'd he end up at Crowne Stable?"

"That was Eugenia's only part. My plan was to come back the next day and bury him under my barn, but Eugenia came across the body and thought we ought to get it away from the barn."

"And Rev. Gibbens?"

"I planned that one after I saw how easy it was to do the first one in."

Leary got up to answer a tapping on the glass door.

"Rev. Daniel Riker is here," the female trooper whispered. "He's adamant that the woman sitting at Tearsall's desk is not the one who chased him into the river. She was a blonde. We showed him several pictures and he picked out Eugenia Jordan every time."

"Thanks." Leary said and shut the door. He waited for a pause in Paula's confessions then said; "We just heard from the minister that escaped. He's insistent that it was Jordan who intended to kill him."

"Yeah." Paul said. "She saw a minister coming on to Mary Ellen Crawford's daughter at a soccer game and wasn't about to let it go the way it went for her sister. She did go after him, but he got away."

"Who put Jordan in the river?"

"Can't figure. But since my twin died and my mom can start a new life, it's the reason I decided to come forward. I didn't want the world thinking Eugenia did the whole preacher thing."

"Brilliant ride tonight."

"You bought a brilliant mare," he managed to say when Hugh Becker came up to him.

"Yes, I did. And I had to buy thirty others just to get her."

"Guess we need to talk about moving them to your farm. Will Jake haul them or do you have a farm manager?" He didn't think he wanted to deliver Annie to her new home. Out of his life. He couldn't let that happen. *Kurwa*, he thought, he owned ten percent of her. That had to give him some rights.

"If you give me the details on the horses, Jake and I will go over the list to determine which ones need to go directly to his stable for training. No doubt he'll want the mare right off so he can hit the early shows with her."

No! Ike had all he could do to keep from screaming. "Mr. Becker, I'm a part owner of Aristooke Annie and I intend to have a say in her career."

"What? Part Owner? Nothing of the kind is recorded on her registration papers. What sort of proof do you have?"

"Benalli and I shook on it."

"No contract? I'm sorry if I sound blunt, but a handshake with a man in prison doesn't carry much weight with me."

"He and I had an understanding. Benalli didn't feel as strongly about Annie as I did. He really wanted a stallion to promote his farm. I knew I was looking at a great horse when I saw her trotting across a field in Maine so I offered to kick in my commission and be a part owner."

"And what was her purchase price?"

"What difference does that make? I own ten percent of a

reigning World Champion. I'd say I tripled my investment at the least." Ike's head buzzed. He looked at his nearly empty glass of bourbon.

"Let me get you another drink. Then how about going back to your stalls where we can talk undisturbed?"

Ike nodded, zombie-like. He knew how to sit a horse, but was at a loss at working the nuances of deal-making with men like Becker.

They sank into director chairs in front of the Crowne Stable tack room. Ike looked at the ribbon and trampled blanket of roses that Chet had draped over the towel rack. That didn't come easy. If he had to fight to keep Annie in his life, he'd do what it took.

"I read people well, Ike. You appear to be an honest man and I'd like to do right by you. Suppose we settle on a figure, say $30,000 as the value–the considerably inflated value--of your commission on the mare. That plus the reputation you earned at this show as an up and coming trainer to be reckoned with should put you in a good position to start your own training stable."

"I wouldn't know what to do with that kind of money." He slapped his shirt pocket, in desperate need for a cigarette. "I'm a horse trainer that picked an unlikely candidate for a World Championship and made it happen. This is just her first year of competition." He filled his mouth with bourbon, taking solace in its familiar taste. He knew he had to resort to begging, but he couldn't formulate a plan.

"I know you have a long time relationship with Jake Paggette and I'm not trying to interfere with that. I'm not looking to train all your horses. Just my mare."

"And where would you propose to do that?"

"I have no idea. This is all too sudden."

"You'll want to stay in Connecticut?"

"Nothing is keeping me there." A vision of Eugenia came immediately to mind. Her blond hair swinging as she hurried toward him. Blue eyes bright with happiness. The day she gave him the engraved lighter.

But that was before he learned what a conniving angel of

Satan she really was. Before he found her body in the river. And, as much as he didn't want to believe he slept with a serial killer, the evidence sure pointed to Eugenia Jordan being the murderer of the Connecticut clergymen.

Why was he so attracted to crazy women? Lisa. Eugenia. And up to tonight he looked forward to getting to know Veronica better. Did she really sell Annie out from him?

"How does Veronica Rouseau fit into this picture?"

"Veronica?"

He studied Becker's face. Was the surprise in the man's face fake? Becker wouldn't look at him straight on. *Kurwa!* He could read horses better than this man. He watched him take a drink of scotch.

"I know her. She works in the registry department at AMHA."

"That's public knowledge."

"I'm a major Morgan Horse breeder, Ike. I register a dozen or more foals each year. Veronica tends to process my youngsters' registration papers. She could probably tell you the names of all my horses–and their sires and dams."

"How did you learn that Benalli needed to sell his entire herd?"

"From what I understand, Benalli's attorney contacted AMHA to see what routes were available to sell the large number of horses. They went through the routine of informing him about setting up a going-out-of-business sale that would take months. Apparently he inquired about quicker means. A girl in the registry gave him the names of a half dozen breeders who liked the bloodlines found in Benalli's herd. I was one of those and Attorney Mendocini contacted me. When I learned Aristooke Annie was part of the package, I immediately made an offer. I'm very pleased I moved fast and my offer was accepted.

"Veronica never told you Benalli was selling out?"

"No. How could she? Veronica was already in Oklahoma when the attorney called AMHA."

He swallowed his bourbon, trying to digest what Becker said. Why didn't it ring true? But he didn't know enough to ask more questions. He made a decision to accept it. But he'd keep his eyes open.

"I'm not having an affair with her, if that's what you want to know. So if you've taken a shine to her...."

Ike waved a hand in dismissal.

"She's a damn fine woman." He smiled and raised an eyebrow.

"I've noticed. Let's get back to the mare. I'm not going to let her pass out of my life."

"I'd be crazy not to continue sending my horses to Jake. He wins for Beckmere. With more than one horse."

"Touché." Ike saluted with his glass. "All I'm interested in is the mare."

"It's not the way I've operated any venture, Ike. If I expect Jake's loyalty to do the best for my horses, he has the right to train all my horses. Keeping what may be the best show horse I have out of his hands would be a downright insult."

"You really approved of the way he carelessly overlooked the length of Redmann's shoes so you lost the Championship? And how about the gracious way he accepted defeat?" He couldn't believe he just bad-mouthed one of the breed's top trainers. Just wasn't done. But he wasn't going to lose Annie without a fight.

"I'm not all happy with Redmann being measured over. But what's this about defeat?"

"Take a look. That crumpled World Championship ribbon and stomped-on blanket of roses sat on Redmann first. When he got measured out, the Steward ordered him to give them to me. This is how he returned them."

Becker got up. Fingered the ribbon and straightened the blanket of roses, all the while keeping his back to Ike.

"I have to admit," Becker said, "I don't like the sound of this. But I do owe it to Jake to hear his side. If you're willing to stay here while I hunt him up, I'll be back and settle this one way or the other."

"That's fair." Me and my JD don't have anywhere to go, Ike kept this to himself. "I'll wait for you."

Becker nodded and hurried off.

#

Half hour later Ike heard Becker walking up. Work your magic, *Lajkonik*, Ike prayed.

"Ike. Thanks for waiting."

"Did you find Jake?"

"Yes, but even better I ran into the Steward who gave me all the details. Said she even had to call Security." Dr. Becker shook his head at the idea.

"All right. Here's the deal. I cannot stomach that kind of sportsmanship. Therefore I need to find another top trainer. I don't know much about you except you did do one hell of a job on one horse. Coincidence?"

He sensed Becker was tittering his way. He clenched his jaws to keep from blurting out something that might mess up his future. But while Becker may have qualms about his ability, Ike had big qualms at all the innuendoes concerning shenanigans in Beckmere's breeding shed. But if he got the job, he would be in a good position to investigate.

"I'm willing to take a chance. But I have to get results. You would be in charge of the entire herd. Right now that includes the mare that won the World Championship and the stallion that took reserve to her and–won the World Championship the two previous years.

Let me at them, Ike thought, still looking anywhere but at Becker. He'd let Becker talk till the cows came home as long as he wasn't going to lose Annie.

"Seems to me they are the most likely contenders for next year's competitions. And maybe there is some horse superior to both waiting in the wings.

Kurwa, the man could talk! Ike brushed his mustache with his thumb.

"With that in mind I will offer you a two-year contract contingent upon at least one World Championship each year in any division. That's the best I'm willing to do.

"That works for me."

Becker smiled and held out his hand.

"Just a handshake?" Ike kept both hands firmly wrapped

around his drink.

"Just a handshake till I get my attorney to draw up a contract. "

"It's a deal." Ike offered his hand and looked directly into Becker's eyes.

"A quick head count indicates I now have eighty horses. I don't want to skimp on their care and training. So, I expect you'll need a couple of assistants."

"I'd like to bring Billie, she's my present assistant. She knows our—your new horses inside-out. Good instructor, too. Great with kids."

"She's hired."

"Then there's a talented horsewoman I recently met. Pippa Medford from White Gate Farm. She's a tiny thing. Just what we need to back the colts. I think she'd come with us."

"You talk her into it and she has a job. There's a two-bedroom stable apartment that should work for them. And there is a log cabin on the farm that just right for you. It will require some serious maintenance, but we can address that after you get to see it.

Ike and his new employer talked about salaries and commissions. Ike quickly agreed to everything Dr. Becker offered. As long as there was a basic house and enough money for food and clothes, and Aristooke Annie, what more could a horse trainer want? Ike knew that Pippa and Billie would be pleased, too. Their concept of the dream job was an opportunity to work in a well-run stable with quality horses.

"I'm going to call it a night." Becker stood up and reached for his wallet. "Here's my card. Call me anytime. I know you have a lot to do after you get your horses home to close up the stable. So let's play it loose. When you're ready to move the horses, let me know."

"Thank you, Dr. Becker." He stood and held out his hand. "All this kind of feels like being bucked off a horse. Don't quite know how best to get back on my feet."

"Call me Hugh." He shook Ike's hand. "I'm looking forward to a lot of good years ahead for Beckmere. You'll contact those assistants you spoke of?"

"You bet." He watched the man walk off and then topped off his horses' water buckets and tossed them a flake of hay. "*Lajkonik,,*" he crooned stroking her neck. "No doubt you're responsible for this turn of events. Good night, Champ."

He wondered where Chet might be. Hadn't seen him since the start of the After Glow party. Maybe he got lucky. He smiled at the thought. Hoped his friend hooked up with someone kinder than Tim. Chet deserved it. He picked up his saddle suit jacket and walked out to his rental car. He'd sleep well tonight. Was it too late to call Billie?

Once in the motel room, he dropped on the bed and placed a call to Billie.

"Billie? Wake up. This is important." He paused waiting for her to come to life.

"I've got you a job with all the same horses plus another forty or so." He wished he could watch her face adjust to the news.

"How did you manage that?" Her voice was cautious, unbelieving. "What's the catch? Is the farm like in Alaska or something?"

"Nope. We're moving on to Beckmere Farm. Right in Connecticut." Did she catch the "we?"

"We?"

"You're coming with me–if you want to, that is"

#

"Want to?" Billie jumped out of bed. and danced around. "It's perfect, Ike. Just perfect." Ike wanted her to go with him! Maybe at a new place without Benalli and all the bad stuff she'd have a chance. "Tell me about my Annie," she asked, worrying that maybe Ike didn't bring it up because he didn't win.

"World's Champion."

"I'm so proud of her. I knew she wouldn't let you down."

"I wish you were here to celebrate, Billie. You deserve it."

Oh my goodness...Ike said something nice without being

prompted. What is the world coming to?"

"I've got good news for you, too," she said.

"I'm listening."

"Eugenia's been cleared of actually killing the ministers. It's been on the news." She explained everything and they talked till the cell phone's battery died.

#

He pulled off his boots and jodphur pants. Wanted a shower in the worse way. He stood under the hot spray soaping away the nervous sweat of the championship and the last of his bourbon haze.

He was so pleased Eugenia had been cleared of the murders. But he'd always wonder if she knew she was pregnant. And did she jump? Did someone push her? Guess those questions died with her. Multi-faceted woman, he thought, stepping out of the shower, reaching for a towel.

Was someone knocking on his door? At two in the morning?

"Who's there?" he growled, stepping into a clean pair of shorts.

"Chet."

He's crying, Ike thought, hearing the desolation in his voice. He opened the door. Chet stood before him with a black eye and blood splattered on his torn shirt.

"Did Tim do this to you?

He nodded, holding a small horse towel to his bloody nose.

"Come in here." He took hold of his friend's arm and pulled him inside. "Sit down." He pushed a pile of clothes off a chair. "Do you need ice for that nose?

"That'd be nice.

Ike pulled a tee shirt over his head and walked out to the ice machine reasoning no one would see him in his underwear at this hour. Back in the room, he wrapped ice in a clean face cloth and pressed it against Chet's nose.

"Keep pressure on it till it stops bleeding."

"I know his temper was really bad because he didn't win tonight. Made it worse that he lost to you. He's convinced you and I...."

"Yeah, I know," Ike cut in. "You don't have to go there." He went to the bathroom and rummaged through his shaving kit. "So what are your plans?"

"Only that I finally learned my lesson. I will not go back to him. I only have the money in my pocket. Tim always gave me an allowance."

"How'd you like to come work for me?" He dabbed peroxide on a cut over his eye. "Hold still. I have this great new job on Becker's farm. And, Chet, I'm not going to lose Annie."

"You mean it? You and I." Ouch! Do you have to pour on iodine, too?

"No way." He held up his hands creating a barrier between them. Got to get this straight from the get-go, he thought. "It's not a case of you and me. It's a job with the horses I'm offering."

"A guy can hope, can't he?"

Giving Chet something to look forward to is the least I can do, Ike thought, since I'm really responsible for Tim's anger. He knew the man had to be jealous of him. He sincerely hoped no one else thought he and Chet were a couple.

"What about Jake?"

"Hugh said he taking all his horses away from him. Because of how he handled being measured over and losing. You're looking at Beckmere's new head trainer and I been commissioned to hire whomever I need to run a top show stable. And I need you."

"You really need me? You're not just being nice?"

"I may be a dumb Pollock, but I'm not so dumb that I don't realize I never could have gotten through this week without you."

"What about Veronica?"

"She's got her own job in he Registry in Vermont."

"I detected a pretty nice flame glowing there."

"She's pretty. And she helped a lot, I have to give her that. But I just sense something lurking beneath that good-looking package. It's a long drive back to Connecticut. Hopefully by the time I get home I will have solved the Veronica puzzle."

"I came knocking on your door thinking it was the end of the world. And here you have it all figured out for both of us."

"I'm pretty convince Annie handled it."

"She's a great horse and all, but..."

"She's my *Lajkonik*, Chet. I owe everything good that's happened to me."

"Which means exactly?"

"*Lajkonik* is a legend my mother told me before bedtime. Seems there was an yearly parade in Krakow in the thirteenth century. The feature was a warrior with a hobbyhorse fastened to his waist. This *Lajkonik* pranced around chasing people with his mace. Everyone believed if he touched you it brought good luck through the next year."

"Annie in my life has definitely made it better."

LaVergne, TN USA
02 October 2009
159796LV00002B/2/P